Mr. Darcy's Letter

ABIGAIL REYNOLDS

INTERTIDAL PRESS

Mr. Darcy's Letter

www.pemberleyvariations.com
www.austenauthors.com

To Deirdre,
who has shared my love of Jane Austen
for more than thirty years

Chapter 1

HAD SHE DREAMED it?

Elizabeth raised herself on one arm and rubbed her eyes. She must have dreamed it. It was impossible that Mr. Darcy, of all people, would have offered her his hand in marriage! Had proud, unpleasant Mr. Darcy, undeniably the most eligible gentleman of her acquaintance, made a declaration of ardent love to her – and made it sound like an unforgivable insult? It must have been a dream, or in truth, a nightmare.

But she knew it had not been a dream. Scenes from the previous night flashed before her. Mr. Darcy, coming to the parsonage ostensibly to ask after her health, but actually to declare himself. His offensive comments about her low connections and how marriage to her would be a degradation and how society would look down on him for it. On and on he had gone, until she had finally lost all sense of decorum to anger, and told him he was the last man in the world she could ever be prevailed upon to marry.

She sat up and covered her face with her hands. Oh, yes, she had lost her temper abominably. So had he, of course, but that did not excuse it. He might be a horrid man, but even horrid men deserved a tiny touch of compassion when being disappointed in love. She shook her head again. Mr. Darcy, in love with *her*?

Unable to bear her thoughts, she arose and drew the curtains open. The bright, sunny day seemed to mock her mood. Oh, heavens, she did not know whether to feel more humiliated or complimented. What would her mother say if she ever discovered that wealthy Mr. Darcy had proposed to her daughter --- and she had refused? Elizabeth shuddered.

She did her best to adopt a cheery demeanour for breakfast, which was not difficult since her cousin Mr. Collins maintained a conversation without the least input from anyone else. A few nods and murmurs of agreement were all that was necessary. His wife, Charlotte, seemed not to notice anything was amiss, but Elizabeth was relieved when breakfast ended.

She was totally indisposed for employment, so she resolved to indulge herself in air and exercise. She was proceeding to her favourite walk when the recollection of Mr. Darcy's sometimes coming there stopped her, and she paused just inside the gate to the park to make certain she was alone. Mr. Darcy was the last person she wanted to see right now.

DARCY IMPATIENTLY PEERED down the last path in the grove. If he did not find Elizabeth here, then it was hopeless. Either she had come early for her morning walk and left already, or, more likely, she had never come to her favourite place at all for fear of meeting him. Perhaps he disgusted her so much that she could not bear the thought of laying eyes upon him.

Her accusations from the previous night still echoed in his ears. He had expected joy in response to his proposal. What a fool he had been, not to realize that Elizabeth Bennet hated him! He must have looked like a village idiot, offering his heart and hand to a woman who detested him, who thought him devoid of every proper feeling. He would never forget her countenance as she told him that he was the last man in the world she could be prevailed upon to marry. How could she think him selfish, immoral, and ungentlemanly? Any other woman would be honoured to marry him.

Her behaviour was as unforgivable as it was unforgettable. If he had not been so completely bewitched, he would have realized that Elizabeth was every bit as foolish as her annoying mother. Did she not realize the advantages he could offer her? She would never have an offer from anyone remotely as eligible as him. She would live forever in that miserable excuse for a country town when she might have been Mistress of Pemberley. It had been a narrow escape for him. He had to remember that. Elizabeth could not have made it clearer that she could never manage the duties expected of his wife. So why did he not feel relieved? Why did he still feel as if he had lost something infinitely precious?

A glimmer of white by the wall caught his eye. Suddenly heavy with foreboding, he recognized Elizabeth's light figure, her back to him as she closed the garden gate behind her. Her face was shaded, and all he could see was the bobbing of her bonnet, but he would have recognized her anywhere. No other woman moved with that mesmerizing grace, like a hummingbird dipping its beak in the nectar of a ripe blossom, like a spirit come to earth to torment men's souls. Despite everything, his body still ached for her.

He knew the instant that she saw him, for she became still, as if rooted to the ground. She began to retreat, as if hoping her presence had not been noticed, but he could not allow her to escape, not now. "Miss Bennet!" he called.

She stopped at the sound of his voice, but did not look up. She could have been a doe, poised on the brink of flight, held in check only by the gossamer bonds of good manners. Now was his moment. He forced his feet to move, first one step, then another, till he stood so close to her that her lavender scent wafted over him. She stood, her gaze averted.

She could still take his breath away. Even knowing she hated him, he longed to taste her soft lips under his - or perhaps to shake her until she saw sense. Instead, he held out the letter he had spent the entire night writing. Striving to keep his voice even, he said, "I have been walking the grove for some time in hope of meeting you. Will you do me the honour of reading this letter?"

Elizabeth reached out to take it, but froze with her fingers only inches away from it. Her hand slowly closed onto itself and withdrew. "I cannot accept it." Her voice sounded strangled.

"I do not ask this of you lightly. There are matters in it of utmost importance," he said icily.

She folded her hands behind her back. "Mr. Darcy, you know as well as I that a single lady cannot receive correspondence from a gentleman. Your opinion of my family's manners may be low, but I assure you that I understand that much of proper behaviour."

He flushed. "This is not the time for foolishness. No one will know of it, and I must insist that you read it."

Her eyes widened and she took a step back. "You presume too much, Mr. Darcy. I wish you good day." She turned and hurried away, almost at a run.

Fuming, Darcy called after her, but she did not acknowledge him. He could hardly go chasing after her. He stuffed the letter in his pocket. He would have to think of another way to get it to her.

ELIZABETH DID NOT stop until she had reached the public road where she leaned against a painted fencepost, out of breath. Her resentment of the previous evening returned in full force at Mr. Darcy's imperious behavior. What could he been thinking? For a young lady, receiving a letter from a gentleman was tantamount to acknowledging an engagement. She could be trapped by propriety into an unwanted marriage.

Unwanted by her, at least. Her eyes widened as she comprehended his strategy. If she took his letter and it came to light, she would have to marry him, whether she willed it or not. She had refused him; now he was preparing to take matters into his own hands and disregard her wishes, just as he had disregarded the wishes of Jane and Bingley in favour of his own. Detestable man!

She would be safe here. Even Mr. Darcy would not risk assaulting her on a well-travelled road, since that could damage his reputation as well as hers. She glanced back over her shoulder, half-fearing to see him following her, but there was no one there. She rested her hand over her racing heart and shivered. Suppose she had taken that letter – for all she knew, he could have had someone watching them already to catch her in the act! Or, even worse, perhaps his plan had *not* been to trap her into marriage, but instead to ruin her reputation in revenge for her refusal. Even she had not thought so ill of Mr. Darcy. It had been a narrow escape.

She must avoid him. He was due to leave for London later that day, so if she stayed away for a few hours, she should be safe. The village was probably her best option. She could call on the old widow there. Mrs. Dunning would think Charlotte had sent her, and the proud

Mr. Darcy would never think to look for her in a ramshackle cottage in Hunsford. He would never deign to enter such an abode. She could not imagine he ever had a charitable impulse in his life.

Her indignation did not lessen as she walked along the footpath. She longed for her sister Jane's calm presence to soothe her agitation. She needed to talk to someone about what had happened, but she could hardly confide in Charlotte, given her friend's dependence on Mr. Darcy's aunt. Elizabeth's anger gave way to amusement as she realized who she most wished she could tell of this misadventure. Mr. Wickham detested Mr. Darcy as much as she did, and had even greater reason to resent him. If only she could tell him how she had accused Mr. Darcy of mistreating him! But Mr. Wickham was engaged to Miss King now, and it would be inappropriate for her to confide in him. Still, the mere thought of doing so made her smile wickedly.

After avoiding the parsonage for over two hours, fatigue made her return home; and she entered the house with the wish of appearing cheerful as usual, and the resolution of repressing such reflections as must make her unfit for conversation.

She was immediately told that the two gentlemen from Rosings had called during her absence; Mr. Darcy, only for a few minutes to take leave, but that Colonel Fitzwilliam had been sitting with them at least an hour, hoping for her return. Elizabeth could only affect concern in missing him. Colonel Fitzwilliam was no longer an amiable friend whom she would miss, but a painful reminder of the most proud and selfish man of her acquaintance.

FROM CHARLOTTE'S ODD glances at her during dinner, Elizabeth suspected her attempt to pretend nothing had happened was lacking in success. When Mr. Collins finally returned to his garden after the interminable meal, Charlotte requested Elizabeth's company in the parlour. Elizabeth, wondering at this odd solicitation, was even more puzzled when her friend firmly closed the door behind them. "Why, Charlotte, have you secrets with which to regale me?" she said gaily, hoping to disguise any disturbance in her features.

Charlotte did not smile in response, but instead wrung her hands together. Elizabeth, now concerned that her friend might truly be ill, encouraged her to sit down, but Charlotte refused. "I must speak with you, Lizzy, and I do not know what is right and wrong in this matter."

"This sounds quite serious!"

"It concerns Mr. Darcy. When he called earlier, he drew me aside to speak to me privately, telling me that it was of the utmost importance that you read a letter he had written. He had no way to deliver it discreetly. He begged my assistance in giving it to you privately. I did not know what to say - he is not the sort of man to whom it is easy to deny anything once he has his mind set on it, so I took the letter. It is improper, certainly, but his aspect was so grave that I did not doubt the importance of it. I cannot imagine what he would have to tell you that is of such great consequence, or rather I prefer not to imagine what it might be. He certainly could not depart quickly enough once he had given me it."

"How dare he involve you in his business!" Elizabeth's cheeks grew hot. Mr. Darcy's impudence was beyond measure, to involve her friend in his snare! Charlotte's reputation too could have been ruined by his thoughtless behaviour. He was a despicable man who cared nothing for who might be injured as long as he had his own way.

Charlotte did not meet her eyes, but drew the familiar letter from her pocket and laid it on the spindly table beside Elizabeth. "There, now it is yours to decide, and I will leave you alone and never mention it again. I have no desire to pry into your affairs."

Elizabeth eyed the letter as if it might be drenched in poison. It bore her name on the outside, written in a firm and close hand on the finest paper. Somehow the very elegance of it only increased her indignation. With sudden resolution she said, "You need not leave, Charlotte. I have nothing to hide from you or anyone else." She took the letter gingerly between her fingers and carried it to the hearth, where she bent down and slowly fed the envelope to the flames, watching as it folded and curled, a wisp of dark smoke rising to disappear up the flue. She held it until she could feel the heat of the flame on her fingers, then dropped the last fragments into the grate where they was consumed until even the shape was lost. She only wished she could burn her memories of Mr. Darcy as easily as she had destroyed his correspondence.

Briskly she rubbed her hands together. "Now there is nothing to concern anyone, Charlotte. Whatever he wished to communicate to me is lost forever, and I shall never see him again."

Charlotte bit her lip. "I hope he has not imposed himself upon you in any way. I could never forgive myself if you came to harm while under my roof. I had guessed him to be partial to you, but I trusted he would act the part of the gentleman."

"Nothing of the sort occurred, I assure you." Sensing that her friend would not rest until she knew more, Elizabeth added, "Mr. Darcy and I exchanged words – heated words, I admit – but that is all. I do not know what inspired him to take the ridiculous risk of writing to me, and I do not care."

"Take care, Lizzy. He is a powerful man, and accustomed to having his way. I cannot advise crossing him."

Elizabeth forced a laugh. "Especially as he no doubt has patronage to offer in the church! Never fear; I am sure he will not blame Mr. Collins in any way for the woeful manners of his Bennet relations. He was never in any doubt of my low connections, or of the poorly bred behaviour typical of my family." She could not keep the bitterness from her voice.

"Oh, Lizzy, I am so sorry. I did not think him that sort of man."

"I have no idea what sort of man he is, apart from the fact that he is a man of whom I wish to know no more. But I do wish to hear of everything that happened last night when you dined at Rosings Park. Was Lady Catherine in fine form?"

Charlotte looked unhappy, but accepted the redirection. Nonetheless, Elizabeth was relieved when she could finally retire for the night. She was afraid Charlotte's sharp eyes had seen too much.

DARCY LEANED ON the windowsill of his room at Rosings as he had so often in these last weeks, just able to make out the roof of the parsonage over the stately oaks in the park. Until today, he had spent hours at this window, thinking of Elizabeth, wondering what she was doing at that moment, picturing her alone in her bed, dreaming of holding her soft form in his arms. Now those passionate desires were replaced by frustration. It had been over an hour since he had left his cousin at the parsonage. Was that the cause of this delay? Was Richard even now enjoying Elizabeth's smiles? Or was it possible that Elizabeth was asking him about the truth contained in the letter? He supposed it was unlikely, unless Mrs. Collins had somehow intercepted her to give it to her.

He tore his gaze away from the parsonage and paced the floor. His belongings had been packed and were already on a coach to London with his valet, and there was nothing left to distract him. He could go down to his aunt's sparse library in search of a book, but that would risk meeting Lady Catherine and he did not trust his temper that far. His lips tightened. What in God's name was delaying Richard?

Finally he heard the clicking of boots echoing down the passageway. Richard at last, thank God! Darcy opened the door without waiting for his knock. "Are you ready?" he demanded.

Richard sauntered in and threw himself in an armchair. "What's the rush? We're only three hours from London – more like two hours with your horses."

"I have had enough of Rosings."

"What's this? First you delay our departure time after time, and now you want to leave this very second."

"Things change."

"Obviously! Why did you run off from the parsonage so quickly? I would have thought you would want to wait to bid farewell to the lovely Miss Bennet, or at least to stare at her silently as you usually do. Oh, do stop pacing and sit down, Darcy. You're making me dizzy."

Darcy glared at him. "Did you see her?"

"No, she still hadn't returned."

"Damn," Darcy muttered.

"Ah hah! Were you planning to steal off to see her alone?"

"Hardly." Since Richard showed no signs of leaving, Darcy poured himself a glass of port and swallowed half of it, disregarding the burning sensation in his throat. "I thought she might have spoken to you, that's all."

Richard raised an eyebrow. "About anything in particular? And slow down on that bottle, or you won't be able to manage your greys."

"I told her about Georgiana and Wickham, and said that if she

8

did not believe me, you could confirm it for her."

Colonel Fitzwilliam rose half-way, slapping his hands on the armrest of the chair. "Good God, man, what were you thinking? We agreed to tell no one, *no one*, about Georgiana and Wickham. One word in the wrong place could ruin her!"

Darcy's lips were in a tight line. "Miss Bennet's discretion can be trusted, and she needs to know that Wickham cannot be trusted."

"So tell her he isn't to be trusted. You didn't have to mention Georgiana. What could possibly be so important that she would need to know?"

"It was the only way she would believe me about him." The words tasted bitter in his mouth.

"Then she is a fool, and so are you, for entrusting that secret to anyone. Miss Bennet is a pretty young thing, and it's damned obvious that you have a *tendre* for her, but that doesn't change the fact that she has no reason to keep secrets for us, and every reason to gossip."

"She will not gossip."

"Darcy, you are the last man I would expect to be taken in by a charming manner and a pretty face!"

Darcy clenched his fists by his side. "If there is anything in the world I do not doubt, it is that Elizabeth is honest and honourable."

"She does not even like you!"

Darcy paled even further. "I know that."

Colonel Fitzwilliam threw his hands up in the air. "I know better than to try to reason with you in this frame of mind. Do what you will, then."

"I have already done it. She is likely reading a letter from me as we speak."

"You put it *in writing*?" His cousin's tone was scathing.

"I am sorry you disapprove," Darcy said icily. "I intend to leave *now*. You can come now and ride with me, or make your own way back to Town. It makes no difference to me." He stalked out of the room, down the wide marble staircase, and out the front door, avoiding even the requisite farewell to his aunt and cousin.

He was relieved to find his curricle ready for him beyond the oversized portico of Rosings, a groom holding the horses' bridles as they stamped and whinnied. They had lacked for exercise these last few days, and it showed. Darcy was almost grateful that the greys were so restive. Keeping them under control would require all his attention.

At the last moment, Colonel Fitzwilliam scrambled in beside him. Without looking at him, Darcy gathered the ribbons in his hand. The greys took little encouragement to set a brisk pace away from the house. Once they reached the London road, Darcy sprang the horses, sending them charging along at a breakneck pace as if speed would allow him to outrun his bleak thoughts. He did not rein them in until beads of sweat coated their backs.

As they slowed to a walk, the colonel heaved a dramatic sigh and crossed his arms over his chest. "Are you still sulking?"

Darcy did not bother to look at him. "No."

"Then what's the matter? I haven't seen you in a mood like this since…well, since Ramsgate. What happened?"

"Nothing." A vision of Elizabeth, her eyes sparkling with laughter, rose before him. He would never be in her company again, never enjoy her smile, never watch her tilt her head with that grace peculiar to her, never catch her feminine scent of lavender, never see her light up the room with her presence. Never.

"Darcy, you are the worst liar I know. Last night you were almost glowing with excitement, then today you are nothing but thunderclouds. *What happened?"*

Darcy scowled. He knew from experience that Richard would not leave him alone until he answered. "Elizabeth Bennet happened." The only woman he had ever wanted to call his own.

Richard's mouth pursed in a silent whistle. "You really are infatuated with her, aren't you?"

"No, I am *not* infatuated." Infatuation would not cause him to lose sleep for months, nor create an ache deep within himself that would never be filled. "I offered her my hand. She refused."

"You did *what?"* Richard shook his head in disbelief. "And she refused? I don't believe it. She has more sense than that."

"She finds me arrogant, conceited, and selfish." Darcy could not keep the bitterness from his voice, but it was a relief to say the words.

"Hmm. I'm sorry."

"You could at least disagree!"

"Darcy, you don't need me to tell you your virtues. But I can see how, to the eye of a stranger, you might appear arrogant and conceited. Miss Bennet in particular – *I* know you were merely tongue-tied in her presence, but it must have seemed as if you wouldn't deign to talk to her."

Darcy turned wounded eyes on his cousin, then stared silently at the road ahead. "I suppose you think I should have pestered her with pointless compliments and bad poems." One of the greys tossed his head angrily.

"No, you aren't suited to play the role of the swain," Richard agreed, his tone more sympathetic. "You behaved exactly as I would have expected you to. I know it speaks to the depth of your feelings, but Miss Bennet does not know you as I do. Oh, for God's sake, Darcy, loosen your grip before those poor horses bolt. Or better yet, give me the ribbons."

Darcy looked down at his hands in surprise. Richard was right; the ribbons were taut, and his hand ached where he held them. Numbly he let his fingers fall away and passed the ribbons to his cousin.

Richard gave a soft whistle as he shook the ribbons lightly. "This *must* be serious. You're actually allowing me to drive your precious greys."

Darcy slumped back against the high seat. "Be quiet, Richard."

His cousin raised an eyebrow but turned his attention to the driving, unabashedly taking advantage of the opportunity to put the horses through their paces.

After a few minutes, Darcy said abruptly, "She is half in love with Wickham, you know."

"I should have run him through when I had the chance," Richard muttered under his breath.

"That is why I had to tell her about Georgiana."

"I hope she believes you, then. I'd hate to think of a lovely girl like Miss Bennet falling into Wickham's clutches."

Darcy squeezed his eyes shut, but nothing could hide the wrenching picture of Elizabeth in George Wickham's arms. "I could not let that happen to her."

"No, of course not," Richard said with unusual gentleness. "She'll be safe from him, I'm sure of it. She is an intelligent and spirited young lady, and you have warned her."

"I'll kill him myself if he touches her," Darcy grumbled.

"Why don't you come out with me tonight?" Richard tacitly ignored his threat. "I am meeting friends at Lady Rendall's soiree, and the entertainment there is always good."

"Thank you for the effort, but I am not a suitable frame of mind."

"I *know* that, but it'll do you no good to sit at home and brood. You need to meet other women."

Darcy rubbed his gloved hands over his face. "True enough, but not yet." There wasn't a woman alive who could take his mind off Elizabeth Bennet.

"Soon, though," said Richard. "And in the meantime, you know where to find me."

Chapter 2

ELIZABETH COULD HARDLY contain her impatience with the slow pace her sisters set. The day was sunny and warm, one of the rare fine days of early summer in Hertfordshire, and new growth showed in every field they passed, but Elizabeth barely noticed it, her mind fixed on the news Lydia had given her. Mary King had broken her engagement to Mr. Wickham, and he was free once more. Elizabeth chewed her lip. Would he resume his old admiration of her, or had some other pretty face already caught his eye? She hoped not. Even if she could have no future with him, she did not want to miss the opportunity to spend time in his company. And, of course, she had a great deal she could tell him if she so chose!

She did not have long to wait for her answer. No sooner had they reached the outskirts of Meryton than Elizabeth spotted Mr. Wickham's handsome form among a group of officers. Her cheeks grew warm when he excused himself to them and came directly to her side. So he had not forgotten her either!

With an amiable smile, he said, "Miss Elizabeth, it is a delight to see you in Meryton once more. We have missed your charming company."

She raised an eyebrow. For most of that time, he had been engaged to another woman, after all, and she would not allow him to forget that. "It was only a matter of weeks, and I am certain you have found something or other to occupy your time. Training, perhaps?"

He laughed without a trace of embarrassment. "That still leaves many hours a day to feel the absence of a lovely lady."

Lydia cast Elizabeth a grumpy look. "We have been quite well amused without you, Lizzy. Why, you missed at least three private parties and an assembly! Lord, I do not know how you bore it. I am sure Charlotte was pleased to see you, but how dull for you! Stuck in Kent with nothing to do but listen to silly sermons, not an officer to be found!"

"On occasion we managed to find ever so slight amusements to take our minds off our tedious days," Elizabeth said with a sidelong glance at Mr. Wickham. "But tell me, Mr. Wickham, have there been many changes to the regiment since I left?"

He inclined slightly toward her with a warm look. "Very few; one or two new officers, that is all. There will be more change, I fancy, when we move to Brighton."

"Oh, do not mention Brighton to me!" Lydia cried. "If only I could go, too! Meryton will be so dull without the regiment. I swear I will perish from boredom."

Wickham said, "You should speak to Mrs. Foster, Miss Lydia. You are her special friend; perhaps she might invite you to accompany her to Brighton. I could put in a good word for Miss Elizabeth as well." Wickham bowed in her direction.

Lydia squealed. "You are brilliant, Mr. Wickham! Would that not be wonderful, Lizzy?"

Elizabeth hesitated, flattered by his suggestion. Brighton would no doubt be entertaining, but she could not see herself travelling there for no better reason than to follow the officers. It could give Wickham the wrong idea about her. "I beg you not to trouble yourself on my behalf, Mr. Wickham. I have no particular inclination toward Brighton. I have only just returned home, after all."

If her refusal made him unhappy, he gave no sign of it. "Then I must make the most of the time I have with you now. Miss Elizabeth, would you do me the honour of walking with me?" He held out his arm to her.

She laid her hand on the heavy red wool of his coat. It was easy to slip into their old intimacy and to enjoy his undemanding company once more, even if he had no particular intentions toward her. It was enough to know that he admired her. He asked her briefly about her health and whether her journey had been a smooth one, but they were barely out of sight of the others when Mr. Wickham began to engage her on the old subject of his grievances against Mr. Darcy. She indulged him as long as she was able, hugging her secret to herself.

Eventually Mr. Wickham asked directly, "Miss Elizabeth, did you have the opportunity to see Rosings Park when you were in Kent? I travelled there once in the company of old Mr. Darcy, and I remember it well."

"Yes, I had the honour to dine with there on several occasions."

Wickham cocked his head to the side. "Indeed? I would have thought Lady Catherine to be above dinner parties with her parson's family."

"I would hesitate to call them parties," Elizabeth said. "Merely an invitation to Mr. and Mrs. Collins to join her at a family dinner. There was no ceremony, I assure you."

"What did you think of Miss DeBourgh? Is her health at all improved?"

"Not having known her in the past, I have nothing to compare it to, but she seemed well enough, if easily tired. We did not converse much."

"I can imagine! She is proud, like the rest of her family. She will make a fitting bride for Darcy, do you not think so?"

Elizabeth suppressed a laugh at this. How little he knew, and how surprised he would be if he did! "I cannot say, though I saw no particular signs of affection between Miss DeBourgh and Mr. Darcy, who was also visiting Rosings along with his cousin, Colonel Fitzwilliam. Are you acquainted with the colonel as well?" She gave him a sly look to see how he bore the news.

He looked surprised and displeased; but with a moment's recollection and a returning smile, replied that he had formerly seen him often; and after observing that he was a very gentlemanlike man, asked her how she had liked him.

"I liked him quite well. He is an amiable gentleman whose only fault is to have a most unpleasant cousin."

Wickham's smile looked forced. "Unpleasant indeed! Did Darcy stay at Rosings long?"

"Nearly three weeks."

"I hope you did not have to tolerate his company overmuch." He drew her slightly closer to him.

"I saw him almost every day, but he did not often trouble himself to speak. Colonel Fitzwilliam, on the other hand, was very pleasant company."

"*His* manners are very different from Darcy's."

"Yes, very different indeed. It is difficult to believe they are from the same family, although I must admit that I could see a definite resemblance between Mr. Darcy and his aunt, Lady Catherine de Bourgh." Elizabeth looked up at him archly.

Wickham laughed with his old ease of manner. "It is true. Both are proud and care nothing for the sensibilities they might injure, nor for anything beyond their family name. Mr. Darcy has always sought to please Lady Catherine; he stands much in awe of her good opinion and judgment. His fear of her has always operated when they were together. A good deal is to be imputed to his wish of forwarding the match with Miss De Bourgh, which I am certain he has very much at heart."

"He might yet surprise you. His interests seemed to lie in a different quarter."

Wickham seemed surprisingly intrigued by this intelligence. "Indeed? And who might the lucky lady be?"

"*That* I cannot tell you." She found herself unable to speak of Darcy's proposal. No matter how much she disliked the man, he had done nothing to deserve the humiliation of having his rejection broadcast to the world. "It makes no difference, since nothing will come of it." She shivered a bit with distaste.

His face was suddenly sober. "Was there some unpleasantness while you were in Kent? I know he admires you – I could see it in the way he looked at you, the first time we met, but it never occurred to me that…. But now you worry me. He is not accustomed to being denied anything he wants. By God, if he has harmed you in any way, I will kill him."

"No," she hastened to assure him, "it was nothing like that. Nothing at all. I simply did not care for his manners." Even to her own ears, it sounded forced.

Wickham's expression grew severe. "Your silence speaks volumes," he said slowly. "I had not thought him capable of it. You are a gentleman's daughter. Can his pride have grown so overweening that he believes everything is within his reach? It must have. He knows you have no brother to defend your honour."

Now truly alarmed, Elizabeth said, "Indeed, there is no cause for anything of the sort. Certainly he is proud and unpleasant, and he does not feel any rules apply to him, but his behaviour towards me was by no means disgraceful, only ill-conceived."

"Was it?" He steered her off the road, away from other ears and took her hands in his, his hazel eyes looking deep into hers. "It is beyond impertinent for me to ask, but you must tell me, what did he do? I fear he has harmed you, and I will not be able to rest until I know. You know I will never breathe a word to a soul."

Elizabeth flushed. "It is not so shocking as you seem to suspect. He wrote me a letter, that is all. I do not know what his intentions were, and they may have been quite innocent. Perhaps he merely thought that the proprieties governing correspondence between an unmarried gentleman and lady should not apply to someone of his consequence. It would not surprise me, in fact."

"A letter? What did it say?"

She smiled. "That I cannot tell you, sir. I did not read it."

His eyebrows shot up. "You did not read it?"

She removed her hands from his with a rueful smile. "No, I did not. I *do* understand the proprieties, and there is nothing Mr. Darcy might have to say to me that I would wish to hear."

"Still, he must have had a reason to write to you. It would hardly be just to pass the time of day, would it? And a letter would not disturb you this much. There must be more to this. I beg of you, Miss Elizabeth; tell me what he did. I am imagining the very worst." His pallor confirmed his words.

She drew as close to him as she dared, until she could practically feel the warmth of him. She lowered her voice. "He made me an offer of marriage. So you see, his cousin is *not* foremost in his mind."

His lips pursed in a silent whistle. "Darcy deigned to propose to a lady so far beneath him? Wonders never cease! I knew he admired you, but this! My congratulations, Miss Elizabeth, on a most brilliant catch."

She gave his arm a slight squeeze accompanied by a teasing smile. "I refused him, of course."

"You *refused?*" He seemed even more stunned by this than by the news of Darcy's proposal.

"Of course I refused. Given how he separated my dearest Jane from Mr. Bingley, not to mention his infamous treatment of you, I had no choice. I could not possibly marry such a man."

Mr. Wickham shook his head, then eyed her carefully. "He may be an unpleasant fellow, but his estate is a magnificent one. You would never want for anything. You could take your place among the finest in the land. Just think of the advantages you could bring to your family and friends! You would not need to have much to do with him, after all."

She could hardly believe his words. Did he think her so mercenary? Of course, he had been prepared to wed Mary King, in whom he had shown no interest until she inherited ten thousand pounds. But Mary King, while no beauty, would make a good wife. She could not imagine Mr. Darcy making a good husband.

"Mr. Wickham, I must thank you for your concern, but you misunderstand my situation. There is nothing that could tempt me to marry Mr. Darcy. I did not like his behavior when he was here last fall, and I liked it even less in Kent," she said fiercely. "And I did not like him giving me that letter the next day."

"He wrote to you *after* you refused him? Then he has not given up on you. I wonder what he wrote."

She shrugged, not wishing to admit how much time she had spent wondering about what Mr. Darcy's letter had contained, to the point where she almost wished she had read it just to solve the mystery. "It might have been some sort of justification of the cruel part he played between Jane and Mr. Bingley."

"Perhaps there are circumstances of which we are ignorant, such as a promise Mr. Bingley had made to another lady."

"You are suddenly very hot in Mr. Darcy's defense, sir! I might almost think you *wanted* me to marry him!"

He took the liberty of touching her cheek with one gloved finger. "You must know that I only have your best interests at heart,

Elizabeth," he said, his voice caressing her as well. "I do not have the power to follow the leadings of my own heart, or I would wish to…. But that is best left unsaid. Since I cannot offer myself as your protection, I will do anything in my power to see you happy. Even if that means you marrying Darcy."

It was the nearest to a declaration of love she would ever have from him, and she had to blink back tears. "I am honoured, Mr. Wickham."

"You must have already known where my heart has long resided, my dear." His gaze moved down to her lips, then he glanced back over his shoulder. "If we were truly alone, I would tell you as a man should tell a woman."

"Mr. Wickham," Elizabeth said uncomfortably. "I have a reputation to protect."

He smiled sadly. "You are quite right, Miss Bennet. I must beg your forgiveness for allowing my sentiments more sway than is proper."

"It is forgotten." She felt a deep pang of sorrow for his pain, but she knew there was no help for it.

"You are very generous," he said, and then his eyes took on a faraway look. "Would Darcy renew his addresses if he thought you might have changed your mind? Perhaps we can arrange to throw you in his way, and I have no doubt that a few smiles from you will suffice. He must be quite bewitched by you."

"I have no desire to see him at all, much less to have him renew his addresses," said Elizabeth with some exasperation. "I must ask you not to speak of this again."

For a moment it looked as if he would argue further, but instead he bowed slightly. "Your wish is my command, Miss Elizabeth."

To Elizabeth's relief, Lydia and Mr. Denny approached at that moment, sparing her from further conversation. She could not help being aware, though, of Mr. Wickham's thoughtful eyes upon her for the remainder of their walk.

JANE RIFLED THROUGH bunches of dried herbs hanging from the ceiling of the still room. "Is there any more chamomile for mother's sleeping draught?"

"Here, I already took it down." Elizabeth placed several sprigs in front of her sister. "Not that it matters; in my opinion the draught only works because our mother believes it will."

"Then for her to believe that, it must taste as she expects." Jane began to snap the dried chamomile flowers from the stems. "It is no trouble."

"I had an unexpected conversation with Mr. Wickham earlier." Elizabeth's spirits had been in considerable disarray since, and she was glad of the opportunity to unburden herself to Jane. "He tried to convince me that I should have accepted Mr. Darcy."

"Truly? Even though he dislikes him so?"

"Apparently he thinks that wealth would compensate for an ill-tempered husband. I hardly knew what to say."

Jane swept the tiny flowers into a neat pile on the work table. "Perhaps he exaggerated Mr. Darcy's faults for reasons of his own, and now feels guilty that he may have inadvertently destroyed his happiness."

"But why would he criticize his patron's son if it were not true? No, it makes no sense."

"I cannot say. Mr. Wickham does care for you, you know, and perhaps he is concerned about your future after our father passes. He cannot protect you by marrying you himself, but knows that if you marry Mr. Darcy, you will never want for anything."

"A strange way to show his caring, I must say."

"Or it might be something else completely. Mr. Darcy clearly dislikes him. Perhaps Mr. Wickham feared that Mr. Darcy would turn us against him, and tried to forestall it with criticism of his own. After all, he was not known here, and Mr. Darcy could have made his life difficult had he so chosen."

"But there is truth in his expression, I am sure of it!" Elizabeth began to strip dried peppermint leaves off their stiff stalk.

"Truth may be relative. Mr. Darcy's manners left much to be desired, but I never saw any evidence of immoral practices in him, and Mr. Bingley spoke so very highly of him. I always had a value for him because of that." Jane's hands stilled for a moment, and then she briskly began chopping the dried mint.

"Mr. Bingley could never believe ill of anyone. Mr. Darcy's pride is unbearable. You did not hear his words when he proposed to me, how he spoke of the degradation that marrying me would bring, of my low connections, even complaining of the behaviour of our family."

Jane carefully set down her knife. "Did he say anything that was not true?"

Elizabeth turned to stare at her sister. "What do you mean?"

"Mr. Darcy is from a proud lineage and possesses a fine estate. In choosing you, he would be marrying beneath his expectations. Not that I doubt that your sterling qualities would outweigh any other concerns, but financially and in terms of social connections, he could do much better."

"Perhaps he could, but how can you support his condemnation of our family?" Elizabeth said indignantly.

"I do not support it, but I recognize the truth of it. Our mother and sisters would be an embarrassment to him, just as they are to us on occasion, and more so because he spends his time in more elevated circles where they are not known. Here at Longbourn everyone knows our mother has a good heart. Can you imagine, though, how she would be received among the ton?"

Elizabeth's throat was too tight to speak for a minute. "There was still no reason for him to say such degrading things to me. He claimed to love me, yet he insulted me."

Jane was silent as she measured a small amount of water into a glass bottle. "Do you think he meant to insult you?" she said in a low voice.

Elizabeth slowly shook her head. "He seemed to think I should be honoured by his *frankness*, of all things."

"Perhaps he was trying to tell you of the strength of his devotion, since it would overcome all these obstacles."

"Either that, or he was making certain that I understood just how much condescension he was showing in making me an offer at all," said Elizabeth bitterly. Why was everyone suddenly taking Mr. Darcy's side? Did no one understand how he had offended her? "Would *you* then have counseled me to accept him?"

"Oh, no, Lizzy; I would never wish you to marry without affection, or to a man whom you do not respect. He was wrong to speak to you so. But I cannot help comparing..."

"Comparing what?"

"Comparing him to Mr. Bingley," Jane said, the words tumbling out in a rush. "I know that he never returned to me because of those same reasons Mr. Darcy gave, and I understand why he had to do it. But Mr. Darcy, who had more to lose, looked at the same situation and chose to overcome it by making you an offer anyway, honestly stating his objections to the match. Mr. Bingley had neither the courage to make an offer to me or to explain why he could not do so. He simply vanished, leaving me forever wondering." Jane's voice was calm as always, but a single tear trickled down her cheek.

Elizabeth laid a hand on her sister's arm. "Perhaps Mr. Bingley did not wish to hurt you."

Jane turned on her abruptly. "Of course he did not *wish* to hurt me, but hurt me he did. He did not have the courage of his convictions, and I am the one who has to pay for them. Not only did I lose him, but I was left to face the humiliation of our entire acquaintance as everyone pitied me for being jilted."

"I am so very sorry, Jane," Elizabeth said softly. She would have felt the same way, she supposed. There were worse things in the world than honest, albeit hurtful, reservations.

Chapter 3

DARCY'S NIGHT WAS proving to be anything but pleasant. He had known it would be, but after weeks of agonizing over Elizabeth's memory, it was time to move forward. Elizabeth would never be his, no matter how seductively she smiled at him in his dreams. It was time to leave romantic dreams behind and make the marriage he had always known would be his someday. Not to his cousin Anne, of course; he needed a bride healthy enough to produce an heir to Pemberley, but there were more than enough eligible young ladies of the ton who would think it a dream come true to be his wife. Any woman of his acquaintance would be thrilled to marry him – any woman except the only one he wanted.

He had done what was necessary; he had accepted invitations to one of the last balls of the season. He rarely attended balls, and when he did, he preferred to stay in the card room. Now, though, he had a mission. He scanned the ballroom, trying to ignore the matchmaking mamas who desperately sought to catch his eye, and picked out a young lady almost at random, for no better reason than that her hair reminded him of Elizabeth's. Once he was closer to her, he realized his error. The colour was similar, but her hair was thinner and lacked the warm highlights that danced through Elizabeth's hair. Though disappointed, he requested an introduction. The poor girl's eyes grew wide when he asked her to dance, but she kept that fashionable look of boredom on her face throughout the set, so unlike Elizabeth who laughed and smiled as she danced. She agreed with every observation he made, and he was bored to death halfway through the set.

The second young lady had been livelier, flirting lightly with him, but he had recognized the hard, mercenary glint in her eyes, and avoided her attempts to lure him out into the gardens. Desperate, he asked a plain-looking wallflower for the next set, but she was so overwhelmed at the opportunity that he could barely get a word out of her. By that time, every lady in the room knew that the elusive Mr. Darcy was finally in the market for a bride. Why else would he have danced three sets? He no longer needed to seek partners; half of the young ladies present had found an excuse to cross his path, hips swaying deliberately and cleavage presented prominently. It was unbearable.

He could not bear another minute in the crowded ballroom, suffering the covetous looks of the matchmaking mothers. Without even making his farewell to his host, Darcy pushed his way through the crush of people until he reached the merciful fresh air outside. He tersely told a footman that he would not be needing his carriage tonight. He needed the walk to clear his head, and in his present mood, he did not care if he was set upon by footpads. They could only rob him and perhaps hurt him. They did not have the power to tear his soul out of his body as Elizabeth had. Mere physical pain would be a relief.

He remembered dancing with Elizabeth at the ball at Netherfield. The delicate touch of her gloved hand on his had been the spark to his tinder. He stood near enough to see the pulse beating in her neck, calling to him, and it had been all he could do not to kiss that tender flesh. In his imagination, she would tip her head back to allow him access, and he would taste each inch of her sensitive skin until her knees would go weak and he would be her only support, drawing her ever closer into his arms. And that was just while they took their place in the line of dancers. Once the dance began, Elizabeth's sinuous movements electrified him, his eyes eagerly searching out the shape of her legs as her skirt swirled around them. When she began to speak to him, he could hardly comprehend her words, only her musical voice in a siren's call. How could he possibly converse when in his mind, his hands were slipping the dress from her shoulders? Somehow he managed to make some sort of answer, even though her fine eyes were hypnotizing him. He did not want to remember the cold shock he endured when she dragged him out of his erotic reverie with a mention of Wickham.

Wickham. He should have realized the danger of allowing Elizabeth to listen to Wickham's seductive lies. Would she have looked more favourably on his suit if Wickham had not poured his venom into her trusting ears? But no; she had told him at Hunsford that her opinion of him was formed almost immediately.

He could not have Elizabeth, but his letter would have made her safe from Wickham's wiles. Knowing what Wickham had done to Georgiana, Elizabeth would not trust him for a second. At least he had that for comfort, cold though it might be.

THE FIRST ASSEMBLY of the summer in Meryton was both a happy and a sad occasion. Happy, because it was exciting to all gather together once more, and sad, because it was the last assembly the officers would attend before decamping to Brighton the following day. In every corner of the room, it seemed, was a young lady with reddened eyes, talking earnestly to an officer who seemed to hang on her every word. Elizabeth was glad she was still heart-whole – or at least mostly so - and could enjoy the dancing. She had seen Mr. Wickham twice since he had told her of his feelings, both times in company, and there had been no repetition of the near-improprieties of that day, just the usual harmless flirtation they had enjoyed in the past. She was sad that he was departing Meryton, but also somewhat relieved, as she was afraid that if she spent more time in his company, her heart might indeed be in danger.

Mr. Wickham had asked at their last meeting for the first set, a lively pair of dances made more enjoyable by his pleasant company. At the end of the set, he did not give her the formal thanks she had expected, but instead steered her toward the glass doors opening on the balcony, then out into the cool dampness of the evening. Elizabeth averted her eyes from a couple who had been taking full advantage of the privacy the balcony offered, and set her hands on the carved railing. She hoped Mr. Wickham would not try to steal a kiss. It would be tempting to allow it, but her better sense would not take the risk to her reputation.

It seemed he did know better, for he merely leaned back against the railing an appropriate distance away from her and commented on how pleasant it was to escape the stifling confines of the assembly room.

"Yes, it was rather warm," she agreed, "but it is always so at an assembly."

He tilted his head back as if he were inspecting the stars and the crescent moon above them. "You have been in my thoughts a great deal of late, Miss Elizabeth."

"You must have been bored indeed to need such relief," she said archly, half hoping and half fearing what he might say next.

"I am concerned for you, and I fear I have done you a grave disservice."

Was he speaking about Mary King? She could not imagine anything else he had done that might displease her. "If so, I am quite unaware of it, and there is no need for you to apologize for anything."

"Please, you must hear me out. This is difficult for me to say, and it does not reflect well on me." He paused, rubbing his gloved hands together. "It is about Darcy. I have told you that he and I played together as boys. We were fast friends in those days. I recall how we used to play at war – my elder brother would take the general's part, ordering Darcy and me into battle. We would pound those enemy saplings into submission with our toy swords." He smiled at her.

Darcy again! This was not what she hoped to speak of in her last conversation with the charming lieutenant. Uncomfortable, she said, "You need not tell me this, Mr. Wickham."

"I fear I must, and you will soon understand why. As I said, Darcy and I were friends, until he went off to school and came back with a sense of his own superiority and the impropriety of spending time with one so far beneath him. I was crushed, to say the least. He, in turn, discovered that his father had taken to enjoying my companionship in his absence, and it made him jealous. I would deliberately say things to annoy him, and he would ignore me, adding insult to injury. And so our friendship turned into enmity, as is not uncommon between boys as they grow. But it would not have been an enmity had we not previously been friends."

"His pride is insufferable!" Elizabeth said vehemently. "How could he treat an old friend in such a manner?"

Wickham shook his head. "Please do not misunderstand; he did not do anything cruel to me, merely avoided me. I was still old Mr. Darcy's favourite, and he had promised me the living when it should become vacant. But he died first, leaving instructions that it was to be given to me. In truth, I always knew that young Darcy would deny me it. We could not have worked together, he and I, after everything we had been through; he disapproved of me as much as I disapproved of him. To his credit, he gave me a small sum of money in lieu of the preferment, but with such a look of scorn on his face that I have never forgotten it."

"Mr. Wickham, I am not certain why you are telling me this," Elizabeth said softly, though in truth she was touched by his confidence in her.

"I feel I have misled you through my complaints against Darcy. I am still hurt - and my pride is injured - by how he treated me, but I also recognize that he is not at heart an unfair man. Proud and uncompromising, disdainful of those beneath him, yes, but who would not be in his position? He is not a villain, Miss Elizabeth, but in my anger I have given you the impression that he is. It was a petty revenge I was taking, to make people think poorly of him, but I thought it harmless since none of those people were within his circle of interest. No one, until you. You have paid an enormous price for my pride."

"Mr. Wickham," she said, "It was not solely on your report that my impression of his character was formed."

"Please, allow me to finish. I have struggled to find the courage to say these things to you, and hope you will forgive the frankness with which I speak. I am aware that your father's estate is entailed. Your family's circumstances will be straitened after his death, and you will all suffer for it, unless one of you marries well. I do not ever wish to see you suffer in any way, Miss Elizabeth. Darcy could provide for your family. He could give you the most beautiful home in the world, Pemberley. He would treat you well; he is generous and loyal to those he considers his equal. And I, by pouring my poison in your ear, have cost you this. I will never forgive myself for that. The only possible amends within my power is to make this confession to you, to clear Darcy's name as much as I can, and to encourage you to give him a second chance. If he sees you again, his feelings will be rekindled; I know that, because he has never been fickle. Please consider this, Miss Elizabeth, for my sake if for no other reason."

"For *your* sake?"

"For my very selfish sake. While my primary concern is for you and your family, I cannot deny that there is more. If you were to marry Darcy, perhaps he and I might be reconciled, at least enough that I could return to live at Pemberley. I miss my home, my family, my old friends. I have a grandmother who has not long to live, and it would please her more than anything if I were to return home. And I would be able to see you, at least from time to time."

Elizabeth's eyes filled with tears at the thought of his exile. "I am sorry, Mr. Wickham. Your concern is appreciated, but even if I wished for it, I doubt Mr. Darcy would so much as speak to me if he saw me again, much less make me an offer. He may have redeeming features, but he is still the last man in the world I would wish to marry." She could see he was preparing to argue further. "If you will excuse me, the next set is starting, and my partner will be wondering where I am."

Wickham's mouth twisted in a sad half-smile, as if to say he had done his best. "Please consider what I have said. Should you ever change your mind, Miss Elizabeth, do not forget that I am your friend, and you can reach me in Brighton."

With some asperity, Elizabeth wondered whether gentlemen from Derbyshire commonly thought nothing of exchanging letters with unmarried women, but she glanced back at him once after wishing him goodnight. She would indeed miss his company.

LONGBOURN SEEMED VERY quiet after the departure of the regiment, especially since Lydia followed them to Brighton in the company of her friend, Mrs. Forster. Elizabeth devoutly hoped, rather than believed, that Mrs. Forster would keep her youngest sister out of mischief's way. Mrs. Bennet and Kitty were disconsolate at the lack of officers in Meryton, their piteous complaints frequently driving Mr. Bennet to closet himself in his library.

Elizabeth counted herself fortunate to have something pleasant to anticipate. Her aunt and uncle Gardiner had offered to take her with them on a tour of the Lake District, and she was as happy to anticipate an extended time in their sensible company as the chance to visit sights she had always wished to see.

The time fixed for the beginning of their Northern tour was now fast approaching; and a fortnight only was wanting of it when a letter arrived from Mrs. Gardiner which at once delayed its commencement and curtailed its extent. Mr. Gardiner would be prevented by business from setting out till a fortnight later in July, and must be in London again within a month. As that left too short a period for them to go so far, they were obliged to give up the Lakes, and substitute a more contracted tour; and, according to the present plan, were to go no farther northward than Derbyshire. In that county, there was enough to be seen to occupy the chief of their three weeks; and to Mrs. Gardiner it had a peculiarly strong attraction. The town where she had formerly passed some years of her life, and where they were now to spend a few days, was probably as great an object of her curiosity, as all the celebrated beauties of Matlock, Chatsworth, Dovedale, or the Peak.

Elizabeth was excessively disappointed; she had set her heart on seeing the Lakes; and still thought there might have been time enough. But it was her business to be satisfied, and certainly her temper to be happy; and all was soon right again.

With the mention of Derbyshire, there were many ideas connected. It was impossible for her to contemplate it without thinking of Pemberley and its owner. What if their paths should cross in Derbyshire? It was unlikely, given the size of the county, but she could not help worrying over it. Her anger with him had waned with time, especially since Mr. Wickham's confession, and the compliment of such a man's affection was more prominent. Still, she felt no desire to see him ever again.

Her recollections of her behaviour at the time of their confrontation at Hunsford were not happy ones. Regardless of the provocation Mr. Darcy had given, she could not justify her own lack of civility and intemperate words. What would she say if they met? She could only pray that it would never come to pass.

Chapter 4

DERBYSHIRE PROVED TO be a more satisfactory substitute for the Lake District than Elizabeth had anticipated. Having admired the dramatic scenery, the hilly towns built all of stone, and the beauties of Dove Dale, Elizabeth understood better Mr. Wickham's longing to return to the land of his birth. She was herself sufficiently taken with the landscape as to wonder if she, after spending a mere fortnight there, might not long for it for the rest of her days.

After seeing all the principal wonders of the country, the travellers bent their steps to the little town of Lambton, where Mrs. Gardiner had spent her youth. Elizabeth had thought little of the location until her aunt informed her that Pemberley was situated not five miles from Lambton. It was not in their direct road, nor more than a mile or two out of it. Mrs. Gardiner expressed an inclination to see the place again.

"My love, should not you like to see a place of which you have heard so much?" said her aunt. "A place too, with which so many of your acquaintance are connected. Wickham passed all his youth there, you know."

Elizabeth was distressed. She felt that she had no business at Pemberley, and was obliged to assume a disinclination for seeing it. She must own that she was tired of great houses; after going over so many, she really had no pleasure in fine carpets or satin curtains.

Mrs. Gardiner would not stand for it. "If it were merely a fine house richly furnished, I should not care about it myself; but the grounds are delightful. They have some of the finest woods in the country."

Elizabeth said no more, but her mind could not acquiesce. The possibility of meeting Mr. Darcy, while viewing the place, instantly occurred. She blushed at the very idea; and thought it would be better to speak openly to her aunt than to run such a risk. But against this there were objections; and she finally resolved that it could be the last resource, if her private enquiries as to the absence of the family were unfavourably answered.

Accordingly, when she retired at night, she asked the chambermaid whether Pemberley were not a very fine place, what was the name of its proprietor, and, with no little alarm, whether the family were down for the summer. A most welcome negative followed the last question, and her alarm being now removed, she was at leisure to feel a great deal of curiosity to see the house herself. When the subject was revived the next morning, she could readily answer with a proper air of indifference that she had not really any dislike to the scheme.

To Pemberley, therefore, they were to go.

AS THE CARRIAGE approached Pemberley, Elizabeth's mind was too full for conversation, but she saw and admired every remarkable spot and point of view. Pemberley House, situated on the opposite side of a valley, was a large, handsome, stone building, standing well on rising ground, backed by a ridge of high woody hills; and in front, a stream of some natural importance was swelled into greater, but without any artificial appearance. Its banks were neither formal, nor falsely adorned. Elizabeth was delighted. She had never seen a place for which nature had done more, or where natural beauty had been so little counteracted by an awkward taste.

The housekeeper, a respectable-looking, elderly woman, much less fine and more civil than Elizabeth had any notion of finding her, welcomed them into the house. Inside, the rooms were lofty and handsome, and their furniture suitable to the fortune of their proprietor. It was neither gaudy nor uselessly fine; with less of splendor, and more real elegance, than the furniture of Rosings.

And of this place she might have been mistress! With these rooms she might now have been familiarly acquainted. Instead of viewing them as a stranger, she might have rejoiced in them as her own, and welcomed to them as visitors her uncle and aunt. But no, that could never be. The Gardiners would have been lost to her. She would not have been allowed to invite them; and she should have lived such a life of misery with Mr. Darcy as to make any consolation impossible.

She longed to enquire of the housekeeper whether her master were really absent, but had not courage for it. At length, however, the question was asked by her uncle; and she turned away with alarm, while Mrs. Reynolds replied that he was, adding, "But we expect him tomorrow, with a large party of friends." Elizabeth rejoiced that their own journey had not by any circumstance been delayed a day.

Her aunt now called her to look at a picture. She approached, and saw the likeness of Mr. Wickham suspended, amongst several other miniatures, over the mantelpiece. The housekeeper came forward, and told them it was the picture of a young gentleman, the son of her late master's steward, who had been brought up by him at his own expense. "He is now gone into the army," she added, "but I am afraid he has turned out very wild."

Elizabeth tightened her lips. Had Mr. Darcy employed his malice toward his old friend even at Pemberley, in Wickham's own home? No wonder Wickham felt he could not return there. She wondered if the people of Pemberley believed Mr. Darcy's slanders, or whether they recalled Wickham's amiability and question the truth. The housekeeper, either from pride or attachment, had evidently great pleasure in talking of her master, but she sounded truly indignant when discussing Mr. Wickham. And Mr. Wickham had admitted at their last meeting that he had not been fully truthful when speaking of Mr. Darcy. Was that enough to cast doubt on everything he had said?

"And that," said Mrs. Reynolds, pointing to another of the miniatures, "is my master, and very like him. It was drawn at the same time as the other—about eight years ago."

"I have heard much of your master's fine person," said Mrs. Gardiner, looking at the picture; "it is a handsome face. But, Lizzy, you can tell us whether it is like or not."

Mrs. Reynolds's respect for Elizabeth seemed to increase on this intimation of her knowing her master.

"Does the young lady know Mr. Darcy?"

Elizabeth coloured, and said, "A little."

"And do not you think him a very handsome gentleman,

Ma'am?"

"Yes, very handsome." It seemed the only thing she could say in civility, and in truth, Mr. Darcy's appearance was handsome; it was only in his behaviour that she saw ugliness.

"I am sure I know none so handsome; but in the gallery up stairs you will see a finer, larger picture of him than this. This room was my late master's favourite room, and these miniatures are just as they used to be then. He was very fond of them."

This accounted to Elizabeth for Mr. Wickham's being among them. Was that truly the source of Mr. Darcy's dislike of him – a jealousy of his father's affection for a mere steward's son?

"Is your master much at Pemberley in the course of the year?" asked Mr. Gardiner.

"Not so much as I could wish, sir; but I dare say he may spend half his time here; and Miss Darcy is always down for the summer months."

"If your master would marry, you might see more of him."

"Yes, but I do not know when that will be. I do not know who is good enough for him."

Mr. and Mrs. Gardiner smiled, but Elizabeth could think of nothing to say. Mrs. Reynolds' views were no doubt coloured by her employment, but she seemed firm in her opinions.

"I say no more than the truth, and what everybody will say that knows him," replied the housekeeper. Elizabeth thought this was going pretty far; and she listened with increasing astonishment as Mrs. Reynolds added, "I have never had a cross word from him in my life, and I have known him ever since he was four years old."

This was praise, of all others most extraordinary, most opposite to her ideas. That he was not a good tempered man had been her firmest opinion. His comportment had always indicated ill temper, and he himself had said he was of a resentful disposition. Her curiosity was awakened; she longed to hear more, and was grateful to her uncle for saying, "There are very few people of whom so much can be said. You are lucky in having such a master."

"Yes, sir, I know I am. If I was to go through the world, I could not meet with a better. But I have always observed that they who are good-natured when children are good-natured when they grow up; and he was always the sweetest-tempered, most generous-hearted, boy in the world."

Elizabeth almost stared at her. Her thoughts tumbled in confusion. The housekeeper seemed so sincere. It was as if they were speaking of two different gentlemen.

"His father was an excellent man," said Mrs. Gardiner.

"Yes, Ma'am, that he was indeed; and his son will be just like him—just as affable to the poor. He is the best landlord, and the best master that ever lived. Not like the wild young men now-a-days, who think of nothing but themselves. There is not one of his tenants or servants but what will give him a good name. Some people call him proud; but I am sure I never saw any thing of it. To my fancy, it is only because he does not rattle away like other young men."

"This fine account of him," whispered her aunt, as they walked, "is not quite consistent with his behaviour to Mr. Wickham."

"No, it is not. Perhaps she fears that I might report any criticism she makes to Mr. Darcy."

In the gallery there were many family portraits, but they could have little to fix the attention of a stranger. Elizabeth walked on in quest of the only face whose features would be known to her. At last it arrested her—and she beheld a striking resemblance of Mr. Darcy, with such a smile over the face as she remembered to have sometimes seen, when he looked at her. She stood several minutes before the picture in earnest contemplation, and returned to it again before they quitted the gallery, as if by gazing at it she could solve the conundrum of Mr. Darcy.

Chapter 5

ALMOST HOME. HE was almost home. The refrain repeated in Darcy's mind as he rode the last few miles to Pemberley. His horse, recognizing that his stable was near, was eager to canter, and Darcy had no objection. He had not been back to Pemberley since Christmas, over half a year ago, and he had missed it every single day. Just as he longed for Elizabeth Bennet every day, but that was a hopeless cause. At least Pemberley was his, even if he could never share it with Elizabeth. He wondered what she would have thought of it. Would she love its elegant architecture and expansive grounds, or would she find herself hemmed in by the wild hills of Derbyshire? Some women disliked them. Perhaps Elizabeth, with her love of long walks, would enjoy exploring the moors and rugged edges. In his imagination, she stood beside him overlooking a view of Pemberley, the brisk wind playing in her curls.

Why was he even thinking such a thing? He would never see Elizabeth again, unless by some chance she returned to Hunsford for Easter in the future. But she would not do so; he knew that. She would avoid visiting Kent in the springtime just because of the knowledge that he might be there. He should not even admit the possibility to himself that they might meet again. It would not happen, and keeping even the merest flicker of hope alive only caused that much more pain and despair.

He pulled up his horse at the top of the hill as Pemberley came into view. The sight of it nestled beside the lake provided a much needed balm for his heart. Perhaps here he would finally find some peace. When he had been here last, he had not even dreamed he might propose marriage to Elizabeth Bennet, or that he might be refused. He had still thought then that any woman would be fortunate to have him, and that was how it should be. He had never been denied anything he truly wanted. What cruel fate had arranged it so that he would be denied the woman he loved?

He loosened the reins and gave his horse the freedom to gallop the last mile. The dust of the road rose around him. The wind whistling past Darcy's ears cooled the sweat on his brow after the long ride in the August sun, which shone brighter than its usual wont in Derbyshire, as if to gild the landscape for his pleasure.

He slowed his mount only when they neared the stable. He heard a stable boy give a shout, and the stable master himself came out to meet him as he swung down from the saddle.

"Welcome home, Mr. Darcy. We did not expect you until tomorrow, but everything is in readiness, as always."

"I have no doubt of it," Darcy said dryly, slapping the dust from his thighs. Mrs. Reynolds would never allow anything less than perfect readiness. "I have ridden far today, and he will need to cool off."

"Yes, sir." The stable master handed the reins to one of the boys who had run out to observe the master's return.

Darcy removed his hat and tucked it under his arm, then ran his fingers through his hair, letting the air dry the remaining beads of perspiration. It was definitely time for a bath and fresh clothes. He strode along the road as it turned toward Pemberley House, providing a vista over the great lawn and the river.

And of Miss Elizabeth Bennet, standing not twenty yards from him.

Could he be imagining it? Could the long, hot ride and his brooding thoughts of Elizabeth have created the image in his head? No, he could never mistake the true Elizabeth for anyone else. His breath caught in his chest as his eyes met hers, her cheeks overspread with the deepest blush. A thousand questions raced through his head. Why could she possibly be at Pemberley? What had brought her there? Had she known he was coming? And the most difficult question of all - had she wanted to see him, or was her blush one of chagrin at his presence?

If he kept standing there like a statue, she would think him a complete idiot. Marshalling his courage, he advanced toward her. "Miss

Bennet, this is an unexpected pleasure." Even he could hear the tension in his voice.

She had turned away, but, on his approach, murmured words of greeting so softly he could barely make them out. She did not lift her eyes to his face. Was it embarrassment or dislike that made her so uncharacteristically shy? He was swept with a longing to take her into his arms. But instead he said, "Have you been in Derbyshire long?"

"Only three days, sir."

He struggled for something to say. "How you been away from Longbourn long?"

"We left a fortnight ago."

"I hope your family is in good health."

"Very good health, I thank you."

"And how long will you be staying?"

"A few days more." Her lips twitched.

"Your family, are they well?"

"Quite well." Now she was laughing behind her eyes at him.

He was making a fool of himself. What would she think of him, disheveled from the road and unable to make the most basic polite conversation? She would dislike him as much as ever, of course. Surely he could think of something intelligible to say, but it seemed that every thought had fled his mind at the sight of her. Mortified, he took his leave of her, then strode toward the house as quickly as his legs would carry him.

WHAT A FAILURE that had been! When he had dreamed of having a second chance with Elizabeth, it had been to show her by every civility in his power that he was a changed man, that her reproofs had not gone unnoticed. Instead, he had made himself look ridiculous in front of Elizabeth, acting like a besotted idiot who could not manage even the most inconsequential of conversations. The more he wished for her good opinion, it seemed, the more elusive it became.

He would not stand for it. He was Fitzwilliam Darcy, the Master of Pemberley, not a foolish boy mooning after a dairy maid. If he wanted to change her opinion of him, he would do so. He called sharply for a manservant, wishing he had not left his valet with his baggage.

A quarter hour later, he was dressed in clean clothes with boots that shone. He had not taken the time to be shaved; he did not know when Elizabeth planned to leave, and he was determined not to miss her. A footman was able to provide the requisite information, that the gardener was taking the party of visitors on the accustomed circuit of the park. Donning his hat and gloves, Darcy set forth, ready to conquer dragons, or at least to make polite conversation with the one woman he could not forget.

The usual path took visitors along a ridge and down to the river in such a manner that the best vistas were revealed to them. Darcy set out from the far end of it toward the beginning, an oddly disorienting experience. It was as if he were walking backwards, seeing the familiar trees and rocks from a new perspective, but he had no interest in the scenery, apart from that which included Elizabeth.

After the better part of a mile, he caught sight of Elizabeth and her party past a curve in the stream. His heart began to pound. He would have to make this appear to be a casual meeting, as if by accident. No, that was ridiculous. Why would Elizabeth believe that, immediately on his return to Pemberley after a long trip, he would suddenly have the impulse to take a walk in the woods? She would know it was deliberate, but there was nothing to be done for it.

And then, before he could ready himself, she was before him, as lovely and enchanting as ever. She fit as perfectly on the familiar path as he had always known she would. It was fortunate that he had already planned his first words, otherwise he would once again be reduced to a stammering fool. Instead, he managed a pretense of calm. "Miss Bennet, I hope your walk has been a pleasant one."

She lifted her chin slightly, but smiled. "How could it be otherwise? The park here is so delightful, the views charming." She stopped abruptly then, as if in confusion, and a blush once again bloomed on her cheeks.

Surely she could not think he would resent praise of Pemberley from her! "I am glad to hear it. The park has been the work of several generations." He noticed the lady and gentleman slightly behind her. He did not recognize them from his visit to Hertfordshire, and the cut of their clothing spoke of London rather than the countryside. "Will you do me the honour of introducing me to your friends?"

Her fine eyes widened slightly, then the corners of her mouth twitched. "Mr. Darcy, may I present to you Mr. and Mrs. Gardiner? Mr. Gardiner is my uncle who resides in Cheapside. This, as I am sure you must have guessed, is Mr. Darcy."

"I am honored," he murmured automatically with a polite bow, but in truth he was stunned. *These* were her aunt and uncle from Cheapside? He had assumed all of her relations were as uncouth as her mother, but this couple was fashionably and appropriately attired, and their manners, as they accepted the introduction, were impeccable. "I hope you are enjoying your visit to Pemberley."

"Indeed we are," said Mr. Gardiner heartily. "My wife has praised the beauty of Pemberley to me many times, and now that I have seen the original, I can say with certainty that she has not exaggerated."

Darcy turned to Mrs. Gardiner. "This is not your first visit to Derbyshire, then?"

Mrs. Gardiner smiled. "No, indeed. I was raised not far from here, in Lambton."

"In Lambton?" Darcy cursed himself for allowing his surprise to show. She seemed too fashionable to be from a small market town. "Then you must know the area well."

"Yes, and it is a great joy to revisit the sites of my past pleasures."

Mr. Gardiner said, "Your man has been telling me what a fine trout stream you have here."

Darcy seized on the topic. "Are you a fisherman? Then you must fish here as often as you wish while you are in the neighbourhood. I will supply you with any tackle you may need, of course. Will you allow me to show you the parts of the stream where there is the most sport?" Darcy was grateful to have found such a safe topic of discussion.

"You are very generous, Mr. Darcy," said Mr. Gardiner as they began to walk, the two ladies in front, the two gentlemen behind.

Darcy could only half attend to his conversation with Mr. Gardiner, not because his discourse lacked interest, but because of the lovely distraction in front of him. He had not forgotten for a moment her light and graceful walk or the way her hands fluttered when she conversed. As they rounded a turning in the path, the sun shone ahead of her, outlining the delicious lines of her legs through the translucent fabric of her skirt. Darcy swallowed hard and tried to focus his mind on trout lest he find himself in an embarrassing condition, but it was impossible to tear his eyes away from the entrancing sight.

ALMOST AN HOUR later, Elizabeth watched Mr. Darcy walk toward the house slowly, as if deep in thought, as the carriage began to pull away, unsure whether she was glad or sorry to be leaving his disconcerting presence. She barely noticed when her aunt and uncle exchanged a significant glance.

Mr. Gardiner cleared his throat. "I must admit that I found Mr. Darcy infinitely superior to anything I had expected. He is perfectly well behaved, polite and unassuming."

"There is something a little stately in him to be sure, but it is confined to his air, and is not unbecoming. I can now say with the housekeeper, that though some people may call him proud, *I* have seen nothing of it," replied Mrs. Gardiner pointedly.

Her husband nodded his agreement. "I was never surprised than by his behavior to us. It was more than civil; it was really attentive, and there was no necessity for such attention. His acquaintance with Lizzy was very trifling." His tone suggested this was more of a question than a statement, and he cocked an eye at her.

Elizabeth fidgeted uncomfortably with the ribbons of her bonnet. She had never mentioned meeting Mr. Darcy in Kent to them, which must make his behavior even more inexplicable. Still, how could she tell them about furthering her acquaintance with him without mention of how they had parted?

When she said nothing, Mrs. Gardiner made another sally. "To be sure, he is not so handsome as Wickham, though his features are perfectly good. But how came you to tell us he was so disagreeable?"

"He… I do not know. I have never seen him so pleasant as this morning." And she had never expected to feel hot and cold all over, as if the ground was unsteady, merely from being in his presence.

"From what we have seen, I really should not have thought that he could have behaved in so cruel a way as he has done by poor Wickham. He has not an ill-natured look. On the contrary, there is something pleasing about his mouth when he speaks. And there is something of dignity in his countenance, that would not give one an unfavourable idea of his heart." Mrs. Gardiner emphasized her last word.

Elizabeth's cheeks grew warm. Why did her aunt have to be so perceptive? "The last time I saw Mr. Wickham, he said he had perhaps been overharsh in his description of Mr. Darcy. Apparently Mr. Darcy did not ignore his father's will, but instead gave Mr. Wickham a large sum in lieu of the living."

Mrs. Gardiner frowned. "Why would Mr. Wickham have told such a tale? He seemed so amiable, but perhaps the housekeeper's description of him was more accurate than I had thought. But how did he come to make such a confession to you?"

"I do not know what to believe anymore!" Elizabeth exclaimed in frustration. "I have no answers to your questions." Except that there was no possibility she could ever see him without remembering his words of ardent love at Hunsford. Knowing that his enigmatic smile bespoke passion rather than criticism had changed everything between them forever.

Her uncle frowned, and Elizabeth knew that while nothing more might be said at this juncture, the subject was not closed.

Her thoughts seemed to race in circles. Mr. Darcy had indeed been civil beyond any expectation. She had been astonished at his desire to introduce her to his sister, but after that, the remainder of their walk had passed in silence. Elizabeth usually prided herself on her ability to maintain a conversation with almost anyone, but in this case she had been tongue-tied by the awareness that the man by her side had not so long ago confessed to being violently in love with her. That evening in Hunsford had changed everything, making it impossible for her to be indifferent toward him, impossible for her to overlook his physical presence? Now she found herself unable to maintain the same feelings of anger toward him, and was disturbed by the extent to which she had found herself longing for him to… she did not even know what she longed for, and that disturbed her even more.

ELIZABETH AND THE Gardiners had only just dressed for dinner on the following day when the sound of a carriage drew them to a window, and they saw a gentleman and lady in a curricle, driving up the street. Mrs. Gardiner said, "Is that not the Darcy livery? Yes, yes, I can see now that it is, and Mr. Darcy himself is driving! I wonder what would bring him to Lambton?"

Elizabeth, with no small degree of embarrassment, said, "When I was walking with Mr. Darcy yesterday, he asked my permission to introduce his sister to me. I had not expected he would bring her today. She must have only just arrived."

"He wishes you to meet his sister? Why, that is quite an honour!" Mrs. Gardiner exchanged a look with her husband. "He must think very highly of you."

Mr. Gardiner seemed to be studying his niece's expression. "Indeed he must."

Elizabeth blushed. The perturbation of her feelings was every moment increasing. She was quite amazed at her own discomposure. She could give no reason why it was important to her for his sister to think well of her, but it was, and amongst other causes of disquiet, she dreaded lest the partiality of the brother should have said too much in her favour. More than commonly anxious to please, she naturally suspected that every power of pleasing would fail her.

She retreated from the window, fearful of being seen; and as she walked up and down the room, endeavouring to compose herself, saw such looks of enquiry in her uncle and aunt as made every thing worse. This could only confirm their suspicions.

Miss Darcy and her brother appeared, and the formidable introduction took place. With astonishment did Elizabeth see that her new acquaintance was at least as much embarrassed as herself. Since being at Lambton, she had heard that Miss Darcy was exceedingly proud; but the observation of a very few minutes convinced her that she was only exceedingly shy. She found it difficult to obtain even a word from her beyond a monosyllable.

No matter how much Elizabeth tried to put Mr. Darcy's words from Hunsford out of her mind, they kept coming back to her. When he would turn his dark eyes on her with the half-smile she had once thought to be derisive and now knew to be admiration of her person, she felt hot all over and as if everyone present must be able to hear the echo of his voice saying, "You must allow me to tell you how ardently I admire and love you."

Elizabeth's perturbation grew when Miss Darcy hesitantly invited her party to call at Pemberley the very next day. A girl so shy could not possibly wish for the company of near-strangers, so the invitation must be the work of her brother, and she was determined to match his civility.

Later, in an attempt to unravel the mystery of Mr. Darcy, Elizabeth asked one of the maids at the inn about him. "Oh, miss, he is a handsome gentleman, is he not?" the girl exclaimed. "Terrible proud, they say, but who wouldn't be?"

"Sometimes gentlemen of such pride are not the best landlords." Elizabeth watched the maid's reaction closely.

"Oh, no, miss, they say he's a generous landlord to his tenants. They'll hear no ill of him, and sure the cottages on the estate are well-tended and no one goes hungry. Many a soul wishes they could be at Pemberley, either as tenant or servant."

"Would you work at Pemberley if you could?"

"Oh, aye, miss! The pay is terrible good." The girl lowered her voice. "He don't mistreat his maidservants, if you know what I mean, nor does he allow anyone else to. Funny gentleman he is that way, but at least the girls don't fear him. He expects good service, though, mind you. Sends the lazy ones packing, but that don't happen much. Nobody wants to lose their position at Pemberley."

So the housekeeper had been correct in that much. Apparently Mr. Darcy could be generous, at least to those who knew their place. She had never heard complaints from the servants at Netherfield about him, beyond that he was fastidious.

It did not answer the question of what Mr. Darcy wanted from her. Did he think that with due reflection she would have realized the advantages of marrying him outweighed her dislike? Or that he could change her mind by appearing to soften his manners until he had her consent? Perhaps it was some mysterious purpose of his own. His character had never been clear to her. If she had only read his letter, she might have some clue as to what he desired from her. Unfortunately, the only thing more mysterious than that was the question of what *she* desired from *him*.

THE PROSPECT OF seeing Mr. Darcy again the next day filled Elizabeth with an odd combination of anticipation and dread. The ladies' visit to Pemberley began auspiciously enough while the gentlemen were off fishing. On their return, Mr. Darcy chose to seat himself in the chair next to Elizabeth, earning her a glare from Miss Bingley. Fortunately, the Gardiners were both excellent conversationalists and well-mannered enough to ignore the occasional barb from Miss Bingley, although by the time tea was served, Elizabeth had counted at least three occasions when that lady had managed to work Cheapside into the conversation. Mr. Darcy at first seemed oblivious to it, but after one particularly egregious remark about the quality of people in trade, he leaned toward her and said in a voice just above a whisper, "I apologize for Miss Bingley's lack of civility. I am sure her brother will speak to her later about it. I hope you know that both you and your family are very welcome here."

His nearness and the warmth of his breath sent a shiver through Elizabeth, but she was unable to resist the urge to tease. "You do not, then, worry that my aunt and uncle will pollute the shades of Pemberley?"

The corners of his lips twitched upwards. "Hardly. My only fear is that Mr. Gardiner may deplete the entirety of Derbyshire of its population of fish. He is a most accomplished fisherman."

"A pity he is wasted in *Cheapside*, then," she said archly.

"No doubt that accounts for fishermen's complaints of decreasing catches in the Thames." He gave her a warm smile that set her heart beating a little harder. Even she could recognize that look indicated something beyond platonic friendship.

Apparently she was not the only one to notice it, as Miss Bingley raised her voice to say, "Miss Bennet, I hear that the militia has left Meryton. I am sure that is a particular loss to *your* family."

"We are managing to survive tolerably in their absence,"

Elizabeth said civilly, aware that Mr. Darcy had stiffened at Miss Bingley's words. He would not have forgotten their disagreement over Mr. Wickham.

"And what of your particular favourite, Miss Bennet? His name escapes me." Miss Bingley smiled like a predator awaiting its prey.

Elizabeth was tempted to avoid the question, but the increasingly stormy look on Mr. Darcy's face brought out her contrary side. She would not allow him to intimidate her, and after all, there was nothing wrong with enjoying the company of a man her host disliked. She would not blush for her behaviour! "Are you referring, perhaps, to Mr. Wickham? He seemed in good health when I last saw him. He is at present enjoying the pleasures of Brighton, where the regiment is now stationed."

Miss Bingley shot a triumphant glance at Mr. Darcy, but he did not seem to notice. If Elizabeth had not seen the whiteness of his knuckles as he clenched the arms of his elaborately brocaded chair, she would not have known anything was amiss. He did not look at her, either. She followed his glance to his sister.

Miss Darcy's face had paled and her expression was pained. Elizabeth wondered if she might be ill, but it did not seem her place to say anything.

Miss Bingley said, "Brighton is indeed a lively place where one might find all sorts of entertainment." Her tone suggested that those pleasures were somehow disreputable.

"Since the Prince Regent is particularly fond of Brighton, I assume it must have its attractions," Elizabeth said equably.

Miss Bingley's lip curled up. "I suppose the sea is pleasant enough there, but for myself, I prefer seaside resorts with a certain particular charm, ones where you might find a higher quality of visitors, such as Lyme Regis or Ramsgate. Miss Darcy, did you not summer in Ramsgate last year? Did you enjoy it?" Miss Bingley's voice became honeyed as soon as she addressed Mr. Darcy's sister.

"I... it is a pleasant sort of town," said Miss Darcy in a voice just above a whisper. She looked positively white now.

"I have heard the promenade there is particularly lovely," Miss Bingley said warmly. "Did you walk there often?"

Miss Darcy swallowed audibly. "Yes, when the weather was fair." She cast a pleading look at her brother, then rose to her feet shakily. "I pray you excuse me. I am not well." Before the gentlemen could stand, she bolted from the room.

Miss Bingley made to follow her. "Poor Georgiana! I will go to her and see to her comfort."

Mr. Darcy responded in a clipped voice. "I am sure she would prefer that we all remain here." He rang the bell, and when a footman appeared, he said, "Miss Darcy is unwell. Please ask Mrs. Reynolds to attend to her."

Elizabeth wondered at his expectation that the housekeeper would see to his sister's comfort rather than her maid, but perhaps it was one of those vagaries of powerful men who expected everyone to jump to their bidding.

The mention of Mr. Wickham had clearly achieved what Miss Bingley had hoped. Mr. Darcy was now paying no attention whatsoever to Elizabeth, and instead addressed himself to the Gardiners. "I discovered today that Mr. Gardiner is an excellent angler. Do you often have the opportunity to practice the sport, sir?"

"Whenever I am able, which is not as often as I would wish," Mr. Gardiner said. "This morning was a pleasant treat."

Mrs. Gardiner gave a light laugh. "My husband would gladly fish every day, had he the chance. It is fortunately that we live in town where there are few opportunities, or I might never see him at all!"

"I could never tear myself away from you for long, my dear," Mr. Gardiner said gallantly, taking her hand and bestowing a gentlemanly kiss on it.

Elizabeth saw Miss Bingley's sneer and the glance she exchanged with Mrs. Hurst. What did they know of true affection? At least Mr. Darcy did not seem to sneer. She sneaked a glance at him, only to find his eyes fixed on her, his visage stony. He looked so angry that she almost flinched.

Seeing her attention to him, he said *sotto voce*, "Please do not *ever* mention that man's name in front of my sister." While his request had a superficial politeness, the deep anger behind it was evident.

Elizabeth swallowed hard, taken by surprise. After his civility of the last two days, she had almost forgotten how ill-tempered he could be. She would not allow him intimidate her, even if she was his guest. Meeting his eyes steadily, she said, "I will not avoid speaking any name merely to satisfy you. Perhaps it is best that I not be in company with your sister again." She did not need to add *or with you.*

His eyes flashed. "Then *I* shall not trouble you again, but merely ask that you not take out your anger with me upon my sister, who is innocent of my sins." He did not wait for a reply, but stood and crossed to the window where he looked out, ignoring the conversation at hand.

Mrs. Gardiner looked questioningly at Elizabeth, who shrugged her shoulders. Once again Mr. Darcy had managed to mystify her. So much for her vaunted understanding of others! But she regretted having caused him pain; once again, as at Hunsford, she had allowed her anger to overtake her common courtesy. The incivility had started with him, it was true, but she had a choice in how to respond to it. She wished she had made a joke of it, as she had so many of the other odd things Mr. Darcy had said during the course of their acquaintance - an acquaintance that was almost certainly at an end now. To her surprise, she felt a pang of distress. She wondered why he thought his sister would be disturbed by mention of Mr. Wickham. Had her sudden illness in fact been distress over Elizabeth's words?

The conversation had moved to Mrs. Gardiner's childhood in Lambton. In an effort to diffuse the tension between her and the master of the house, Elizabeth asked her aunt if there had been much change to the area since that time.

"It is much as I remember it. The changes have been mostly in my eyes; the houses seem smaller, the streets quieter."

"Except for this one, I am sure," Mr. Gardiner said jovially. "This house could never seem small."

"No, indeed, Pemberley is quite as grand as I remember it," his wife agreed. "though the grounds were somewhat different then. I recall formal gardens surrounding much of the house, with promenades between them. I must confess that I find the current arrangement more pleasing and natural. One would hardly know there had ever been anything apart from parkland here."

Mr. Bingley smiled. "When I first came here, it was more a mixture of natural plantings and formal designs."

Miss Bingley said, "Mr. Darcy did much of the design work himself."

Elizabeth saw her chance. "It is lovely. I have rarely seen a house so well situated to its surroundings. I find it hard to imagine anything more perfect."

Darcy turned slowly, as if he were in discomfort, until he faced her. "All things change, Miss Bennet. We can only hope that they change for the better. But Miss Bingley gives me too much credit; it was my mother's idea to develop a more naturalistic setting. She found formal gardens old-fashioned and stifling. The current park has been the work of many years, but elements of the original remain. The rose garden you saw when you first visited, the rock garden, and the maze have been here for generations."

Miss Bingley said, "The maze is one of the largest in this part of England, is it not?"

Mr. Darcy's lips tightened in response to this blatant attempt at flattery. "I cannot say. I know only that it is large enough that I lost my way there more than once as a child. I am not over fond of mazes, but it is part of the heritage of Pemberley."

Miss Bingley hastened to assure him that she also did not enjoy mazes, but Darcy was not looking at her. Elizabeth was all too aware that his eyes were fixed on her, his expression incomprehensible but fierce. "Miss Bennet, did you take the opportunity to walk through the maze on your tour of the park?"

She wondered why he was deliberately addressing her, given his obvious discomfort. "I am sorry to say I did not. I have a partiality for woodland walks, and there were enough lovely ones here to keep us well entertained. But I saw it from the outside and it seemed very... well-tended." She was not often at a loss for words, but what was there to say about a maze she had not been through? Why did he care?

Miss Bingley hastened to interpose herself. "Ah, yes, Miss Bennet. I had forgotten you are a *great walker*, even when the ground is muddy and *other* ladies might remain inside."

Elizabeth counseled herself not to lose patience. "Indeed, and when my sister lay ill at Netherfield, it would have taken far more than mud to keep me from her side."

Mrs. Gardiner seemed to sense the tension in the room, and without understanding the cause, applied her well-bred skills to the occasion by launching into a lively description of the gardens they had seen at Blenheim and Chawton, and of Capability Brown and his astonishing transformations of parkland. Mr. Gardiner added some observations of his own, and the conversation proceeded without further difficulty until Mrs. Gardiner, to Elizabeth's great relief, announced that it was time for them to return to Lambton.

Mr. Darcy and Mr. Bingley volunteered to see them to their carriage, but the former insisted on a detour to the library to show Mr. Gardiner a rare tome on the subject of fish of Northern England. It took him several minutes to locate the particular volume he sought. Elizabeth hung back by the door, watching Mr. Darcy's elegant hands turning the pages, her spirits still low from their disagreement. But after a minute, Mr. Darcy left Mr. Bingley with the Gardiners to examine the remainder of the book. Elizabeth caught her breath when she realized he was taking purposeful strides in her direction. But that was nothing to the surprise she felt when he took her by the arm in a forceful movement and drew her into the anteroom.

She was sufficiently shocked by this uncharacteristic behaviour that she knew not what to say. Once she had seen his grim expression, she was glad to maintain her silence.

Darcy spoke in low tone, his face near her ear. "I must know. Did Mrs. Collins give you my letter?"

Elizabeth swallowed hard. "She did."

"You did not believe what I had written." He sounded half-savage.

"I did not *read* what you had written. I burnt it."

"You burnt it?" His voice dripped ice.

"It is not proper for an unmarried lady to read a letter from a single gentleman." Good heavens, she sounded as prim as Mary.

"So you went back to Meryton completely ignorant of Wickham's misdeeds? He cannot be trusted! If he harmed you in any way, I will kill him, I swear it."

Elizabeth could not help being amused by his similarity to Mr. Wickham at that moment. "He did nothing to me. He was a perfect gentleman."

Darcy drew in a deep breath, clearly fighting for control. "You do not know what he is capable of."

Her temper flared. "What I do not know is why you persist in slandering him. Was not refusing him the living he was promised enough?"

"Is that what he told you? I do not suppose he thought to mention that three years earlier, he had told me he had no intention of taking orders, or that I gave him three thousand pounds in lieu of the preferment - money that he squandered before returning to me and demanding the living he had been promised."

Elizabeth could not believe her ears. It was consistent with the story Mr. Wickham had told her at their last meeting, but three thousand pounds? That was a fortune. Otherwise, the two stories matched, but what proof did she have from either of them? "I do not know what to say."

He drew even closer and said in a fierce near whisper, "I suppose he also did not tell you about how he imposed himself upon my sister last summer and convinced her to believe herself in love with him and to agree to an elopement, when his only object was her dowry of thirty thousand pounds? His plans were foiled by the merest chance."

Now she was truly shocked. "I am grieved to hear it. But is it not possible that he cared for her?"

Darcy's mouth twisted. "He cared enough to orchestrate his meeting with her and to arrange to be rid of her chaperone. She was then but fifteen years of age, and he almost twice that. When I confronted him, he made no pretense of affection for her. He wanted her fortune, and the chance to revenge himself on me was an added incentive. If he had succeeded, his revenge would have been complete indeed. And *this* is the man you chose to believe over me. You would have learned that months ago if you had read my letter."

Elizabeth turned her face away, unable to look into those fierce dark eyes any longer. She wanted to believe it was untrue, but Mr. Darcy would never make up such a story about his own sister, and

Miss Darcy's reaction that very afternoon was confirmation of his words. How could she have misjudged the situation so badly and blindly believed Mr. Wickham's story? She, who prided herself on her discernment, had shown absolutely none. To think that she had thought herself half in love with Mr. Wickham! Nausea twisted her stomach as she realized how easily he might have taken advantage of her. And today, out of her ignorance, she had foolishly injured an innocent girl's sensibilities.

Stricken, she covered her eyes with her hand. "I am so very sorry. Please give Miss Darcy my deepest apologies for my thoughtless words." She was horrified to discover her voice was trembling as she tried desperately to hold back tears.

The tight grip on her elbow eased and was replaced by gentle touch on her shoulder. He said softly, "Please, you must not blame yourself. He is a master at manipulation."

His sudden tenderness was her undoing. She bowed her head as a silent sob tore through her. "I have been such a fool. How you must despise me!"

"No, never that." His voice was just a whisper now as he stroked her shoulder. "Never while I live, Elizabeth." Then his arms enfolded her, holding her close.

As tears burned her eyes, she leaned her face into his shoulder. The circle of his arms seemed her only haven in a world turned upside down. His firm lips pressed against her forehead felt like a promise, and the warmth of his breath brushed her ear as he murmured, "My dearest, loveliest Elizabeth. Do not cry, my love; all will be well."

At first his words barely registered, only his comforting tone, but slowly his whispered intimacies sank in. She tilted her head back to look at him, unable to comprehend how he could say such things after all she had done to him. But his dark eyes held no anger now, only a different sort of fire.

A sense of pressure built within her, as the heat of his body against hers seemed to churn her very lifeblood into a torrent. His hand cradled her cheek, sending a shock of sensation through her that left her knees weak. His lips silently formed the syllables of her name. Half-mesmerized, Elizabeth could but watch as his head descended toward her. Then his lips were brushing her own aching ones, and she forgot to breathe as powerful sensation raced through her.

A sharp cough broke the spell. Darcy abruptly pulled away, stepping in front of her as if to mask her presence with his body, but not before Elizabeth saw Mrs. Gardiner's stunned expression.

"Ah, there you are, Mr. Darcy," her aunt said loudly, moving to block the doorway. "Have you seen Elizabeth?" Her hands made shooing movements in Elizabeth's direction.

Elizabeth stumbled slightly, her cheeks burning, then hastened to follow her aunt's silent directive by slipping into the passageway. She heard Mr. Darcy's voice behind her, his voice less than steady. "Perhaps Miss Bennet has returned to the drawing room."

She hurried in the direction he suggested, swiftly drying the remnants of her tears. Hopefully the afternoon light would be dim enough to hide the redness of her eyes. Fortunately, the drawing room was now empty; she did not think she could have faced Miss Bingley at that moment. As she heard voices approaching, she pretended interest in a porcelain figurine on the mantelpiece. Elizabeth knew she should attempt to show some animation, but she felt as frozen as if she were the one made from porcelain.

Mrs. Gardiner engaged Mr. Bingley in a lively discussion of the latest plays at Covent Garden, giving Elizabeth time to recover her composure. Darcy seemed to be paying no attention to her at all, offering every courtesy to her aunt and uncle. She braved a quick glance at him, but she could ascertain nothing from his expression. With some amusement she realized that a man of such pride must be at least as mortified as she was, not least because her aunt was protecting his good name. She did not believe he had planned to kiss her - it was quite out of character for a man so controlled – but it did answer the question of whether he retained tender feelings for her. The question was what she wished to do about it.

He did not address her directly until he offered his arm to walk her to the carriage. Resting her hand on his sleeve suddenly seemed a much more intimate thing, especially with the feelings his kiss had awoken in her still alive within her. In the dimness of the hallway he bent his head towards hers. His warm breath intimate against her ear, he said softly, "I must speak with you. May I call on you tomorrow?"

Despite her confusion about him, her treacherous body responded instantly to his words, reliving the feeling of being in his arms. "If you wish." It was a struggle to say even that much.

He chuckled softly. "Oh, I wish, Miss Bennet. I certainly wish."

They emerged onto the portico and there was no time to say more. He bade her a formal good day as he handed her into the carriage, but his eyes spoke volumes, and then only to wish her a good evening, and for just a shadow of a moment, she felt his fingers tighten on her hand.

The carriage was barely out of sight of the house when Mrs. Gardiner said, "Well, Lizzy, I believe it is time for you to tell us more about your Mr. Darcy."

Chapter 6

AN EXULTANT DARCY watched the carriage disappear behind the trees. Elizabeth had kissed him and agreed to receive him tomorrow, even though he decidedly did not deserve it after his idiotic loss of control. What was it about Elizabeth Bennet that brought his normally sanguine temper to a boiling point within minutes? He could not believe he had grabbed her arm, hard enough that he later saw her rubbing it absently. If that had not been enough, he had taken advantage of her distress. She would have been within her rights to think him a complete brute and a seducer to boot. He would have to begin tomorrow's call with an apology. God, but tomorrow seemed a long time away!

He had not realized that the sight of Elizabeth in tears would undo him to such an extent. Yes, he had first put his arms around her to offer her comfort, but that noble sentiment disappeared almost as soon as he felt her soft form against him, the fodder of so many of his fantasies. Her scent of lavender had made his head swim, and he had hardly realized what he was saying to her as long as she permitted him to explore her forehead and hair with his lips. And then she had looked at him with those fine eyes, and he was completely lost to reason. If Mrs. Gardiner had not interrupted them, he was not sure he would have been able to stop with a relatively chaste kiss, not when his body ached for her with a passion beyond any he had ever known. And Elizabeth had allowed him to kiss her.

He knew he should be castigating himself for his behavior, but it seemed beyond his ability. His only regret was disappointment that Mrs. Gardiner had hidden their indiscretion. Why could she not have done what any other woman in her position would have? If she had allowed her husband or even Bingley to see them, there would have been no choice in the matter, and he would be engaged to Elizabeth at this very moment. He would have the right to hold her in his arms and to beg her forgiveness for his outrageous behavior.

"Darcy? I say, Darcy!" Bingley jostled his elbow. "Are you planning to stand out here all night? My sisters will be waiting for us."

Darcy shook his head. "Please give them my regrets. I must check on Georgiana. I will join you at dinnertime." The prospect of an evening in the company of the Bingley sisters had no appeal, especially in comparison to the opportunity to dwell on the memory of Elizabeth in his arms.

ELIZABETH DECLINED TO join her aunt and uncle on their calls the following morning. She did not know when Mr. Darcy planned to call, but she did not wish him to find her absent. Her thoughts regarding him were agitated. When would he come? What would he say? And most importantly, what answer would she give him? Her aunt had given her to understand that after her behavior the previous day, there was only one answer that she could give. Instead of rebelling against the idea, Elizabeth found a strange contentment in it. Mr. Darcy still puzzled her, but she was certain now that she wished to understand him better.

There was a light tap on the door and one of the barmaids entered and bobbed a curtsey. Ever since Mr. Darcy had called on Elizabeth at the inn, the staff there had treated her and the Gardiners with an almost excessive degree of attention. Yesterday it had amused Elizabeth, but today nothing could amuse her.

"Miss Bennet, if you please, there are letters for you," the girl said.

Elizabeth took the two envelopes and was happy to see Jane's familiar script on both of them. One had been missent; hardly a surprise since Jane had written the direction so ill, which was unlike her. She must have had to rush to get it ready for the post. Elizabeth turned them over in her hand, thinking of her dearest Jane and how much she missed her. How she would have loved to talk to her at this very moment! Jane would have known the right thing to say to make her feel more certain of herself. But for today, she would have to be grateful to have a letter from her.

She handed the barmaid a coin, then crossed to the window seat where the light was better and opened the first letter.

IT HAD TAKEN longer for Darcy to leave Pemberley than he had expected. First he found himself taking unusual care with his appearance. Then he stopped to check on Georgiana who required repeated assurances on his part that no one would have suspected anything based on her hasty departure the previous afternoon.

The sun was already well into the sky by the time he mounted his stallion and set off toward Lambton. He was too impatient to follow the winding road, so he set off across the broad moorland at a trot. Soon he would see Elizabeth.

He paused at the top of a hill to get his bearings, then wheeled his horse to the right toward the London road. In the distance he could see an open carriage travelling down it at an almost recklessly fast pace. Someone must be in quite a rush. He set a course parallel to the road on the other side of the stream to avoid being covered with dust when the carriage barrelled past him.

The carriage was almost upon him when something caught his eye. It was Mr. and Mrs. Gardiner, conversing in an urgent manner, while the figure across from them could be no one but Elizabeth. He caught a glimpse of her dark hair, but her face was lowered into a handkerchief. She appeared to be crying.

The knowledge of why she must be crying struck him like a bullet. He had been deceiving himself. She had not wanted to see him today, but had said the only thing she could to escape from his company. Her civility was nothing more than that; her opinion of him had not changed since the night of his disastrous proposal. And now he had made it worse, behaving like a savage, first in his reaction to what she said about Wickham, damn his eyes, and then again outside the library. She would never forgive him, even if she acquitted him of cruelty to Wickham.

He had distressed her even more than he had in the past, and now she was fleeing his very environs. He reined in his horse and watched the back of the coach disappear down the road towards London. His heart felt as if it was pounding out of his chest, loud enough that anyone within a mile would hear it.

For a moment he considered pursuing them, but that would be folly. She was obviously desperate to avoid him, and what could he possibly say to her in front of her aunt and uncle that would make any difference? It was too late. The damage was done, and Elizabeth was gone. There would be no more second chances.

Slowly he turned back toward Pemberley, but now he let the horse meander at a walk. He was in no hurry to return and to face his guests, to pretend that his heart had not been ripped out of his chest. There was no rush; he had his entire life ahead of him to regret his errors and to learn to live without the woman he loved.

"I HAVE BEEN thinking it over again, Elizabeth," said her uncle as they drove from the town, his voice raised to be heard over the pounding of hoofbeats and the rattling of the carriage wheels, "and really, upon serious consideration, I am inclined to judge that you did not do Mr. Darcy enough credit. He did not strike me as the sort of man to flee from a bit of scandal. He should be given a chance to decide for himself whether to continue the acquaintance under the circumstances; and after his behavior yesterday, he does have a certain responsibility toward you, whether he likes it or not."

Elizabeth shook her head miserably. "If Lydia had run off with any other man, I might have agreed to discuss it with him; but Mr. Darcy detests Wickham and everything he stands for. He would never agree to ally himself to our family now, even were Lydia and Wickham to marry, an outcome which I think very unlikely. Wickham will use her and abandon her; my family will be shamed and ostracized; and I will not drag Mr. Darcy into it."

"You think his affection for you is so shallow and transient as that?" her aunt asked. "I cannot think so myself."

"I do not doubt his sentiments, but there is only so much that sentiment can overcome."

Mr. Gardiner said, "Perhaps once we reach Longbourn, I will write to him and explain the circumstances. Then he can make his own choice in the matter."

Tears filled Elizabeth's eyes once more. "Please, promise me that you will do no such thing. He will find out soon enough about our disgrace, and I simply cannot bear the thought…" But at that point sobs overtook her and she could say no more. She buried her face in her handkerchief as her aunt and uncle exchanged concerned glances.

DARCY DID NOT know how he maintained a civil demeanour during the next fortnight. He did his best to behave in his usual manner. He spoke gently with Georgiana, avoided the worst of Miss Bingley's sycophantic compliments, played billiards and fished with Bingley, and went through all the motions of being the Master of Pemberley. But that was all on the surface, covering a vast sea of emptiness inside.

Through the goodness of heaven, he had been given a second chance with Elizabeth Bennet, a chance to prove to her that he was worthy of her. He had failed abjectly. No longer could he think that her anger and scorn at Hunsford had been an aberration caused by some misalignment of the stars. He had not learned anything from that episode. No, the truth was that he was a man who by nature hurt the woman he loved, the woman whose opinion he most cared about. All the effort he had put into improving his manners with others had been inadequate when faced with the reality of the emotions Elizabeth Bennet released in him. Now she was gone forever.

It was as if the world conspired to remind him of his failings. At church, the sermon delivered by old Mr. Emmons spoke of humility finding favour in the eyes of God. Pride goeth before a fall. He had learned that lesson quite well, thank you, and there was very little he felt proud of in himself these days. But, ever in mind of his duty as Master of Pemberley, he kept an attentive expression on his face throughout the service, his back ramrod-straight. Beside him, Georgiana sat with the Book of Common Prayer open in her lap, listening intently as always. She had been subdued since Elizabeth's visit, frequently apologizing to him for things that were not her fault, as if she thought him angry at her.

The interminable service finally ended, although it was no more interminable than anything else these days. As he left the family pew, Darcy nodded to tenants, stopping briefly to speak to Mrs. Brown whose husband had died unexpectedly a few weeks past. He shook the curate's hand and complimented him on his sermon. Outside the church, he waited while a little girl curtsied and gave Georgiana a bouquet of wildflowers. Georgiana, who had always been good with children, spoke courteously with her and thanked her for the lovely flowers.

"Mr. Darcy, sir." A boy, his voice breaking, spoke at his elbow.

Darcy did not recognize him as one of his tenants, but perhaps he had just come through his period of growth which often made children half-unrecognizable. "Yes?"

"I'm Jimmy, from Lambton. I've sommat for you." He fished in his pocket and brought out an envelope, somewhat crumpled and the worse for wear from spending time in a pocket that was not as clean as might be.

Darcy took it automatically, seeing his name written across it in a flowing hand. "Who is this from?"

The boy leaned closer to him, bringing a stink of stables. "From a lady what stayed at the inn there."

A lady at the inn? Elizabeth! Could it be? He had never seen her handwriting, but it looked like a woman's hand. "When was this?" He spoke more sharply than he intended.

"A fortnight ago, mebbe more. I tried to bring it to you, sir, but the footman wouldn't let me in to see you. The lady said I had to give it to your hand only, private like, nobody else. She made me promise, and said I should burn it if I couldn't give it to you." He glanced around surreptitiously.

Darcy, his heart pounding, but conscious of Georgiana's eyes on him, pulled out a handful of shillings and gave them to the boy. It was far more than the service deserved, but he did not care.

The boy's eyes popped as he felt the weight of coin in his hand. "Thank you, sir. Much obliged, Mr. Darcy," he stammered.

Darcy nodded to him absently, still trying to grasp the existence of a letter from Elizabeth. He longed to tear it open and read it, but this was not the time or the place.

As if reading his mind, Georgiana touched his arm lightly. When she had gained his attention, she indicated the area behind him with a move of her head. Glancing over his shoulder, he saw Miss Bingley approaching and stuffed the letter inside his coat. The last thing he needed was to have to explain its existence to Miss Bingley. It was quite bad enough that he had been forced to listen to her barely disguised insults of Elizabeth for the last two weeks. He arranged his features into a polite mask.

Afterwards he could scarcely recall the trip back to Pemberley House. Bingley filled the air with nonsensical talk, but all Darcy could think of was his letter. He could almost imagine he could feel the pressure of it through his waistcoat and shirt. Certainly it felt as if he had something burning hot hidden there.

Once back at the house, there was the necessary delay as they all took refreshment, but as soon as possible, Darcy made his excuses.

Miss Bingley fluttered her eyelashes at him. "Why, Mr. Darcy, it is Sunday, the day of rest. Surely your business can wait?"

"Oh, leave him be," her brother said. "You know there is nothing more aweful than Darcy on a Sunday with nothing to do."

"So I have heard," Darcy said dryly, "on many occasions." But his mind was too full of Elizabeth to invent a clever excuse, so he limited himself to a correct bow and departed. Miss Bingley would fuss at Georgiana and Mr. Bingley, but he could wait no longer. He headed to his study and closed the door.

He sank into the leather chair that had been his father's before him and carefully laid the envelope on his desk. He ran his finger over the letters of his name. Now that he was alone, part of him did not want to discover what was in the letter. It was hard to imagine it being anything pleasant after their last meeting, but Elizabeth was not the sort to berate him in a letter. Besides, what could she say to him that was worse than what he had already said to himself?

With a sharp movement he broke the seal and unfolded it, smoothing the parchment with his hands. It was dated the morning of Elizabeth's departure.

Dear Sir,

It is ironic, is it not, that having refusing to read an illicit missive from you months ago, I now find myself in the position of resorting to the same tool and hoping that you will retain enough respect for me to read this, rather than consigning it to the fire as I did. I will be well served if you refuse, though; it is no more than I deserve, but this is the only means available for me to communicate to you my most sincere apologies for my past follies. I can give no explanation for my gullibility and ready belief in Mr. Wickham's tales when in truth I had no reason whatsoever to take his word over yours, apart from a misplaced faith in my own cleverness. It was inexcusable for me to abuse you to your face with his lies. You may rest assured that I will take this lesson in my own fallibility to heart.

I had intended to tell you this later today, but it was not meant to be. This morning I received letters from my sister with an urgent request for me to return home as soon as possible. I will not trouble you with the dreadful nature of the intelligence the letters bore except to say that it bears witness to the truth of many things you said to which I refused to listen. It will be some time, if ever, before my family recovers from the setback it currently faces, for which I must claim my own not insignificant part of responsibility. Under the circumstances, I doubt we will meet again, which is why I have taken the liberty of writing this letter.

My deepest regrets in this matter are for the way in which I unwittingly upset Miss Darcy yesterday. I was wrong in every way, and she paid the price. I can only hope that, being young, she will recover quickly, but I wish I could do something to remedy my error. Since I cannot, I hope you will share with her any part of the truth that you feel might help, including how foolish I have been.

I am grateful to have had the opportunity to see Pemberley. It is indeed a delightful place, and I wish you much happiness there and elsewhere.

E. Bennet

Darcy read the letter, then, in disbelief, he read it through again. What on earth could Elizabeth feel she needed to apologize for, to apologize to *him* of all people? He was the guilty party. But even beyond that, he was horrified by the degree of distress that came through her words. What could have happened at Longbourn to cause such unhappiness? This must have been why she was crying in the coach. It was nothing to do with him at all. He was swept with a simultaneous wave of relief and a fierce desire to rescue Elizabeth from whatever trouble she faced. He looked back at her words, searching for any hint as to what had occurred, but could see nothing. What had he said that she had refused to listen to, and how could it relate to whatever was happening at Longbourn? Why did she bear responsibility for it? He stared at the letter as if by force of will he could make more words appear on it.

He would not have believed that lively, spirited Elizabeth Bennet was capable of this degree of self-castigation. There was a darkened spot on the paper as well - could it have been a tear? He stroked it lightly with his finger, as if he could somehow offer her comfort thus.

But now she did not expect them to meet again. Did that mean she had no desire to see him? He suspected it did. He had ruined his last chance with her. He looked again at the words she had written. Was this all he would ever have of her? It could not be, but he did not know what to do about it. Why had he not ridden after her coach? He tried to imagine what bad news she might have received. She would have told him about an illness or a death, leaving financial reversals and scandal. Elizabeth had never seemed to value wealth. If she had, she would have accepted his proposal in Hunsford without a second thought. Scandal was more likely, but it would take something quite severe to cause this response.

One thing was for certain. He must do something to relieve her suffering. The question was what he could do.

Chapter 7

DARCY LEANED OVER the billiard table and took a shot. The ball missed the pocket by a good inch, but that was hardly surprising. His mind was not on the game, but on the company. This was his first chance to speak alone with Bingley since receiving Elizabeth's letter. Chalking his cue, he said casually, "Bingley, do you ever think of Jane Bennet?"

Bingley's customary smile faded. "Of course I do. I am not as fickle as that, you know."

"I was not suggesting you were fickle," Darcy said calmly. "However, even the most violent love can fade with time."

"*You* have never been in love, then." Bingley walked around the table, looking at it from various angles, setting up his shot.

Darcy thought darkly that he knew too much of love, but a heart-to-heart discussion was not his plan for the day. "It seems the Bennet family is facing some sort of difficulty."

Bingley straightened, his brows coming together. "What do you mean?"

Darcy chose his words with care. "I have been given to understand that Miss Elizabeth Bennet was in great distress the morning she left. She had earlier received a letter, and something was said about trouble at home and that they might never recover." Darcy did not want to take the risk of mentioning the letter from Elizabeth; it would be far too difficult to explain.

"Is something the matter with Jane?"

"I know nothing more." He attempted to sound disinterested, as if this were not something which had been haunting him. "I did learn one thing from Miss Elizabeth, though. Apparently I was mistaken in thinking Miss Bennet indifferent to you. Miss Elizabeth says her sister's attachment to you was quite strong, but little displayed. It seems she has not been in her usual spirits since you left Netherfield."

The colour left Bingley's face. "Jane cares for me? But she made no effort to show it. Caroline never even received a response to her letter. I do not believe it."

He would have to tell him the truth, mortifying as it might be. "In fact, your sister did receive a response, more than one. Miss Bennet came to London last winter and called upon your sisters there. Caroline even returned her call some weeks later."

Bingley's shot went wild. "What? That cannot be true."

"It is true," Darcy said steadily.

"How do you know this?"

Darcy heaved a sigh. "Caroline confided in me because she knew I opposed the match as well. Mistakenly, I might add."

"And you did not tell me? Do you value my judgement so little?" Bingley's knuckles were white where he gripped the side of the billiard table.

"Bingley, I am telling you this now because I realize I was wrong. I should have told you then." Darcy wondered if their friendship would survive this revelation. Perhaps it depended on what had happened at Longbourn. If the crisis were indeed serious, he did not know that he could forgive himself. In Bingley's shoes, he would be livid.

"You.... I cannot believe you did this to me! You knew how much I cared for her!"

Darcy said nothing, only met his friend's furious eyes.

"And why are you telling me this now?"

Darcy was half-tempted to tell him the truth, that he was revealing this out of his own selfish desire to discover what was happening at Longbourn. He could not go quite that far. "Hearing this news brought it to my mind, and made me realize how much pain I may have caused."

"You say that so calmly, as if it is of no matter!"

His control cracked. "It matters. I understand perfectly if you cannot forgive me. You would be quite justified."

"I... oh, devil take it, Darcy, that is not what I meant. You know that. It is just that I cannot bear to think of my Jane in distress over me. But this is my fault. I should never have left her, never have listened to you and my sisters. She must hate me for abandoning her." He shook his head as if trying to assimilate this new knowledge. "She truly cared?"

"Apparently so, if we are to believe in Miss Elizabeth's knowledge of her sister, and I cannot think why she would fabricate such a story." At least Bingley had not asked him how in the world he had come to speak with Elizabeth about such personal matters. It was fortunate for him that Bingley was such a trusting soul.

"I must find out what the problem is. I cannot leave Jane to face difficulties by herself. Perhaps there is something I could do to help."

It was what Darcy had wished to hear, but he would not tell Bingley that. If Bingley chose to go back to Jane Bennet, it would have to be his own decision. Darcy could not trust himself to advise his friend. He had done such a poor job of it in the past. He wanted the information Bingley could gather, but did not want to take advantage of him.

"I could go back to Netherfield," Bingley continued. "I still hold the lease, and nothing could be more natural than for me to go there. It should be easy enough to find out what the matter is - someone is always willing to talk about the misfortunes of others. But are you sure that she cares about me?"

"I am certain that Miss Elizabeth believes she does, and I think it is unlikely she would be wrong about her sister's sentiments." Darcy wondered how many times he would have to repeat himself on this subject.

"Then I will go to her. I will tell my man to have my bags packed and ready to leave in the morning."

"Your sisters may require longer than that to ready themselves to depart."

"I doubt they will want to come. Caroline hates Netherfield. She only tolerated it because you were there. And she loves being at Pemberley. Can they not remain here? I know it is a burden, but you need not talk to them much if you do not wish."

"They may stay here as long as they choose. It is not a burden at all," Darcy protested automatically, knowing Bingley would not believe him. But Bingley seemed to require another hint. "But you cannot go there by yourself. It would look odd."

Bingley raked his hand through his hair, leaving it standing half on end. "What do I care how it looks?"

"You might not care, but Miss Bennet might take it amiss if you appear out of the blue without family or retinue. You will not help her by adding to gossip."

"She will…. No, you are right, Darcy. I will have to persuade at least Caroline to go with me. Perhaps you could accompany me. Then Caroline will be eager to go."

The idea tempted Darcy more than he cared to admit. He could see Elizabeth, breathe her perfume, and find out for himself what had caused her precipitate departure. But she would not thank him for appearing; that was clear from her letter. It would be wiser to wait until he knew the situation, and then he could decide on his approach. He refused to think about what it would mean if she still wanted to have nothing to do with him. Surreptitiously he touched the pocket where her letter was hidden. He had not been able to bring himself to leave it in the study.

But first he must keep Bingley from making a bad situation worse. "Would it not be simpler to plan it ahead? I know you are anxious to ride to Miss Bennet's rescue, but the sensible thing is to wait."

"I cannot wait if Jane may be suffering!"

"It need not be long. You could begin preparations immediately." Darcy only wished he could make an excuse to go with Bingley. "Will you inform me of what you find?"

"Of course," Bingley said distractedly.

"I will do my best to convince your sisters that a return to Netherfield would be agreeable, though they will still oppose any alliance with Miss Bennet."

Bingley scowled. "No doubt they will, but I was fool enough to listen to them last time about Jane Bennet. I will not make that mistake again, you may be sure of it."

Darcy thought privately that they had both been fools. The image of Elizabeth weeping in the carriage came before him, and he swallowed his longing to fly to her side. This must be done properly if he was to have any chance at all. He took aim at another ball, trying to pretend he cared at all where it might go.

"Darcy." Bingley's voice held an unusual harshness that made Darcy straighten slowly and look at his friend.

"Yes?" he said evenly.

"What else are you hiding from me?"

"About Jane Bennet? Nothing." At least he could say that much honestly.

"Then how do you come to know such a remarkable amount about Miss Elizabeth Bennet's affairs? And for God's sake, tell me the truth this time!"

Darcy stood stock still for a moment. "If you insist," he said slowly. "But it is a very long story, and not a happy one."

BY THE NEXT day, Darcy was re-thinking his advice that Bingley should wait. Patience was not in his friend's personality. He was accustomed to following his whims no matter where they led him, and often enough they had led him into trouble from which Darcy had been forced to extricate him. Now Bingley paced the halls of Pemberley like the proverbial caged tiger.

His sisters had formed a silent conspiracy against him. Miss Bingley said, "I cannot believe you wish to return to that godforsaken place, Charles. There is nothing there for you."

Bingley glared at her. "This is my decision, Caroline, and if I choose to go to Netherfield, I shall go to Netherfield. You may either join me or find somewhere else to live."

Caroline's eyes narrowed, but she managed an ingratiating smile. "You do not mean that. Of course I will go wherever you go, but I question the wisdom of this plan. Mr. Darcy, tell him what a foolish idea this is."

Darcy's lips thinned. "I was the one who suggested it to him. He has leased the estate, and he might as well have use of it. The hunting there is excellent."

"Does that mean you will be joining us there?" Caroline asked with a servile smile.

"No, it does not." Darcy did not leave any room in his manner for debate. "I will be travelling to Rosings to visit Lady Catherine. Georgiana will be accompanying me." It was the one place he was sure Miss Bingley would not try to follow him.

Beside him Georgiana gasped, her face pale. He should have warned her of this, given how much she hated going to Rosings. He would make sure it would be a short visit, but there was no reason to tell Miss Bingley that.

Georgiana plucked at his sleeve timidly. She whispered, "Could I not go to Mr. Bingley's country house instead? I have always wished to see it."

Were he not keeping a stern countenance for Bingley's sake, Darcy would have smiled at the weak excuse. "Would you prefer that, then? I am sure Miss Bingley would invite you." It might reduce her opposition to her brother's plans if she thought she were pleasing Darcy by doing it. At his sister's nod, Darcy raised his voice. "Georgiana tells me she has always longed to see Hertfordshire."

Miss Bingley's face lit up at the opportunity. "Would you like to join us there, Georgiana? If it is agreeable to your brother, that is. He may have other plans for you."

"No, not at all," Darcy said smoothly. "If you would enjoy her company, she is more than welcome to join you. I know I need have no worries if she is in your capable hands." He would no doubt pay for that bit of flattery when Miss Bingley redoubled her efforts to attract his attention, but if it brought her into compliance with her brother's wish to go to Netherfield, it was well worth it. He would sacrifice far more for Elizabeth's sake.

He would speak to Georgiana later. Perhaps there would be a chance for her to spend time with Elizabeth. It would be good for both of them.

IF ONLY SHE had read his letter. If only she had read it. The refrain repeated itself inside Elizabeth's head until she wished she could tear the thought out and free herself from it. If she had read Mr. Darcy's letter in Hunsford, she would have known Wickham to be a scoundrel and not to be trusted. She could have warned her family against him.

Her father would never have allowed Lydia to go to Brighton if he had known she would be in company with such a man. The means to save her family had been right in her hand, and she had burnt it unopened.

She distracted herself as best she could, taking her turns sitting with her mother, listening to Mary's moralizing, and caring for her young cousins. She was grateful for Mrs. Gardiner's continued presence, since her aunt's good sense provided a much needed balm. Walking to Meryton provided an occasional change of pace, though Elizabeth could not say it was always a pleasant one.

She went once with Jane to purchase some ribbons for Kitty, although it was hard to imagine the use of a newly decorated bonnet when none of them were invited anywhere and their neighbours would be embarrassed to be seen by them. Mrs. Long was in the shop when they arrived, and lost no time in asking after "poor Lydia" and exchanging a smirk with the merchant. Jane's smile never faltered, but Elizabeth was hard put to make a pleasant acknowledgment when she knew the intention behind it.

Mrs. Long said, "We all think of her every day and hope for the best, but as you know, Lydia was always a wild girl. I told your mother time and again that she needed to teach her proper manners, but *she* never saw anything wrong with it. I imagine she regrets that now. Is she still taken to her bed?"

"She is improving, thank you," Jane said. "It is kind of you to think of her."

"That horrible Mr. Wickham! Did you know that he is in debt to half the tradesmen in town? Of course, I always knew he was a scoundrel. Why, I told your mother so when I first met him."

Elizabeth said, "Odd, I always thought you were partial to him, but I must have been mistaken."

Mrs. Long lifted her nose. "Have you ever heard anything further of Mr. Bingley, Jane? What a pity it was that he left so suddenly."

Elizabeth had heard her ask this question many times, and she marveled at Jane's ability to handle it with grace. It was hard to think well of neighbours who took such pleasure in Jane's disappointed hopes.

"Mr. Bingley?" Jane repeated steadily. "No, I have not heard from his sister these many months."

"Do you think he has any intention of returning to Netherfield?" Mrs. Long persisted.

"I cannot begin to guess. Lizzy, what think you of this blue ribbon? Would it match Kitty's dress, do you think?"

Elizabeth glared at Mrs. Long, seething. It was times like this when one learned who one's friends truly were. "I think it would be quite perfect."

Chapter 8

JANE'S SPIRITS WERE as low as Elizabeth's, but they each endeavoured to hide their distress behind a mask of cheerfulness. Kitty, never having been particularly troubled by Lydia's elopement, was the first to begin visiting the few friends who would still receive members of the Bennet family in their present scandalous condition. One day she came home from Lucas Lodge with her cheeks bright from running. "You will never guess what Maria Lucas told me!" she cried.

Elizabeth feared the news which so pleased Kitty might be less pleasant to her, but said, "I cannot guess; so I hope you will take mercy on me and tell us."

"The housekeeper at Netherfield has received instructions to prepare the house for the arrival of Mr. Bingley!" she announced triumphantly, with a knowing look at Jane. "He is expected to arrive in a day or two, and will stay several weeks for the shooting."

Jane's face grew white and her hands trembled on her work, but she said in an even voice, "You need not look at me. This news does not affect me with either pain or pleasure. Mr. Bingley is coming to the house that he has legally hired, and that is an end to it. It means nothing else."

Elizabeth was unconvinced, but did not wish to upset her sister any more than this intelligence must have already done. It had been many months since her sister had mentioned Mr. Bingley's name, but she knew Jane had not forgotten him. She had not told Jane about seeing Mr. Bingley at Pemberley for fear that it would distress her, but if that gentleman was coming to Netherfield, he would likely mention their meeting. It would be best to confess first. Once Kitty had left the room, she said, "Did I tell you that I saw Mr. Bingley when I travelled to Derbyshire? He was visiting Mr. Darcy at Pemberley. I had thought he was going to Scarborough next, but he must have changed his plans."

Jane looked at her in surprise, then almost immediately turned away to her work. "No, I had not realized you had seen him." Her needle punctured the fabric with unusual force. "Did he... was he well?"

"We had little opportunity to talk except in company, but he did mention that we had not met since the 26th of November. He asked whether all my sisters were still at home, but I expect there was only one he wished to hear about."

Jane frowned. "It does not matter. I cannot imagine that he retains any feelings for me, and even if he did, our present circumstances would prohibit him from making an alliance with me. I am sure we shall meet as indifferent acquaintances, nothing more."

"Of course." Elizabeth longed to tease Jane about her complete lack of indifference. She thought it quite likely Mr. Bingley would wish to see Jane, but she feared her sister might be correct about the effects of the current scandal. It was possible Mr. Bingley would not even visit them; most of their friends had steered clear of Longbourn since Lydia's flight, not wishing to be tainted with the shame of the Bennet family. Without question, the marriage prospects of all the Bennet girls had been substantially damaged by Lydia's actions, and she doubted anyone would now consider them eligible for a gentleman of Mr. Bingley's stature.

The thought of Mr. Darcy crossed her mind, as happened more often than she would have wished. He was completely out of her firmament now. Her hope had been that he would never hear of Lydia's shame, but if Mr. Bingley discovered it, he would no doubt share it with his friend. She could only imagine what Mr. Darcy would think when he discovered that the sister of the woman he almost married had run off with Mr. Wickham of all people. He would think he had a near-miraculous escape. Her throat felt oddly tight. She was not certain *she* could meet Mr. Darcy as an indifferent acquaintance, not after the way she had treated him. He could not possibly still retain even the smallest amount of affection for her.

"You did not tell me much of your visit to Pemberley, Lizzy,"

Jane said in a voice as close to an accusation as Elizabeth had ever heard from her.

Elizabeth understood Jane's desire for a change of subject. "Our aunt wished to see the estate, and we were assured the family were away. Mr. Darcy arrived while we were touring the gardens. Later he introduced me to his sister and invited our uncle to fish with him. Miss Darcy asked us to tea while the gentlemen fished, and afterwards they joined us. Miss Bingley and the Hursts were there as well. Miss Darcy is a shy young thing, but seemed quite sweet."

"I recall Caroline hoped that Miss Darcy would marry Mr. Bingley," Jane said softly. "It sounds as if they spent a lot of time together."

"I saw no sign of any attachment between them. Mr. Bingley paid more attention to me than to her. She is very young." But not too young to think herself in love with Mr. Wickham, though she could not tell Jane that. Mr. Darcy had told her that in confidence, and she would not violate his trust.

"Did you not worry that Mr. Darcy might seek to trap you, as he did with the letter?"

Elizabeth's cheeks grew so hot that she put her hands to them. "Oh, do not remind me of the terrible things I said about him! I was quite wrong. He was not trying to trap me at all."

Jane raised her eyebrows. "Still, it must have been uncomfortable to see him again."

"I have never been so embarrassed in my life! I felt it must look as if I were throwing myself in his way, but he was very civil." More civil than she deserved, that was for certain. "It was odd - all the while we were touring the house, his housekeeper kept praising Mr. Darcy, telling us how sweet-tempered and generous he was, and I did not believe a word of it. She told us that Wickham had turned out quite wild, and I thought she was just parroting her master's beliefs. I was so ready to think ill of Mr. Darcy that I did not pay attention to the evidence in front of my eyes. I have treated him most unfairly. You told me so long ago, and I did not listen."

"I always had a greater value for him than you did, it is true, but he is not perfect. He insulted you at the assembly, and he denied Mr.

Wickham his inheritance, though now that we know more of Mr. Wickham, perhaps Mr. Darcy had his reasons in denying him a position in the church."

"His reasons go beyond that, Jane. It turns out Mr. Darcy gave Wickham, at his request, three thousand pounds in lieu of the living. Had I bothered to confirm Wickham's story, I would have known much sooner that he was not to be trusted."

Jane's mouth formed a silent circle. "You cannot be blamed for believing Mr. Wickham. We all did. His appearance of goodness was so convincing, and there was no reason to think he would lie. You must not blame yourself, Lizzy."

If only she could take Jane's words to heart! "Still, I was very unkind to Mr. Darcy, and he did not deserve it."

"Do you think better of him now?"

"I suppose I do. He was neither proud nor reserved during our visit, and his housekeeper showed a side of him I had never known. Nobody in Derbyshire had anything but praise for him. He went out of his way to show me attention, even after all the terrible things I said to him at Hunsford. I would have thought him quite a different man, except that we did quarrel a bit at the end." Not to mention sharing a kiss she would never forget.

"You quarreled? I cannot believe it."

"Oh, we did indeed, when he discovered I had never read his letter. He had not been trying to entrap me at all, but to warn me about Mr. Wickham. Because I had not read it, I said something that angered Mr. Darcy." Elizabeth shut her eyes, remembering the angry lines of his face when she mentioned Wickham's name. "I was a fool not to see Mr. Darcy for what he was. I had no reason to think him dishonest except that I disliked him, and that was only because he had insulted me when we first met."

"You sound as if you have regrets," Jane said almost timidly.

"Regrets?" Elizabeth gave up any pretense of work and put her embroidery aside. "I regret that I was uncivil and unkind, yes." She felt a tension in her stomach from a very different regret, a regret that she would never see him again and that his kiss would never be more than a memory for her.

"But not for refusing him?"

"How could I? I did not like him at all at the time. I have more respect for him now, but I still do not know if we would have suited each other. And Pemberley - I had no idea how grand it was. I have never seen a house more perfectly situated. The grounds are lovely, and the interior demonstrates fine taste and restraint. I cannot picture myself as mistress of such an estate." It was such a contrast to the bleak future that loomed before her now, thanks to Lydia's foolishness. "What I regret most is having given Mr. Darcy so much reason to think ill of me."

"Oh, Lizzy. I do not think you would be so pained if you did not like him at least a little," said Jane gently.

"Like him? I suppose I liked him well enough at Pemberley. It is astonishing how many flaws in a man can be forgiven by the knowledge that he admires me!"

"Lizzy, I pray you be serious. I think you have developed a fondness for him."

Elizabeth sighed and picked up her work again, not wanting to meet her sister's eyes. "It would not matter if I had fallen violently in love with him. He will never have anything to do with me or our family now, especially given that Mr. Wickham is involved in Lydia's disgrace. I fear you are right that we are not suitable matches for gentlemen any longer."

Jane looked off out the window and nodded sadly. "Much has changed, but we will make the best of it. We still have our home and each other, and perhaps the matter of Lydia may come to a better resolution than we currently suppose."

Elizabeth would have liked to believe her, but knowing what she did of Mr. Wickham's character and past, she thought it highly unlikely. But it was Jane's way to look at the brightest side, and she would not take that small comfort away from her sister.

Chapter 9

THERE WAS STILL no word of Lydia at the end of the week. Any remaining hope disappeared as the days went by, till even Kitty had stopped racing to the door at the sound of hoof beats in front of Longbourn. So there was little excitement when she reported from the window seat that a curricle was pulling up to the house.

"Who is it?" asked Jane.

"A man and a woman. No, wait! It is Mr. Bingley and a lady whom I do not know. Not that sister of his, thank the Lord."

Jane half-rose from her chair, her eyes wide as those of a frightened doe. Then she sank down again, smoothing her hair and straightening her dress.

Elizabeth crossed to the window. "That is Miss Darcy," she said with amazement. "What could she be doing here? Jane, dearest, you are not facing the hangman's noose! Come, we must greet our guests with smiling faces." She silently thanked heaven that her mother had gone to Meryton to visit Mrs. Phillips. She could not imagine how Mrs. Bennet's ill manners would appear to Miss Darcy.

A knock sounded and they waited while Hill admitted the guests. Mr. Bingley appeared in the sitting room door with a hesitant smile which turned to a beaming one when his eyes rested on Jane.

Elizabeth was grateful for the rituals of polite society that took them through the next few minutes. She welcomed the guests, introduced Miss Darcy to her sisters, and took Jane's role in asking Hill for refreshments. Jane was pale and distracted, but the roses returned to her cheeks when Mr. Bingley took his old accustomed seat by her side.

Bingley said, "How wonderful it is to see you again! We arrived only last night, but Miss Darcy could not wait to see her new friend." His jovial manner suggested that Miss Darcy was not the only one eager to come to Longbourn.

"I hope your journey was pleasant. Did you come directly from Pemberley?" Elizabeth said. It was not the question she most wanted answered, but it was as close as she could get.

"Yes, though we took three days to make the journey. My sister does not care for long days in a carriage." Although Mr. Bingley was answering Elizabeth's question, he looked only at Jane, whose eyes were on the floor.

"Miss Bingley is at Netherfield as well?" Elizabeth enquired, but what she really wanted to know was if Mr. Darcy was there. Would Miss Darcy be at Netherfield without her brother? If he was there, why had he not come to call? She feared she knew the answer. She told herself firmly that she would not regret him, ignoring the little voice which said it was too late for that.

"Yes, though she is indisposed this morning. Mr. and Mrs. Hurst had to travel on to Scarborough and could not join us, but they both send their best regards. And you are all well, I hope?"

"Very well, thank you," Elizabeth said, while Kitty and Mary, awed by the elegance of Miss Darcy, merely nodded their heads in agreement.

"Is Miss Lydia still in Brighton?"

If it had been anyone else, Elizabeth would have supposed this to be mocking, but Mr. Bingley was so transparently happy that she could only believe he somehow remained in ignorance. She saw Mary open her mouth to speak, and hurried to intervene. "Mr. Bingley, Miss Darcy, would you care to take a turn around the garden with Jane and me? Miss Darcy has never seen them, and we have made many changes since last year." She flushed, knowing this excuse was patently ridiculous, as Jane had not even poured the tea yet. She could not allow Mary to make the situation worse by moralizing.

Bingley looked surprised, but accepted the invitation. As soon as they were outside Longbourn, he offered his arm to Jane who took it after a moment. Elizabeth walked ahead with Miss Darcy, leading them toward the small wilderness where they might be guaranteed some privacy.

Miss Darcy made several admiring comments about the walk, although Elizabeth knew it was nothing to Pemberley. Elizabeth was marshalling her courage to a desperate act, and hardly replied. When they reached a small clearing, she turned back to Mr. Bingley and Jane.

"I am sorry to be ungracious to anyone, least of all such valued guests, but I must inform you of a matter which may cause distress to you."

Jane gave a little gasp and pulled away from Mr. Bingley, taking a handkerchief from her pocket. "Lizzy..." she said beseechingly. Bingley, who had looked only mildly curious until now, stepped toward her as if to comfort her.

Elizabeth steeled herself to continue. It would only be worse to wait. "In a country neighbourhood such as this, you would learn of this soon enough. It cannot be concealed, and I prefer you hear it from us directly. My sister Lydia is not in Brighton. She has left her friends - has eloped; has thrown herself into the power of ... one of the officers. They went off to London and have not been heard from since. It seems the officer was not inclined toward marriage." She would not mention his name, not in front of Miss Darcy. She had suffered enough already at Wickham's hands.

The girl clapped her gloved hand to her mouth and looked with some desperation at Mr. Bingley, whose mouth was drawn. "I am grieved," he said with deep simplicity. "Is there anything that can be done to ameliorate your circumstances?"

Jane turned away and covered her eyes with her handkerchief, and Elizabeth knew she must be weeping.

"I thank you on behalf of my entire family, but there is nothing. I raise this issue so that you be aware of it. Our family is not welcome in many circles now, and it is possible our shame may extend to our visitors in the minds of some people." She felt a heavy weight settle inside her stomach.

"I... your family will always be welcome at Netherfield," Mr. Bingley declared. "And with your permission, I will also continue to call at Longbourn."

From the corner of her eyes, Elizabeth could see Jane's shoulders shaking silently, and she bit down on her own lip to stop her tears. "We will always be glad to see you. But, delighted as I am to see Miss Darcy, I cannot believe Mr. Darcy would allow her to visit Longbourn if he knew the circumstances."

The girl shook her head. "I appreciate your concern," she said in an almost inaudible voice, "but my brother would not wish me to abandon friends in time of need. That is not his way."

"Perhaps you should ask him," Elizabeth said, throwing caution to the wind.

"If it will relieve your concern, I will write him and ask, but I know his answer," she said.

So he was not at Netherfield. The weight in Elizabeth's stomach threatened to swallow her. "Now I believe it is time for me to take Jane back to the house."

Bingley cleared his throat and said timidly, "If I might have a moment?" He went over to Jane and bent his head toward hers, speaking softly enough that only Jane could hear. Jane nodded once, but kept her head bent.

"We will be just ahead," Elizabeth said, though she doubted either was listening. With a gesture to Georgiana, they started down the path back to the house. "I am truly sorry. I am repaying your hospitality with unpleasantness, I fear."

"No! Not at all. I appreciate your honesty. There is sometimes too little of it in the world. I know my brother would feel the same way if he were here."

"Is he still at Pemberley?"

"No, he had to travel to Rosings to visit my aunt, then to London. He has been very restless these last few months."

Elizabeth's throat tightened. Was it because he was thinking of her? Not that it mattered now, but her reaction to seeing Georgiana today brought her to a realization that had been long in coming. When she had been in Derbyshire, she had thought that she still possessed to power to make Mr. Darcy renew his addresses to her, should she choose to use it. But she had not wished to, not until she learned the truth about Mr. Wickham - and then it was too late. She had lost him before she had a chance to let him win her heart. She knew now that he would have found little difficulty in that endeavour, but Lydia had ruined her chance for a future with Mr. Darcy or any respectable gentleman.

Fortunately, as Elizabeth would have been hard put to say a word, Georgiana seemed to share her brother's ability to walk in silent companionship. Nothing was said by either until they reached Longbourn House. Behind them, Elizabeth could hear the scuffling of gravel indicating that Jane and Mr. Bingley were behind them, but she chose not to look back.

In the sitting room, Mary gave Elizabeth a reproachful look. Elizabeth mentally shrugged. What difference did it make if she did not follow the customary form for a visit? It was not as if they could be shamed any further.

Jane's eyes were red but otherwise appeared her usual serene self once more, though Bingley seemed more troubled as he hovered over her. Elizabeth was relieved that their guests did not stay long, and joined Jane in walking them out to their carriage.

"I hope we will see you again soon," she told Miss Darcy as the girl tied her bonnet under her delicate chin. "I was sorry that our acquaintance was interrupted when I had to leave Lambton so precipitously."

"As was I," Georgiana agreed. "My brother has spoken of you so often and so highly that I feel as if I have known you for a long time."

Elizabeth felt colour creeping into her cheeks. "He is too kind to me, then." She turned to Mr. Bingley who was releasing Jane's hand from his own. Elizabeth offered him her hand as well, but he took it in an uncharacteristically clumsy manner, using both of his hands. Elizabeth assumed he must be off balance from the difficult visit, but then she felt something flat press against her glove. She opened her mouth to speak, but Mr. Bingley gave her a significant look, so she merely stepped back, holding whatever it was he had handed her in such a secretive manner.

As she joined Jane in waving to the carriage as it pulled away, she took the opportunity to slip the paper, for such it was, into her pocket for safe-keeping. She was exquisitely aware of its presence. The possibility that it was from Mr. Darcy had her pulses fluttering;

although nothing could come of it, it would be gratifying to know he was thinking of her and cared enough to find a way to respond to her.

As soon as she could, she escaped to her room and sat on her bed. She took out the paper and held it for a moment, savouring the brief time of hope it gave her, then she examined it. It bore her name in the close, firm hand she still remembered from the envelope she had burned long ago. Her mouth grew dry. Carefully she slit it open. It was dated four days earlier at Pemberley House.

> *My dear Miss Bennet,*
>
> *The arrival of your letter was a great relief to me. Although I am grieved to hear that you are facing unknown difficulties, it was at least comforting to know that your precipitate departure was not occasioned by offense at my manner of expressing myself. It is I who must apologize for my behaviour that afternoon. I can offer no excuse beyond strength of feeling and surprise at discovering you had not read my letter, but those hardly suffice.*
>
> *I have spoken with Bingley regarding my misapprehension of your sister's feelings for him, and it was only a matter of minutes before he developed an intense desire to visit Netherfield once more. I hope his presence will bring about a happier outcome than it did the last time he was there.*
>
> *I do not know what called you home so urgently, but I can plead a real, though unavailing, concern as to your present well-being. If there is ever a way in which I may be of service, it would be an honour to do so. I will ask Bingley to endeavour to deliver this to your hand unobtrusively, and his discretion can be trusted. I will only add, God bless you.*
>
> *Fitzwilliam Darcy*

On finishing the letter, Elizabeth leaned her head against the bedrail. He had not forgotten her. Even if a true connection between them was impossible now, it helped to know he was thinking of her without ill feelings. He was indeed a good man. If only she had realized it sooner!

She folded the letter and tucked it away in her vanity drawer along with her most prized possessions.

GEORGIANA AND BINGLEY spoke little during the carriage ride, each involved with their own thoughts. Georgiana felt deeply for Miss Elizabeth, whose suffering was apparent behind her brave front, but beyond that, she could not help dwelling on her own lucky escape from the same mistake that Miss Lydia Bennet had made. She could not blame another girl for making the same error in judgement she had made, but her imagination travelled beyond reality and to what her brother would have endured, had he not interrupted her elopement with Mr. Wickham. He would be suffering as Miss Bennet did now, subject to gossip and the world's derision, his life forever changed by her foolishness. His own prospects would be affected and his pride mortified. She had so easily been fooled into a decision that could have ruined both of their lives.

If Miss Elizabeth's sister was not in fact married, it could be another disaster not just for her friend, but for her brother as well. Georgiana had never seen him take such an interest in a young lady before, and it had given her hope that he might marry someday soon and fulfill her longing for a sister. At first she had thought Miss Elizabeth a perfect match for her brother, with her wit, laughter and liveliness - she even made Fitzwilliam laugh at himself! She did not allow Miss Bingley to intimidate her, a skill Georgiana wished she could emulate. After Miss Elizabeth had spoken so warmly of Wickham, Georgiana had wished her far away and never to be heard of again, until Fitzwilliam explained that he was at fault for not exposing George Wickham to the people of Meryton. She understood all too well how charming Wickham could be when he chose.

But be that as it may, a scandal enveloping the Bennet family would put an end to any hope of her brother marrying Miss Elizabeth. Fitzwilliam was generous, but he would not endanger the Darcy family name, not the way she had with Wickham. But she had learned her lesson. She would never allow herself to trust a man again unless she had her brother's blessing to do so.

Back at Netherfield, they found Caroline anxiously awaiting their arrival. She took Mr. Bingley's arm the moment he exited the carriage. "Charles, I must speak with you right away about a matter of utmost importance. Will you come to the drawing room?"

"As you wish," Bingley said, sounding as if his wish was quite different, but as usual, he obeyed his sister.

Georgiana said timidly, "Perhaps I shall wait in my room, then?"

Caroline turned a beaming smile on her. "No, of course you must join us. This is something you should hear as well. I would not wish you to be left in ignorance."

Georgiana was sure she would rather be left in ignorance of anything that delighted Caroline this much, but she followed her to the sitting room.

Bingley said, "Now, what is this all about, Caroline?"

"Well," Caroline said, perching on the edge of her seat, her hands folded in her lap. "While you were out at Longbourn I had a visit from Lady Lucas, who shared the most interesting information with me. And before you caution me against believing whatever I hear, I have checked with several of the servants here, and they all agree with her story." She lowered her voice dramatically. "It seems that Miss Lydia Bennet has continued in her wild ways. She has run off with an officer. Of course, it is hardly surprising, given the way her family behaves, but it does rather change things, does it not?"

"I do not see why," Bingley said sharply. "I was already aware of this matter. Having an ill-behaved sister does not make Miss Bennet or Miss Elizabeth Bennet a jot less agreeable, and I intend to continue to enjoy their company."

"Charles, you cannot mean it! Their whole family is disgraced, and no one in the area wishes to share the taint of acknowledging them. We would look like fools if we maintained the acquaintance. I am sure Mr. Darcy would agree, even if he does admire Eliza Bennet's *fine eyes*. He would not want his sister spending time with women of such questionable morals." She smiled triumphantly.

"That is up to Darcy, not to you. He would not run from his friends in their time of trouble," Bingley said angrily.

"Oh, Charles, you know that he has always disapproved of the Bennet family! He considers them ill-bred and unworthy of his attention."

"That would explain why he went to such an effort to introduce

83

his sister to Miss Elizabeth at Pemberley," Bingley said with heavy sarcasm.

"He did not know of this latest escapade. I am sure…"

"*I* am sure it is time for you to stop speaking for Darcy, who is quite able to make his own decisions without regard to you!"

Caroline took a deep breath and put on her sweetest smile and most cajoling air. "Come, Charles, I am certain that this has come as much of a shock to you as it has to me. It is terrible what those Bennet girls must be going through. Jane is such a sweet girl, and you know how much I like her. But we have our own social status to consider. An association such as that could affect the invitations we receive next season, and could cost us the acceptance we have finally begun to win in the ton. You know I only wish to protect you."

"Oh, leave be, Caroline!" Bingley jumped to his feet and strode out the door.

Georgiana wished with all her heart that she could follow him, but she remained where she was, just as a well-bred young lady was expected to. Perhaps if she were quiet enough, Caroline would forget her presence. But it seemed that luck was not with her.

"Men!" Caroline cried with exasperation. "Sometimes I swear they seem by far the most irrational creatures. He knows what I am saying is true, but he does not want it to be true, so he ignores it. Heaven knows what trouble he would get into if I were not here to save him."

Georgiana made a non-committal noise, hoping Caroline's anger would burn itself out. It was not the first time she had seen Caroline deriving pleasure from the misfortune of others, but she hated it. She could see how it could be twisted to work against herself as easily. Who could be sure that Caroline was not saying cruel things about her behind her back? She was not under the impression that Caroline's attentions to her came from any kind of liking so much as a desire to please her brother.

Caroline tapped her fingers on the arm of her chair. "If only I had known this before you called at Longbourn! It will be more difficult to extract ourselves from the acquaintance now. But you need have no worries, Georgiana. I will make certain you are not forced into their company, regardless of what Charles may do. I owe that much to your brother. He would never have allowed you to come here had he known."

Georgiana was well practiced at failing to respond to comments she disliked in such a way that the speaker always took her silence as assent, and she put that skill to good effect now. It was almost amusing - finally there was something that Caroline and Elizabeth agreed on. They both thought her brother would not approve of the connection. How odd that now that they were finally in agreement, they were both wrong! She was sure of it.

"I confess I am not the least bit surprised. The Bennet family was always a disgrace. If it were not for how pretty the older girls are, no one would ever have tolerated them. Your brother often commented on the family's ill breeding."

Would Caroline say she was ill-bred if she knew the truth? With a carefully studious expression, Georgiana stood. "Thank you for your warning. I will go now to write to my brother for his opinion on the matter. I will be sure to tell him of your concern for me." She knew Caroline would never understand that this would worsen his opinion of her.

In truth, Georgiana had no intention of informing her brother about this matter. It would be far too painful for both of them, and she did not wish to be the bearer of bad news about Miss Elizabeth Bennet. Far better to speak only of the journey and her impressions of Netherfield.

Chapter 10

JANE AND ELIZABETH were walking together in the shrubbery behind the house when they saw the housekeeper coming towards them. Instead of the expected summons to their mother, Hill said, "I beg your pardon for interrupting you, but I was in hopes you might have got some good news from town, so I took the liberty of coming to ask." "What do you mean, Hill? We have heard nothing from town," Jane said.

"Dear madam," said Mrs. Hill, in great astonishment, "don't you know there is an express come for master from Mr. Gardiner? He has been here this half hour, and master has had a letter."

Away ran the girls, too eager to get in to have time for speech. They ran through the vestibule into the breakfast room; from thence to the library. Their father was in neither; and they were on the point of seeking him upstairs with their mother, when they were met by the butler, who said, "If you are looking for my master, ma'am, he is walking towards the little copse."

Upon this information, they instantly passed through the hall once more, and ran across the lawn after their father, who was deliberately pursuing his way towards a small wood on one side of the paddock.

Jane, who was not so light, nor so much in the habit of running, as Elizabeth, soon lagged behind, while her sister, panting for breath, came up with him, and eagerly cried out, "Oh, Papa, what news? what news? Have you heard from my uncle?"

"Yes, I have had a letter from him by express," Mr. Bennet said heavily.

"Well, and what news does it bring? good or bad?"

"What is there of good to be expected?" he said, taking the letter from his pocket; "but perhaps you would like to read it." Elizabeth impatiently caught it from his hand. Jane now came up.

"Read it aloud," said their father, "for I hardly know myself what it is about."

Gracechurch-street, Monday, August 24.

My Dear Brother,

At last I am able to send you some tidings of my niece, but not such, upon the whole, as to give you satisfaction. Two days ago Lydia appeared at my door appearing quite weary and less than presentable. She is not married. After some prevarication, Lydia admitted that Mr. Wickham had abandoned her several days previously without a word of where he was going and apparently no intent of return, and that she had been forcibly evicted from the rooms they had taken owing to lack of payment. She walked all the way to Cheapside with only the clothes upon her back. Mr. Wickham had apparently taken the last of her funds when he left. Lydia retains some hope that he will return to her, but it seems quite clear to me that we have seen the last of that man.

Lydia has been in very poor spirits since her arrival here. I have never seen her like this before. She hardly ever speaks to us; she barely eats, and only that when we remind her, and she sits by the fire all day doing nothing. My wife is doing her best to comfort her, but without success. You may wonder at my waiting for two days to contact you, but I have been reluctant to do so until we made a plan for Lydia's future. Since Lydia's flight is known in Meryton, she cannot return to Longbourn. I have a clerk, a young man of no wealth or family but of great ambition, and I have spoken with him regarding Lydia. He is willing to marry her in exchange for preference at the firm, plus her settlement of a thousand pounds. Although this is not the sort of match we would have considered for her in the past, it is likely the best we will find now. He is a hardworking lad who should be a steadying influence on Lydia, and he will not be able to mistreat her under my eye.

The difficulty, as my dear wife points out, will be in obtaining Lydia's consent to the scheme, as she refuses, though without giving a reason. As I see it, she has little choice, but the final decision is likely to rest on your authority. If she believes this is her only option except the streets, I think her native self-interest will prevail. I shall send this by express, that no time may be lost in bringing me your answer. If, as I conclude will be the case, you send me full powers to act in your name throughout the whole of this business, I will immediately give directions to Haggerston for preparing a proper settlement. There will not be the smallest occasion for your coming to town again unless Lydia proves obstreperous; therefore, stay quietly at Longbourn, and depend on my diligence and care. Send back your answer as soon as you can, and be careful to write explicitly. Yours &c.,

    Edw. Gardiner

"Indeed, Jane, she is alive," Mr. Bennet said with heavy irony, "albeit ruined in reputation and prospects. We must indeed be thankful."

"At least she had the sense to seek out our uncle," Jane offered.

"It does not seem she had any choice. And now I must rely on your uncle and his connexions to sort out her future, and be completely useless to my own daughter."

"And have you answered the letter?" said Elizabeth.

"I accepted his terms. What other choice do I have?"

"Poor Lydia. She will not like being married to a clerk," Jane said. "But perhaps she will learn to love him."

Elizabeth said, "Not unless he has a red coat. I hope the poor man knows what he is getting himself into. But she must marry him."

"There is nothing else to be done. I wonder just how much *preference* your uncle is giving him," said Mr. Bennet.

Elizabeth exchanged a glance with Jane. "May we take my uncle's letter to read to our mother?"

"Take whatever you like, and get away."

Inside the house, they found that Mary and Kitty were both with Mrs. Bennet: one communication would, therefore, do for all.

"Well, this is nothing new," Mrs. Bennet announced. "Lydia is a healthy girl, so I always knew she was alive and well. But I am sure there is some sort of misunderstanding. Your uncle always fears the worst. Mr. Wickham is a gentleman and must have left only on a matter of business, and when he returns, they will be married and we shall all celebrate."

Elizabeth said, "I fear Mr. Wickham is not a man to be trusted. He has used our dear Lydia abominably, and the sooner we accept that, the sooner we can move forward."

"Nonsense, Lizzy! You are just cross with him because you liked him too well yourself, and he chose Lydia."

"Believe me, I wish nothing at all to do with Mr. Wickham."

"Such nonsense! But I must dress and bring the news to my sister Philips that Lydia is found."

Jane exclaimed, "No, mama! We must not tell anyone until we know the outcome."

"Pish tosh. Kitty will help me get ready."

Elizabeth hurried down to her father and informed him of her mother's intentions. "She must not go. If we are to have any chance of preventing this from becoming public knowledge, we must keep our silence now. Once the world knows for a fact that she has been with Mr. Wickham, it will not matter if our uncle finds a husband or employment for her. We must leave it a mystery until we know the outcome and can explain it accordingly."

Mr. Bennet took off his glasses and set them on his desk. Rubbing the bridge of his nose, he said, "If you know of some miraculous method to prevent your mother from talking, I beg of you to share it with me, for I have been seeking such a thing these last twenty years and more."

"I pray you, be serious! This could impact us all."

"Ah, Lizzy, do not lose your sense of humour! Only silly people will be frightened off by such nonsense. Now go; I want my library to myself again."

Elizabeth left, but not without resentment. Her father had not heeded her warnings about sending Lydia to Brighton, and she had taken that calmly. Now, knowing what she had personally lost from Lydia's foolishness, it was harder to put it aside. She thought of Mr. Darcy walking by her side through the grounds of Pemberley, and of the intent look in his dark eyes as they spoke. It had taken her a long time, but she finally understood the truth of it. She was in love with him, just when it was too late.

THE LETTER TO Mr. Gardiner was duly sent, and the wait for a reply began. The questions in town became more pointed, but it seemed that somehow Mrs. Bennet had restrained herself from gossiping, since no one seemed aware that Lydia had been found. Mr. Bingley and Miss Darcy called at Longbourn on more than one occasion, but the invitation to Netherfield Mr. Bingley had promised did not materialize, and no word came from Caroline Bingley, despite an invitation to tea being sent. Jane lamented, "If only I could ask him if Caroline is avoiding us! I would not like to think it of her, if nothing else but that it makes matters most difficult for Mr. Bingley. I am glad to see him, but how can anything possibly happen in face of such familial disapproval?"

"It depends on whose opinion he values most, his sister's or yours," said Elizabeth. "From what I see, your views carry a great deal of weight." But Jane refused to get her hopes up.

One morning Kitty set out to visit Mariah Lucas, as was their regular habit, but on this occasion she returned in less than an hour just as the family was taking their afternoon meal, her eyes swollen and tear-tracks running down her cheeks. Mrs. Bennet looked up at her irritably. "Whatever is the matter, Kitty? Have you no consideration for my poor nerves?"

"Oh, mamma," Kitty said, her voice shaking, "I am sorry. I will retire now."

Elizabeth frowned at this uncharacteristic behaviour. Jane laid her napkin carefully on the table and came around to stand with her arm around Kitty. "What is the matter? Has something happened to Mariah?"

Kitty shook her head. "No, I do not think so, but I did not see her." She gave a hiccoughing sob and buried her face in Jane's shoulder.

"What is it, then?" Jane prompted gently.

"There is no need to make such a fuss!" Mrs. Bennet declared. "Kitty, how you try my nerves!"

Kitty whispered something in Jane's ear which caused Jane to stiffen and to look at her in disbelief. "She did not, did she?"

"She did. She told me not to return."

Jane put both arms around her weeping sister and turned her head toward her father. "It seems Lady Lucas told Kitty that Mariah was not at home, and was unlikely to ever be home at such a time as Kitty might call."

Mrs. Bennet cried, "Lady Lucas? That is nonsense. You must have misunderstood her, Kitty. She would never exclude us. It is impossible."

Kitty's voice was barely audible. "She said that since Lydia is unmarried, it is not appropriate for Mariah to visit with me."

"Has she heard the news somehow, then?" Elizabeth asked sharply.

"Apparently," Jane said, biting her lip.

Mrs. Bennet picked fretfully at the tablecloth. "I did not tell anyone except my sister Phillips, and I swore her to secrecy. I would not do anything to endanger Jane's chance to secure Mr. Bingley."

Mr. Bennet's eyes narrowed. "Then how is it discovered?"

"Perhaps the servants…" Elizabeth said with deep dismay. This was a disaster.

"Hill is the only one aware of the truth, and I sincerely doubt she would jeopardize her position by speaking out of turn," said Mr. Bennet. "I will talk to her this afternoon. Perhaps she can shed some light on this."

Kitty said miserably, "It was not Hill. It was me."

"You?" Elizabeth said in disbelief. She set down her fork, her appetite vanished.

"I only told Mariah, and she solemnly swore she would never tell another soul!"

A shocked silence met this remark, then Mr. Bennet pushed back his chair, leaving a full plate of food in front of him. "I will be in my library." He walked out with a weary stride.

Scarcely was the door closed behind him than Mrs. Bennet began a tirade about Kitty's indifference to her nerves and to her family's future, Lady Lucas' treachery, and their future once they were thrown into the hedgerows by Mr. Collins. "I hope you shall be proud of yourself then, Kitty!"

Jane appeared near tears. Mary began a moral platitude, but before she could get half-way through it, Elizabeth interrupted to beg to be excused. Without waiting for permission, she left the table and took Jane by the arm, tugging her toward the door. Jane followed without struggle, though she glanced over her shoulder at the still-sobbing Kitty.

Once they were safely in their rooms, Elizabeth closed the door behind her and leaned back on hit, closing her eyes. "This is most unfortunate," she said. Oddly, the thought that crossed her mind was that she wished she had said a proper goodbye to Mr. Darcy when they met for the last time.

Jane sniffled, and Elizabeth opened her eyes to the expected site of her sister sitting on the bed, her face in her hands. "If Lady Lucas will not receive us, then no one will," she said despairingly. "We will be pariahs. Our reputations are destroyed."

Elizabeth sat on the bed beside her and took her hand in both her own. Jane's fingers were ice-cold. She only wished she had some words of comfort to offer. But if it was known that Lydia was found and unmarried, it would not matter. It would be too late. The only thing to do was to start looking toward a new future. "I am thinking that perhaps we should go to London for a time. Some of this may blow over after a few months."

"Do you think so?"

Elizabeth in fact rather strongly doubted it, but there was always the chance that some far worse scandal would take the attention of the Meryton gossips and they might be readmitted to society, albeit with a lowered status. Her greater hope was that in the new environment of London where Lydia's disgrace was not public knowledge, Jane's beauty might attract a new suitor. "I think there is always hope," she said stoutly. "And if not, you will simply have to suffer my company for the rest of your life, which could be considered tragic, but I prefer to think of it as comedy."

Jane giggled through her tears. "Hardly tragic, dearest Lizzy. But you are right, one door closes and another may open. It is just..." Her voice caught and she fell silent.

"Just what?" Elizabeth asked gently, though she suspected she knew the answer.

"Just that it will be a future without Mr. Bingley in it. I know there never was any real hope once Lydia ran off, but he has been so attentive."

"It gave us all hope, and I am sure his friendship will not be among those we will lose. But friendship is hardly a consolation, is it?"

Mrs. Bennet's voice, now raised to a shriek, penetrated the upstairs and their door. Jane sat up a little straighter. "Poor Kitty. I really should go to her rescue. She meant no ill."

"No, she simply kept Lydia's secret when she should not have, and now has not kept our secret when she should have. I have not the least sympathy for her, I fear."

"Oh, to think how happy we were just a year ago! How could things come to such a pass?"

Elizabeth recalled the harsh words Mr. Darcy had used regarding her family when he offered for her in Hunsford. His words about her connections being a degradation and the unfortunate behaviour of some of her family sounded almost prophetic now. Did the man have to prove himself correct in every instance? The conceit almost made her smile, but then she thought of how she would never have a chance to tell him so, and her heart ached.

Chapter 11

FOR TWO DAYS the Bennet ladies stayed at home with no callers or word from the outside world. Mr. Bennet stayed in his library, while Mrs. Bennet had taken to her rooms with tears and lamentations of regret, invectives against the villainous conduct of Wickham, the treacherousness of Lady Lucas, and complaints of her own sufferings and ill usage; blaming everybody but the person to whose ill-judged indulgence the errors of her daughter must be principally owing.

"If I had been able," said she, "to carry my point of going to Brighton, with all my family, this would not have happened; but poor dear Lydia had nobody to take care of her. Why did the Forsters ever let her go out of their sight? I am sure there was some great neglect or other on their side, for she is not the kind of girl to do such a thing, if she had been well looked after. I always thought they were very unfit to have the charge of her; but I was over-ruled, as I always am. Poor dear child!"

Elizabeth's tolerance for these outbursts was less than Jane's, and her natural impatience with remaining indoors was making a calm composure difficult to maintain. When she found herself snapping at Mary over an unimportant attribution, she decided it was time to take action. She was usually the first of the family to wake in the morning, so the next day when she arose, she put on her bonnet and gloves and set off to Meryton with a basket over her arm.

The cool, fresh air on her cheeks was invigorating, and for the duration of her walk with no one but the singing birds for company, it was almost possible to forget the heavy atmosphere at Longbourn, her mother's fits of nerves, Mary's moralistic platitudes and Kitty's tears. With a lightened heart, she reached High Street, already full of people and lined with shops she had known all her life.

There were no signs that anything was amiss when she stopped at the grocer for fruit. He greeted her as pleasantly as always and picked out the best peaches for her. The butcher's boy nodded in response to her greeting. But Mr. White, the plump, balding butcher, seemed uncomfortably friendly, almost flirtatious with her. He had admired her for years, but surely he could not think she would have lowered her sights so far as to consider a suit from him! She was relieved to escape his shop, and decided to leave that particular shopping errand to Hill in the future.

Most of the townsfolk seemed to have no particular interest in her, and she began to think they might have assumed matters were worse than they were in reality. With a little extra spring in her step, she continued on. Outside the stationer's shop she encountered Mary King and greeted her pleasantly. Mary started to speak in return, then the hand of the gentleman beside her grasped her shoulder. Elizabeth saw it was Mary's uncle. He neither acknowledged her nor touched his hat, instead drawing Mary past her and away. Elizabeth kept her cheerful smile fixed to her face, even when she felt Mary surreptitiously press her hand as she passed by. Mary was not the sort to cut an acquaintance, but it was clear that had been her instructions.

A sick feeling formed in the pit of Elizabeth's stomach, but she would not allow herself to be intimidated, even as other acquaintances failed to meet her eyes. She made a point of traversing the full length of the town before turning back, her head held high. She had almost reached the edge of town when she heard a girl call her name. She turned to see Miss Darcy alighting from an open carriage which also included Miss Bingley.

Georgiana hurried over to her with a hesitant smile. "It is a pleasant day for an outing, is it not?" she asked shyly.

Elizabeth felt a rush of affection for the girl. "Very pleasant indeed."

"Miss Bingley wanted to go to the silversmith, and I decided to come along. Now I am glad I did."

Elizabeth wondered how much Georgiana knew of what had happened. If Miss Bingley had any say in the matter, she was sure Georgiana had been informed of every horrible detail as well as a few that never happened. She wondered how painful it might be for the girl, given her own history. The frown on Miss Bingley's face in the carriage showed clearer than words her opinion of Elizabeth.

"It is a pleasure to see you, too. May I hope everyone at Netherfield is well?"

"Oh, yes, quite well, thank you." Georgiana faltered. No doubt she wished to avoid the minefield of asking about the Bennets.

"And your brother? Have you heard from him lately?" Elizabeth held her breath. She did not know why she was so anxious for any news of Mr. Darcy. Perhaps she just wished for a reminder that they both lived in the same world.

"He writes me faithfully twice a week. He is such a good brother! I had expected him to stay longer at Rosings, but he has already returned to London. He was pleased to hear that I was visiting you." Georgiana's cheeks were tinted a pale pink.

The heaviness that had been in Elizabeth's stomach since her encounter with Mary King turned into a happy warmth. "When you write him next, please do give him my best regards." He could make of that what he will, but it felt right to say it.

"I was thinking of calling at Longbourn tomorrow," Georgiana said tentatively. "If you are not otherwise engaged, that is."

Elizabeth's happy feelings floated away. She knew Mr. Darcy would not thank her for jeopardizing his sister's reputation. Her mouth felt dry and she had to force herself to speak. "As fond as I am of your company, I am not sure that is a wise idea."

Georgiana's face fell. "As you wish," she half-whispered.

With a pang of guilt, Elizabeth said, "I hope you know I speak only in your best interests, not out of my own desires."

Miss Bingley removed herself from the carriage and approached them. Without so much as a nod at Elizabeth, she said, "Georgiana, please return to the carriage immediately. This woman is not fit to associate with you. Your brother would be angry with me if I allowed you to...."

But she never had a chance to finish what she planned to say. Georgiana drew herself to her full height, taller than both of the other women, lifted her chin, and said coolly, "What my brother wishes me to do is between him and me, and I know he would be very disappointed in me if I did not show the kind of loyalty to my friends that he himself would." Her resemblance to Mr. Darcy at that moment was uncanny.

Elizabeth was half tempted to laugh, half tempted to applaud Georgiana's declaration of her independence. She compromised with an amused smile. She would not leave the poor girl dangling, though, after her brave words. "Miss Darcy, I was thinking of taking a walk along the river tomorrow. There are some lovely views near the old stone bridge. Would you care to join me?"

Georgiana smiled, first timidly, then radiantly. "I would be very happy to do so."

ELIZABETH HAD PLANNED her walk for the early afternoon, but she was not surprised when she was forestalled by the arrival of both Miss Darcy and Mr. Bingley at Longbourn that morning. Mr. Bingley's face was lined as if he had been suffering sleepless nights.

When he came to the sitting room, he announced that Georgiana had invited him to accompany her and Miss Elizabeth on their riverside walk, and wondered whether any of the other Bennet sisters might choose to join them. Mary declined, stating the necessity to continue her studies, and Kitty owned that she would prefer to remain indoors. It was taken as a given that Jane would be joining the walkers, although she had said nothing.

They set out first in the carriage, which Mr. Bingley directed to the old stone bridge. He sat facing the three women, making determined small talk. Elizabeth kept her eye on Jane whose expression was the same one of amiable distance that had caused Mr. Darcy to think she did not care for Mr. Bingley. It was strikingly different from the smiles Mr. Bingley's presence had provoked in her these last weeks.

The path along the river was only wide enough for two to walk abreast, so Elizabeth set forth with Georgiana, while Bingley and Jane followed behind, soon allowing the others to outstrip them. As they strolled, Elizabeth asked Georgiana about her childhood at Pemberley, taking a guilty pleasure in every mention of Mr. Darcy's name. It was clear that Georgiana idolized her brother. In the meantime, the other couple lagged further and further behind to the point of being out of

Elizabeth's sight for several minutes. She hoped rather than expected that this would lead to a happy conclusion.

When the path reached the road and it was time to return to the carriage, Elizabeth kept Georgiana in conversation for several minutes without walking, attempting to let Bingley and Jane catch up to them, rather than imposing themselves unexpectedly by meeting in passing. When the other couple finally appeared, Jane's face showed signs of strain. Elizabeth set off on the return journey at a quick pace, thinking that Jane might wish to return home as soon as possible, and this time the four walked together.

When they returned to Longbourn, Mr. Bingley handed Jane and Elizabeth out of the carriage, but did not accept Jane's half-hearted invitation to refreshments, pleading another engagement. Elizabeth, now quite worried, was glad she would have the opportunity to talk to her sister sooner rather than later, but the carriage was not quite out of sight when Jane said, "Please do not say anything, Lizzy. I wish to be alone." She walked off hurriedly in the direction of the wilderness where Elizabeth had first acquainted Mr. Bingley and Georgiana with the intelligence of Lydia's flight. Elizabeth watched after her in concern, but could not justify ignoring her sister's request.

NEARLY TWO HOURS later, when Jane had not yet returned to the house, Elizabeth collected Jane's blue wool shawl and headed out toward the wilderness. Her sister's favourite hiding place was on the old swing they had all played on as children, and Elizabeth thought this her most likely destination. As she expected, Jane sat on the warped board of the swing, rocking back and forth with her feet dragging along the ground. She looked up when Elizabeth came through the line of trees.

"We have enough invalids in our family at the moment," Elizabeth said. "I would not wish you to take a chill." She draped the shawl around her sister's shoulders.

Jane sighed and pulled the soft fabric tightly against her. "I thank you. The breeze was indeed becoming cool." Her voice seemed somehow empty.

"Do you wish to talk about it? Or shall I leave you again?"

Jane shook her head. "There is nothing to tell. He has loved me all this time, and only left because he was persuaded that I was indifferent to him. He returned to Netherfield hoping for a new beginning with me, and while he wishes we could marry, he understands it is impossible as things stand. If he married me, he would be harming the prospects of his sister and any children that might ensue from such a marriage. He said he was willing to go forward with it anyway, but even I could tell he was half-hearted about it. When I refused, he seemed more relieved than anything else."

"You refused? Oh, Jane, why? If he is willing to marry you, you should snap up the opportunity for happiness!"

Jane pushed off with her feet so that the swing was higher, then released it to swing forward and back again, forward and back. "I know I should have accepted for mamma's sake, but I love him. If we were to marry, he would lose all the progress he and his father before him made in society. I am not willing to bring that sort of ruination and pain upon him for the slight exchange of my love." She bit down hard on her lip, as though trying to keep from crying.

"That is hardly a slight exchange, as Mr. Bingley must know as well."

"And then there would be having to deal with Caroline's unending hatred because by marrying me, Mr. Bingley would have ruined her chances to make a good marriage. Shall I put myself forward at her expense? She would gain nothing if we married, and lose a great deal. It is not worth it. Mr. Bingley would end up resenting me for what I had done."

"Jane, only you would refuse a proposal from the man you love because it might hurt the chances of a woman who has already tried to destroy yours!" Elizabeth's argument was only half-hearted, since she knew that Jane would never be able to take a step like that to harm another.

"He did not truly wish me to accept. If he had, he would have pressed me further. As soon as I said I understood, he said nothing more."

"He is a man easily influenced by others, not always for the better." She wondered if Mr. Darcy's influence played a role this time as well. The thought made her heart ache, but she could not blame him if he advised his friend against the marriage now.

"It is true," Jane said. "But he is still the most amiable man of my acquaintance." She began to weep again, and Elizabeth had no comfort to offer beyond her handkerchief. Her eyes were filling with tears as well. She knew too much now about the pain of love that would never be fulfilled.

JANE WAS SUBDUED all evening and into the next day, but she kept her own counsel. Elizabeth hated to think of what Mrs. Bennet's reaction would be when she discovered Jane's suitor had decamped. The question became more pressing when a letter arrived for Elizabeth from Netherfield. She opened it to find an elegant sheet of paper written in a flowing hand, and before she even read it, she guessed what it was likely to contain. If she was to judge by the stricken look on Jane's face, her sister knew as well.

> *My dear friend,*
>
> *I am disconsolate to tell you that Mr. Bingley and his sister have unexpectedly decided that our party is to return to London tomorrow morning. I would wish you to know this is none of my desire. Becoming further acquainted with you has been my greatest pleasure here in Hertfordshire, and I am saddened at the interruption. When the plan first arose, I wanted to come tell you of it myself, but Miss Bingley says that we must prepare for our departure and that the carriage cannot be spared. I hope we will be able to meet again soon, and in the meantime, may I ask if you would be so generous as to correspond with me? I wish you all the best, and that your current situation may have a happier outcome than present expectation. Thank you for your friendship.*
>
> *Yours in haste,*
> *Georgiana Darcy*

"They are leaving tomorrow. Georgiana does not say anything about a planned return."

Jane nodded jerkily, put aside her work, and left the room.

Chapter 12

THE BUTLER BROUGHT Darcy an envelope on a silver platter. "An express from Miss Darcy, sir," he said.

Darcy ripped open the envelope, fearful of what it might contain, but it was only a notice that there had been a change of plans and she intended to arrive in London the following day. He tossed it aside.

"Will there be a reply, sir?"

"No, no reply." Darcy waved him away moodily.

So he would see Georgiana tomorrow. At least then he would finally get some answers. Bingley, despite his promise to keep Darcy informed of the situation at Longbourn, had not bothered to contact him at all. Georgiana's letters had been cheery and made several mentions of Elizabeth, but nothing about any problems with the Bennet family. He had concluded that in fact the crisis at Longbourn did not exist, and had been manufactured for his benefit by Elizabeth as an excuse for avoiding being in his presence again. It was a bitter pill; he had hoped from her letter that she thought somewhat better of him than that, at least that she would be willing to tell him the truth.

He poured himself a generous snifter of brandy. Why could he not simply forget about Elizabeth Bennet? He had been attracted to women before, sometimes to the point of infatuation, but always he had been able to move on. Elizabeth did not even like him, for God's sake! What would it take for him to leave her in his past?

THE NEXT MORNING Darcy woke with a headache, but it was beginning to pass by the time Bingley's carriage arrived at his door. He came out to meet them. Georgiana embraced him warmly, but looked a little sad. Bingley looked as if he felt worse than Darcy did, and if Darcy was not mistaken, there was a distinct odor of drink coming

101

from him, despite it not yet being mid-afternoon. Only Miss Bingley appeared her normal self.

"Bingley, Miss Bingley, would you care to come in to refresh yourselves?" Darcy asked.

Bingley half-lurched out of the carriage. Darcy caught his arm before he could lose his balance.

Miss Bingley ignored her brother's antics and said, "Why, thank you, how kind of you to invite us."

"Not you, Caroline," Bingley said, his speech a little slurred. "You go home. I want to talk to Darcy. Privately."

Miss Bingley stiffened. "Very well, Charles, if that is what you wish." She sounded as if she was speaking to a misbehaving child. "Mr. Darcy, if he should cause you any difficulty, just send me a message and I will have someone collect him immediately."

Darcy nodded to her, though he did not care for her tone. Without waiting for any further invitation, Bingley stumbled into the house and followed his usual route to the sitting room. When Darcy caught up to him, Bingley was already pouring himself a glass of port.

"Is it not a little early in the day for that?" Darcy asked mildly. A few hours in a carriage with Miss Bingley might be enough to make a man wish for a drink, but this was excessive.

Bingley sat down heavily on the brocaded sofa, the port threatening to slosh out of his glass. "Won't do. I can't marry her. Wish I'd never gone back. Still the most beautiful woman I've ever met."

"It did not work out?"

"How could it, after what happened to her sister? I couldn't do it to my family. Couldn't take the scandal at all, so I left her all alone. I'm a coward, that's what I am."

Darcy could have sworn the floor shook under him. "What happened to Miss Elizabeth?"

"To her? Nothing. It's the other one, the one I wrote you about."

Darcy wanted to wring the information out of him. "I have not heard a word from you since you left Pemberley."

Bingley looked up at him through bleary eyes. "I wrote you. Sent it to you at Rosings. A few days after we arrived."

Darcy counted days in his head. He had stayed at Rosings only for two nights before having a disagreement with Lady Catherine severe enough to make him choose to leave rather than to remain in her company. The letter would have arrived just after he left Rosings, but it should have been forwarded to him in London, as Georgiana's letters had been. Then again, he would not put it past Lady Catherine to deliberately withhold his letters from him out of spite. She would not dare to try anything with letters from Georgiana, but he could imagine her delight in refusing to send on Bingley's letter. "I did not receive it. What has happened?"

"The youngest sister - Miss Lydia - ran off with an officer. Eloped. But they never married. He abandoned her in London. It was your old friend Mr. Wickham, in fact."

Wickham again! A murderous impulse seized Darcy. How dare he lay his hands on Elizabeth's sister? "What happened?" he asked darkly.

"To Miss Lydia? No idea. She turned up at the uncle's house in town, and that's the last anybody knows of it. The family is in complete disgrace. No one will receive them because of the shame. And I cannot marry Jane because of her fool of a sister. It's not right."

Darcy knew all too well how cruel society could be, especially in country neighbourhoods. How Elizabeth must be suffering! So there *was* a reason why she had left Pemberley in such a hurry. "And the family has done nothing to preserve Miss Lydia's reputation?"

Bingley raised haunted eyes. "I do not know. I am not in their confidence. Georgiana might have some idea. She spent a great deal of time with Miss Elizabeth. Caroline refused even to speak to any of the Bennets. It was horribly unpleasant."

Darcy could only imagine. "Bingley, you must remain here. I will have someone bring you some food, and I will return after I have spoken to Georgiana."

But Georgiana had little more to offer, apart from telling him how brave Elizabeth was when she told them what had happened and how devastated Jane Bennet seemed. Darcy returned to Bingley who was staring morosely into the fireplace, an empty glass by his elbow. Bingley roused himself enough to answer Darcy's questions, but little more.

"So did you propose to Miss Bennet?"

"Not really. At first we were all waiting, and then when it seemed her sister was lost forever, I spoke to Jane. I told her I had loved her all along and could think of nothing I would like more than to have her for my wife. She told me she would not put me through the scandal of marriage to someone like her. Good God, Darcy, she wept! I would have done anything for her, but I knew she was right. If we married, it would ruin Caroline's prospects, take away from our position in society which is perilous enough as it is….no, I could not do it, and she was the one who was brave enough to say so. That was two days ago. God alone knows what will happen to her now. I cannot bear to think on it. What a fool I was to walk away from her a year ago! If I had married her then, all this would have been avoided."

Darcy stood by the fireplace, oblivious to the heat pressing against his legs, his fingers tapping on the mantelpiece. "Perhaps Wickham can be prevailed upon to marry the girl. That would be something."

"I have no idea. The word was that he had abandoned her."

"Where is she now?"

"At her uncle's house in Cheapside."

"On Gracechurch Street, if I recall correctly," Darcy said absently. Perhaps there was something he might be able to do after all.

DARCY DID NOT find it difficult to locate the Gardiner residence. While Gracechurch Street stretched for many blocks, a few carefully placed questions brought him to the correct house. He rapped on the door and gave his card to the manservant who opened it.

The man returned quickly and said that Mrs. Gardiner would see him, and asked him to wait in the sitting room. It was tastefully decorated, although a careful eye could detect a certain frugality compared to the houses he usually frequented. He examined an attractive small watercolour on the wall, recognizing it as a landscape near Lambton. Memories of Elizabeth there welled up in him.

Mrs. Gardiner was dressed neatly and practically, clearly not expecting to receive guests, but she greeted him with as much graciousness as if she were welcoming him to a manor. "This is a lovely surprise, Mr. Darcy. My husband is out, but I am glad to have the opportunity to return your kind hospitality. I hope your sister is well?"

He bowed slightly, wishing that Mr. Gardiner were there. It would be easier to talk to a man about such things. He hardly knew how to begin speaking to a woman.

"She is quite well, thank you. She has just returned from a stay at Mr. Bingley's estate in Hertfordshire, and she brought some intelligence which has caused me concern."

Mrs. Gardiner's smile faded slightly as she motioned to him to sit. "I am sorry if it has created any inconvenience for you."

Darcy noted how neatly she had avoided stating that she knew what he was speaking of. "It is a delicate matter, but one which concerns me in that I bear a certain responsibility for it."

She raised an arched eyebrow, then rang the bell. When the manservant appeared, she asked him to fetch Mr. Gardiner from the warehouse. When he departed, she said, "Perhaps you could enlighten me, as I am unaware of any matter which touches on you, Mr. Darcy."

"I am, as you may guess, speaking of the matter of your youngest niece. You may be aware that my family has a long history of dealings with Mr. Wickham. I was aware he was not a man to be trusted, but I chose to say nothing of the matter in Hertfordshire because I thought it beneath my pride. In hindsight, I failed in my responsibility to the people of Meryton, and allowed a situation to arise which has harmed people of my acquaintance." In particular, the woman he loved.

She looked at him for a long moment, then smiled warmly. "Is it then your personal responsibility, Mr. Darcy, to warn the entire world of every potential blackguard? I am sure you must know more than one."

Her gentle teasing reminded him of Elizabeth, and his stiffness eased slightly. "You are graciousness itself, madam, but the fact remains that I have a gentleman's duty to ameliorate a desperate situation when it is one I could have prevented."

"I suspect, then, that this is a discussion you should be having with my husband. He should be here in a few minutes, as the warehouse is not far. May I offer you some refreshment in the meantime?"

Darcy accepted her offer gratefully, and they chatted about Derbyshire while she poured out tea. The tea was excellent, clearly expensive, not like bitter leavings more commonly found in such households. He wondered how often it was served there, and whether it was brought out especially for him. But he had to admit that if he had not known their address and Mr. Gardiner's occupation, he would have taken them for fashionable people. Certainly they exceeded much of the *ton* in civility and amiability.

A heavy set of footsteps presaged Mr. Gardiner's arrival. That gentleman stopped short at the sight of their guest, but recovered himself quickly and made the usual polite inquiries.

Mrs. Gardiner said, "Mr. Darcy has come with some concerns regarding our present difficulty and how to ameliorate it. If you will excuse me, I will withdraw to allow you to discuss this."

Mr. Gardiner held up a finger to indicate that she should wait. "If this matter concerns our niece, I would prefer that you stay, as you have better insight into her than I. Mr. Darcy, do you object to my wife's presence?"

"Not at all," he said. He explained his circumstances again, and added, "I have already begun some inquiries into Mr. Wickham's present whereabouts. If I can locate him, there is a chance I can persuade him to make matters right with Miss Lydia."

"Any intelligence you can offer would be greatly appreciated. I am not sure, however, that he has any ongoing interest in Lydia, from what she had told me."

"Perhaps not," Darcy acknowledged. "Forgive me for speaking bluntly, but Wickham will do almost anything if I make it worth his while. He is very fond of money, and always short of it. This would, of course, be at my expense."

"That is generous of you, and although I would prefer to be of some help to my niece, I believe we can address that question later if Wickham has been found. Otherwise...."

"If I cannot locate him, I do have other resources which may lessen the impact on the Bennet family. There are men who would be willing to marry your niece with sufficient financial incentive."

The Gardiners exchanged glances. Mr. Gardiner said, "I agree with your sentiment, and in some ways I would be happier to see Lydia wed to someone other than Wickham, but we have run into some difficulties in that regard as well. There is a young man in my firm, a clerk who is educated but has no wealth or family to speak of, who was willing to consider the idea in exchange for preference at the firm plus a dowry, but Lydia refuses to have anything to do with him or any other man who is not Wickham. The potential bridegroom is not willing to marry her against her will, and I have yet to convince Mr. Bennet that harsher measures should be taken to win her compliance. We have threatened to put her out on the streets, but is not a situation in which I wish to find myself unless she makes it impossible to do anything else." He shook his head and sighed.

Mrs. Gardiner said, "She is quite out of spirits, poor girl. She seems very troubled by her experiences, but she must marry, or else leave her family forever."

"I see our minds run in similar directions. Can you tell me what Miss Lydia would wish for in a husband, given the limitations of the current circumstances?"

Mr. Gardiner looked to his wife, who said, "She had dreams of marrying an officer, one who would take her to balls and assemblies, a man she could show off to her friends and acquaintances. That last is obviously impossible, but a soldier might be more agreeable to her. She remains fixed on Mr. Wickham, and sees marriage to him as the only way she could ever return to Meryton or her old life. It is true enough; even if she marries someone else, she could not go back, since everyone knows it was Wickham she ran off with."

"Has she told you where she saw him last? That might prove of assistance in trying to locate him."

"He left their lodgings while she was out shopping. At first she thought he had merely gone out himself, but then she found that all his belongings were missing, along with the little money she had left. I can press her for more details if that would help."

Darcy nodded. "It might. So we have the beginnings of a plan."

LOCATING MRS. YONGE did not prove as difficult as Darcy had feared. A few coins changing hands at her old lodgings was sufficient to obtain her new direction, which was in a neighbourhood of London where Darcy would be disinclined to go without a footman for protection. She had clearly fallen a long way since her days as Georgiana's governess. Darcy found a vindictive pleasure in the thought.

When Mrs. Yonge first opened her battered door to him, he almost did not recognize her. Her appearance, once refined if impoverished, was now slovenly, and it was not difficult to recognize the odor of alcohol that permeated the air. At first she refused to speak to him, but coin of the realm again proved the necessary lubricant. She allowed him into the house, which apparently was some sort of boarding house. "What is it you want then?" she asked.

"I am looking for George Wickham."

"He isn't here."

"When did you see him last?"

"What's it worth to you?"

Darcy silently handed over a handful of coins which she examined without apparent pleasure.

"He was here till a few weeks ago with some girl he picked up. Then he left. He took near ten pounds of my money with him, damn him. All my savings. Didn't pay his rent, either."

"If I am able to find him, I will make sure your money is returned to you."

Mrs. Yonge laughed derisively, showing teeth that had begun to yellow. "You won't find him."

"Where did he go?"

"He left on a ship to Canada. Seems his old militia mates were getting hot on his trail and he didn't think he was safe in England."

Darcy silently damned Wickham. This was one thing he had not expected. "Are you certain?"

"As certain as one ever could be with George Wickham."

There was little he could say to that.

COLONEL FITZWILLIAM OFFERED Darcy a glass of port. "So, what is on your mind? I can tell from your expression that this is not a social call."

Darcy did not bother to deny it. "I need your assistance to locate a soldier. I do not know what regiment he is in. Would you be able to find him?"

"That should not be too difficult. Who do you wish to find?"

"You will not like this. I am looking for Captain Wickham."

The colonel choked on his port. "Why on earth would you want to find *him?* Can't help you, anyway. He deserted. They've been hunting for him for weeks. And he was a lieutenant, not a captain, damn his eyes."

"My apologies. I should have made myself clearer. I want the *other* Wickham," Darcy said.

Chapter 13

IT WAS THE first piece of luck Darcy had on the entire quest. Captain Wickham was in England, not on the Continent, and was no farther than Gravesend, where his regiment was in training after taking significant casualties in France. Darcy paid a quick call on his commanding officer with a letter of introduction from Colonel Fitzwilliam, and received immediate direction to the quarters where he might find Captain Thomas Wickham. There he was informed that the Captain was at dinner, but a helpful orderly took him to the officers' mess.

Darcy heard him before he saw him, his deep voice carrying across the table, telling an off-colour joke. The big man in the red coat stopped in mid-word when he saw his visitor. "I say, Darcy, this is a surprise. What brings you here?" He frowned, as if he expected ill tidings. "Who is it? You might as well tell me at once."

For a moment Darcy did not understand him. "Your family is all in good health, to the best of my knowledge. I would like a few minutes of your time, if that is possible." Darcy spoke as neutrally as he could manage.

"Anything for an old friend." He shoveled another bite of meat into his mouth before standing and motioning to Darcy to follow him.

Darcy would certainly not have called him a friend of any sort.

Captain Wickham's quarters consisted of a small room with a cot bed. "It's not much," he said, "but we won't be here long. Which brings up the question of why *you* are here, Darcy. A little out of your element, aren't you?"

"As usual, I am trying to clean up one of your brother's messes, and in this case, I need some assistance from you."

The man guffawed. "That's a rich one, Darcy. I owe him nothing and you less. Your father bought me this commission, and you had nothing to do with it."

Darcy leveled his best Master of Pemberley stare on him, but the captain seemed singularly unaffected by it, probably from having known him before he could walk. "I am hoping to find a solution that will be to our mutual advantage. I am prepared to pay you for the inconvenience. I assume you are still fond of money?"

He grinned. "Some things never change. So what is it you want me to do? The brat won't listen to me, you know that."

"Does he ever listen to anyone? No, I have a proposition for you. I have a girl who needs to marry, and a soldier named Wickham fits the bill best."

The captain stared at him in disbelief. "Marry? I have no intention of marrying, Darcy. Find yourself another fool."

"Perhaps I will, but may I tell you the terms before you refuse?"

"Make your best offer then, Darcy. It will have to be pretty damned good." He sprawled into the one chair in the room.

"She is a gentleman's daughter. One of your brother's leavings, of course. She thinks highly of men in red coats, and cannot return home unless she is married, since the whole affair is public knowledge. If she were to become your wife - Mrs. Wickham - everyone would assume it was you she had run off with and she would be accepted in society again. She comes with a dowry of a thousand pounds and an annual allowance to you of two hundred pounds during her lifetime. I will double that. She is sixteen."

He scratched his chin thoughtfully. "Tempting, but not tempting enough. I have no desire to be saddled with a woman."

Darcy drew out a parcel of paper tied with string. "Five thousand pounds, and your brother's debts, which I have bought up. Enough to put him in debtor's prison for life, however long that might last. They would be yours on your wedding day." Despite the man's current disdain for George Wickham, Darcy knew he had once loved his younger brother.

The captain's eyes narrowed and he tapped his foot. "Make it ten thousand pounds and perhaps we can talk. If she's pretty, that is."

"You will find it no chore to bed her. Six thousand pounds and five hundred per annum provided you treat her well, and you agree to put on enough charm that she wants to marry you."

"Five hundred per annum. Tempting, but what is in it for you?"

"She is the daughter of a friend whom I have no desire to see disgraced. Think about it. You could leave the army and be a man of means. You will never have another opportunity like this."

"Must be a *very* good friend." Thomas Wickham pushed himself out of the chair and stuck out his hand. "You have a deal."

DARCY WOULD HAVE liked to pace the length of the Gardiners' sitting room, but he forced himself to sit still. Not only was it better manners, but he could not abide how Lydia Bennet cringed whenever he so much as looked at her. As if he had ever done anything to hurt her! But it was very strange to see a silent and frightened Lydia Bennet. He almost wished she would show some of the lack of decorum he associated with her.

Instead, he said, "George Wickham will not return. He is already aboard a ship to Canada, and no one knows how to reach him once he arrives there, which will be in several months. He is gone. He used you."

Lydia said in a barely audible voice, "I cannot marry that clerk."

"You must either wed or leave your friends and family forever."

"I have no choice but to leave them. If I do not marry Mr. Wickham, I can never go home again."

"If you do not marry, you will be on the streets where anyone can misuse you. You may well be with child."

Now it was Mrs. Gardiner's turn to flinch at his harsh tone, but she made no argument. "It is true, Lydia. You are running out of choices."

"I cannot be a clerk's wife and scrub floors all my life. I would rather die." She flung herself down on the sofa and began to sob.

Darcy seriously doubted she would follow through on her dramatic statement, but was grateful not to have to press the point. "Fortunately, you still have one choice left. George Wickham has a brother in the regulars. I have acquainted him with your situation, and he feels bound to honour the promise his brother made to you, especially as you may be carrying a child of his blood. He has agreed to meet with you, and if he likes you, he will marry you," Darcy said.

Lydia's sobs stopped abruptly, but she did not raise her head.

Mrs. Gardiner took on the role of persuasion. "There is nothing like going to a ball on the arm of a handsome officer, you know. If he is anything like George Wickham, he is no doubt delightful." She looked like it pained her to say so. "More importantly, you would be Mrs. Wickham after all."

Darcy thought sourly that Thomas would no doubt be *quite* delightful with six thousand pounds riding on the outcome. "All I ask is that you meet him."

"Would it not be lovely to have an officer call on you? Perhaps if you like him, he could take you to the theatre or to Vauxhall," Mrs. Gardiner said coaxingly.

A flicker of her old spirit showed in Lydia's eyes. "You would allow that?"

"That would be a great advantage of accepting his suit," Mrs. Gardiner agreed.

Lydia said shakily, "I will consider it."

TWO DAYS LATER Darcy took Thomas Wickham to Gracechurch Street in a new, well-fitted red coat, shaved and dressed by Darcy's own valet, and carrying a bouquet of flowers.

"I feel like an actor," the captain complained.

"A well-paid actor," Darcy said pointedly, but in truth he was more relaxed with the man than he had expected to be. Although his manner and appearance still reminded him unsettlingly of George Wickham, Thomas seemed to have matured into a decent man, jovial where George had been overly charming and manipulative. It was a strange day, Darcy decided, when he felt that a man who could be bribed into marrying a fallen woman was a relatively honest fellow. "I hope you will treat her well."

Darcy rapped sharply on the door and performed the introductions. The captain produced the bouquet and offered it to Lydia with a flourish. He said admiringly, "Darcy, you should have told me how lovely she is."

Darcy gritted his teeth but kept a smile on his face. This was for Elizabeth. He could tolerate anything for her sake.

ELIZABETH LONGED TO be anywhere but Longbourn. Mrs. Bennet was still keeping to her rooms except for those times when she emerged to berate Jane for failing to secure Mr. Bingley or to blame Elizabeth for their present predicament by not marrying Mr. Collins. Jane put a brave face on during the day, but at night Elizabeth could hear her crying into her pillow. Mary had more than enough to moralize over in Lydia's dilemma, predicting dire outcomes for all of them. Kitty, who had come through the earlier parts of the ordeal unscathed, had sunk into a deep loss of spirits after being turned away from Lucas Lodge and left only to the company of her sisters. Mr. Bennet had begun to take his meals in the library, saying sour faces ruined his digestion. The cook, who had been with the Bennets since Elizabeth was a child, left to seek employment in a respectable household, though Elizabeth suspected the scandal might well have been just an excuse. Cook had complained often about Mrs. Bennet's constant demands upon her.

If only Lydia were not at the Gardiners' house in London, Elizabeth would have begged to go there simply to escape the prison-like atmosphere at Longbourn. Visiting anyone but close family was out of the question. She knew Mr. Collins would not permit her to visit Charlotte under the current circumstances. Even walking to Meryton was a bitter experience; every time she showed her face there, the one person she could be certain of seeing was Mr. White, the butcher. He had lost no time in making his intentions clear, and that Miss Elizabeth Bennet could not now hope for any better than him. Nothing she said could discourage him.

Letters continued to arrive for Mr. Bennet from Mr. Gardiner, but all he would tell Elizabeth was that nothing had changed. Then one day he invited Elizabeth and Jane into his library and handed them a letter.

Jane read it aloud.

> *My Dear Brother,*
> *There has been a startling new development in the matter of*

Lydia. Last Saturday we received a quite unexpected visitor in the form of Mr. George Wickham's elder brother. He is a captain in the regulars, and through various channels he learned of Lydia's plight. He came to offer what support he might to compensate for his brother's shameless behaviour. I did not know at the time the precise nature of the remediation he planned to offer, but he seemed a pleasant and respectable fellow. He has not had much to do with his brother for some years now, owing to a parting of the ways over the younger Mr. Wickham's profligate habits, but he retains a certain fondness for him. He spent quite some time with Lydia discussing her options and warning her of the dangers of hoping for her lover's return, and as she seemed more inclined to take his counsel than that of ours, I allowed him the privilege, if it can be called such. It was quite a shock to both my wife and me when two days later, Mr. Thomas Wickham (for so he is named) announced that Lydia had done him the honour of accepting his hand in marriage. The particulars I reserve till we meet, but you can imagine our shock.

"Could such a thing be?" Jane asked, her eyes wide. "That she should be married, and to Mr. Wickham's brother? Why would he agree to such a thing?"

"Read on, and you shall discover the answer," said her father.

All that is required of you is to assure to your daughter, by settlement, her equal share of the five thousand pounds secured among your children after the decease of yourself and my sister; and, moreover, to enter into an engagement of allowing her, during your life, one hundred pounds per annum and a discharging of his brother's debts which would otherwise fall upon him, thought to equal no more than a thousand pounds. These are conditions which, considering every thing, I had no hesitation in complying with, as far as I thought myself privileged, for you. We have judged it best that my niece should be married from this house, of which I hope you will approve. A license has been obtained, and we hope to perform the ceremony next week. Your's, &c.

Edw. Gardiner.

"So the man is mercenary, it seems," Elizabeth said.

"Perhaps there are good reasons," Jane said. "After all, he is responsible enough to wish to help Lydia. Perhaps he fell in love with her, but knows he could not support her without help."

Elizabeth shook her head with a smile. "You will always think the best of everyone! But whatever his reasons, their marriage would be a godsend for Lydia. Even the name - she will be Mrs. Wickham. It will help quell the rumours."

Her father said, "Yes, yes, they must marry. There is nothing else to be done. But there are two things that I want very much to know:— one is, how much money your uncle has laid down to bring it about; and the other, how I am ever to pay him."

"Money! my uncle!" cried Jane, "what do you mean, Sir?"

"I mean that no man in his senses would marry Lydia on so slight a temptation as one hundred a year."

"That is very true," said Elizabeth, "though it had not occurred to me before. Oh! it must be my uncle's doings! Generous, good man; I am afraid he has distressed himself. A small sum could not do all this."

"No," said her father, "The man is a fool, if he takes her with a farthing less than ten thousand pounds. I should be sorry to think so ill of him in the very beginning of our relationship."

Elizabeth fought back a smile. "Well, our uncle thinks well of him, and that is a good sign. Come, let us tell our mother the news."

MRS. BENNET COULD hardly contain herself. As soon as Jane told her of Mr. Gardiner's hope of Lydia's being soon married, her joy burst forth. She was now in an irritation as violent from delight, as she had ever been fidgety from alarm and vexation. To know that her daughter would be married was enough. She was disturbed by no fear for her felicity, nor humbled by any remembrance of her misconduct. That she was marrying a complete stranger was of no matter.

"My dear, dear Lydia!" she cried: "This is delightful indeed! She will be married! I shall see her again! She will be married at sixteen! My good, kind brother! I knew how it would be. I knew he would manage every thing. How I long to see her! and to meet her Mr. Wickham too! But the clothes, the wedding clothes! I will write to my sister Gardiner about them directly. Lizzy, my dear, run down to your father, and ask him how much he will give her. Stay, stay, I will go myself. Ring the bell, Kitty, for Hill. I will put on my things in a moment. My dear, dear Lydia!—How merry we shall be together when we meet! Oh! here comes Hill. My dear Hill, have you heard the good news? Miss Lydia is going to be married; and you shall all have a bowl of punch to make merry at her wedding."

Mrs. Hill began instantly to express her joy. Elizabeth received her congratulations amongst the rest, and then, sick of this folly, took refuge in her own room, that she might think with freedom.

Poor Lydia's situation must, at best, be bad enough; but that it was no worse, she had need to be thankful. She felt it so; and though, in looking forward, neither rational happiness nor worldly prosperity could be justly expected for her sister, in looking back to what they had feared, only two hours ago, she felt all the advantages of what they had gained.

Chapter 14

DARCY BLINKED AT his sister's pleading expression. This was not what he had expected when Georgiana had timidly said she would like to ask a favour of him. "You wish to have a cat? I thought you wanted one of Lycisce's puppies."

"They are very sweet, but I would prefer a cat, one who would be a pet, who would stay with me. It would be good company. I would keep it out of trouble."

He had never been able to deny Georgiana anything her heart desired. It was fortunate that her desires tended to be quite modest. "If you would like a cat, I see no harm in it. But you have never mentioned a fondness for cats before."

"I had never thought much about them, but there was a cat at Longbourn who was so very sweet. He particularly loved Elizabeth and was forever twining around her ankles. Twice he sat on my lap, and I found it soothing. I cannot explain it better."

Darcy could picture it - Elizabeth laughing over the antics of a small cat. The image gave him a warm feeling. There was nothing like Elizabeth when she was filled with delight over something. It was almost as if she shone with liveliness and intelligence. He felt a sudden longing for her presence, but that was useless. She wanted nothing to do with him. He felt a sudden fierce jealousy of the unknown cat who had the extraordinary privilege of twining around a pair of graceful ankles that had caused him more sleepless nights than he cared to admit. "I see no problem with a well-behaved cat, if you wish it."

Georgiana still looked anxious, so Darcy said, "Is something the matter?"

"I have been wondering... when I was at Netherfield, Miss

Bingley said you would not approve of my associating with Miss Elizabeth Bennet under the circumstances. I thought you would not mind, but lately I have not been so sure. I did not mean to do anything you would disapprove of." She gave him a pleading look.

"Disapprove? No, not in the least. I am glad you would not abandon a friend just because she faced difficulties."

She released a pent-up breath. "Oh, good. I have been so worried. You frown every time I mention her name, and I thought perhaps you were angry with me."

"I frown? That is ridiculous," Darcy said.

Georgiana gave a little giggle. "You are frowning right now."

With embarrassment he realized she was right. He was not about to tell a sister ten years his junior that whenever he thought of Elizabeth, he felt a piercing pain that nothing could remedy, and fierce shame over his own failings. "It is nothing against Miss Elizabeth. I am worried for her situation, that is all."

"Oh, of course." She brightened immediately. "I should have realized. I do wish there were something we could do to help. I understand her sister's position so well. I never told her about my own connection with Mr. Wickham, of course."

"Elizabeth already knows." The words slipped out before he had time to think through the implications. "I warned her against him when she was at Pemberley. Wickham made a great many friends in Meryton. I should have made my warnings more general when I was there."

Georgiana paled. "Do her sisters know as well? They never acted as if they were aware of it."

"Not as far as I know, unless Miss Elizabeth told them, and I trust in her ability to keep a confidence."

"Oh." Georgiana nodded slowly, and he could see a look dawning over her face. He suspected it meant she was putting together a number of puzzling things and coming up with an all-too-accurate solution. She was becoming a woman more quickly than he expected.

"I must be going," he said abruptly.

"Perhaps I will see you later, then." She put her hand on his arm timidly. "I am so sorry, Fitzwilliam."

He knew she was not speaking of her behaviour.

ELIZABETH RAN A brush through Jane's long silky hair as they sat on her bed. "Jane, would you think me terribly selfish if I asked to go to London for a time?"

"Selfish? Of course not. You are never selfish."

Elizabeth laughed. "That is correct. Thank you for the reminder that I am absolutely perfect."

Jane swatted at her. "You know what I mean. Why do you want to go?"

"The Gardiners are taking on a great deal of work on Lydia's behalf. Perhaps I could assist them with the children to lessen the burden on them."

"That is a very kind idea, and not in the least bit selfish."

"The selfish part is that I would be happy to escape our current situation. I need a place where I do not see Lydia's shame in every face. But that would leave you here on your own."

"That matters not. I can be content anywhere, as you know." She sounded wistful, as if she had forgotten what it meant to be content. "I would rather be here."

Elizabeth took several more strokes through Jane's hair, then handed her the brush and turned her own back. "But would it worsen the gossip if I went there, since Lydia is there?"

"I would not think so. No one would know, in any case, since no one will acknowledge us. Once it is known that Lydia is to marry, we can always say that you went to help with the wedding. There is nothing shameful in that."

"I suppose not. I will ask our father tomorrow."

THE LONDON POST coach was crowded and rocked precariously on the rutted road. Elizabeth was glad to be on the side rather than squeezed in the middle of the bench, and even happier that no one she knew from Meryton was on board. For the first time since she had left Derbyshire, she felt free of the miasma of shame and hopelessness. Even the strong odor of onions from the heavyset gentleman opposite her could not dampen her spirits.

She decided to enjoy her freedom. Soon enough she would have to deal with Lydia, and from her uncle's communications, her sister had turned into someone she no longer knew.

The difficult part would be to keep her own pain private. Lydia had taken so much from her that could never be replaced. She leaned her head against the side of the coach and closed her eyes, recalling Mr. Darcy and that half-smile she had so often observed on his face when he looked at her. If only she had known sooner that it was admiration rather than critical, how different things might have been! If only she had not listened to Wickham's lies. She had been a fool to believe a tale of woe so easily spun to a near-stranger.

She could no longer deny harboring tender feelings toward Mr. Darcy. She began now to comprehend that he was exactly the man who, in disposition and talents, would most suit her. His understanding and temper, though unlike her own, would have answered all her wishes. It was a union that must have been to the advantage of both; by her ease and liveliness, his mind might have been softened, his manners improved, and from his judgment, information, and knowledge of the world, she must have received benefit of greater importance. But no such happy marriage could now teach the admiring multitude what connubial felicity really was. A union of a different tendency, and precluding the possibility of the other, was soon to be formed in their family.

What a triumph for him, could he know that the proposals which she had proudly spurned only four months ago, would now have been gladly and gratefully received! He was as generous, she doubted not, as the most generous of his sex. But while he was mortal, there must be a triumph.

She should be grateful in the knowledge that he would not now completely scorn her, at least if his sister was to be believed, and she thought his honour would demand as much. But it could be nothing more. He could not but shrink from such a connection. All his initial objections still applied, and in addition, hers was a family now allied with the man he had so justly scorned.

Mr. Gardiner's manservant met the coach in London and escorted Elizabeth via hackney coach to Gracechurch Street. It seemed quite unchanged since her last visit there in May. It was she who had changed. She felt as if she had aged years in the last few months.

No sooner was she in the door than her nieces and nephews came tumbling down the stairs to meet her, each with their own news which must be delivered instantly to their dear cousin Elizabeth. Once she had heard all the details of the frogs in the yard, the new schoolbooks, the critical question of precisely when one should graduate from the nursery to the schoolroom, and other matters of great important, Mrs. Gardiner came to greet her with a warm embrace.

"I am glad you are come, Lizzy," her aunt said. "I am greatly in need of sensible company."

"I can only imagine. But now I am here to spare you any excess dealings with young ladies of a less sensible nature!"

Her aunt took her arm and said in a quiet voice, "I am worried about Lydia. She is not at all herself. When she first arrived, she looked so wild I barely recognized her. I actually feared for a while that she might do herself some harm."

"Has she spoken of what happened to her?"

"She avoids the topic, but she is frightened. We have discovered that there were apparently several days between Mr. Wickham's flight and the time she left their lodgings, and it was location quite unsuited for a young lady of gentle upbringing. I fear she may have been misused during that time. She refuses to speak of it, but she is frightened."

"Frightened? That is quite unlike the Lydia I know."

"It is indeed. Fortunately, she is improving a little. At least she seems to trust Thomas Wickham."

"And is he a man to be trusted?"

Mrs. Gardiner paused. "Yes, I believe he is. Even if he is only marrying her for pecuniary reasons, he seems a decent man."

"Does Lydia like him?"

Her aunt sighed. "I believe so. He flatters her constantly."

"Oh, dear," said Elizabeth with heavy irony. "How pleasant for everyone."

TO ELIZABETH'S SURPRISE, Lydia seemed unusually happy to see her, embracing her and holding her tightly, even sniffling a little. "Oh,

Lizzy," she cried. "I have missed you so much!"

Perhaps, Elizabeth thought, the idea of never seeing her family again had made Lydia value them a little more, since she had never before shown this sort of affection. "I hope you are well." She could not bring herself to say anything kinder.

Lydia shrugged and looked away anxiously, causing Elizabeth to reflect on her aunt's earlier words about her sister suffering possible misuse. She wondered if Lydia had finally realized that the world did not exist specifically to provide her with enjoyment. "Do tell me about your husband-to-be. I know nothing of him beyond his name and rank."

Lydia seemed calmer at the thought of her intended. "You will meet him soon enough. He is as amiable and handsome as his brother, and always the gentleman. He has been in the regulars since he finished at university and has fought in actual battles! He will not tell me stories of them because he is afraid of damaging my sensibilities."

As if Lydia had any delicate sensibilities! But perhaps it was best for her betrothed to maintain some illusions about his future wife, at least long enough to get them to the altar.

"It is extraordinarily generous of him to offer for you. I hope you realize that."

Lydia burst into tears. "I do know. I was so frightened, Lizzy. You cannot imagine."

It was astonishing to see her youngest sister in the grips of an emotion other than excitement or sulkiness. Perhaps she really had learned something from her experiences. "I am sorry Mr. Wickham – the younger one, that is – treated you so poorly."

"He was so charming and thoughtful of me in Brighton, but as soon as we reached London, he changed. He was always impatient, as if he were waiting for something, but I never knew what it was." Lydia mopped her eyes with a handkerchief that bore signs of recent use. "He promised to show me all the delights of London, but instead all he did was to take me walking every day, up and down the same street near Hyde Park, even when it was raining. I should have known something was wrong, because he said he was going to introduce me to one of his friends who worked at a fancy townhouses there, but when he tried to see her, he was practically thrown out. I was such a fool!'"

Elizabeth could not argue that point.

She took only a few moments to freshen up after speaking to Lydia, and felt all the fatigue inherent in long day of travel in close quarters. Feeling unequal to an evening with the family, she determined she would instead take a small tray in her room and go to sleep early. She started down the steep, narrow steps to inform her aunt of her decision. Halfway down, she heard the front door close. The manservant was accepting the hat and gloves of a man in a dark coat who stood with his back to her. His height and the breadth of his shoulders reminded her of Mr. Darcy, and she scolded herself for allowing a man she would never see again to dominate her thoughts. Just then he turned around.

It *was* Mr. Darcy, with a look of astonishment that no doubt mirrored her own. In shock, Elizabeth tripped over the next to last stair and reached out to the banister for support. Before she could steady herself, Mr. Darcy lunged forward and she felt warm hands grasp her waist. Mr. Darcy guided her down the last step until she stood only inches from him, her cheeks burning.

She felt unable to breathe. Through a dry mouth, she said, "I think there is nothing so important for a lady as a graceful entrance, do you not agree?" His hands, resting on her hips, seemed to burn through her dress, and she felt a queer sensation in the pit of her stomach, as if she were still aboard the bouncing coach.

He looked sterner than she remembered him being at Pemberley, but after a moment, she saw the corners of his lips twitch. "It was very kind of you, Miss Bennet, to arrange matters so that I would feel useful the moment I arrived." He looked down, as if he had just realized his hands were still upon her, and removed them. Elizabeth could not tell if it was wishful thinking, but she thought he seemed reluctant to release her.

It was not until that moment that she realized the oddity of the circumstance. What on earth was Mr. Darcy doing at her uncle's house on Gracechurch Street? True, he had met Mr. Gardiner in Derbyshire, but such a trifling acquaintance between gentlemen of such differing circumstances could hardly be expected to be maintained in Town. For a dizzying moment she thought he must be there for her sake, but that could not be. He had been as astonished to see her there as she was to see him.

Just then Mr. Gardiner came down the passageway to the entrance hall. "Darcy, I had not expected to see you so soon, but it is of course a pleasure." He then took in Elizabeth's presence and said quite unnecessarily, "Lizzy, I had not realized you were here yet. Welcome." His eyes flicked back and forth from Elizabeth to Darcy and back again with a half-puzzled expression.

Elizabeth realized both she and Mr. Darcy had the air of having been caught in some act of mischief, and she blushed even more furiously at what her uncle must be thinking. In an attempt at lightness, she said, "It seems to be my day to be surprised and surprising at every turn."

"Well, do come in, Darcy. Lizzy, how was your journey?"

"It was quite free of difficulty," she said, not wishing to have Mr. Darcy know that she had travelled alone by post. "I arrived about an hour ago."

Mr. Gardiner ushered them both into the sitting room. "I am glad you are here. It is good to be reminded that we have a sensible and well-mannered niece. We were in grave danger of forgetting that such a thing existed."

Elizabeth sent him a warning glance. Surely he was not going to discuss Lydia in front of Mr. Darcy, of all people.

Darcy said, "Speaking of Miss Lydia, I believe that her intended will be arriving shortly to take her for a drive."

Elizabeth's jaw dropped. How did he even know Lydia was there?

"That will please her. She seems in better spirits, but is still not herself," Mr. Gardiner responded, shaking his head. "Soon enough it will no longer be my responsibility."

Mr. Darcy seemed not at all surprised by these comments. Both men had the air of continuing an earlier conversation. To her amazement, Darcy crossed the room to the chair which was commonly Elizabeth's during her visits. Self-consciously she seated herself on the sofa across from him.

She jumped when he addressed her. "Miss Bennet, may I hope that you have left your parents in good health?"

If this was to be a repeat of their first meeting at Pemberley, Elizabeth was prepared this time. With an arch smile, she said, "Yes, thank you. My parents are both in good health." Their spirits were another matter, but fortunately he had not asked about that. "And Miss Darcy, is she well?"

"Quite well. You seem to have made quite an impression on her while she was at Netherfield. And your sisters?"

"They are also well. To the best of my knowledge, everyone in our immediate circle is in good health." She gave him a teasing look, and could have sworn she saw his face redden.

"Lizzy, you may speak freely in front of Mr. Darcy," her uncle said. "He knows that all is not well."

Elizabeth's mouth dropped open, then she quickly shut it. What was her uncle thinking? Discussing intimate family matters with Mr. Darcy?

"Miss Bennet, you may be assured that anything you say will be held in confidence," Darcy said with a stiff formality.

She darted a shocked glance at him. His sister must have told him the truth of what had happened to Lydia, but then why had he come to Gracechurch Street? She would have expected him to avoid it. "My mother is better since the recent news, and no longer keeps to her room all day. My father spends all his time in the library. Jane... well, Jane is suffering a certain amount of distress, but as usual, masks it from the world. Kitty has lost her spirits since being turned away from our neighbours' houses. Mary is unchanged in essentials."

Mr. Gardiner nodded soberly. "I am not surprised. Your father's letters these days are limited to brief instructions to me, so I have been concerned as to what he might not be telling me."

Elizabeth was sorely tempted to point out to her uncle that Mr. Bennet was not the only member of the family who had apparently been keeping his own counsel. She stole a glance at Mr. Darcy and discovered his eyes resting on her as they had so often in the past, but she could not make out his expression.

Mrs. Gardiner bustled in with a tea tray. "Good afternoon, Mr.

Darcy. I hope you will stay to dine with us?"

"You have family visiting," he said, gesturing toward Elizabeth. "I will not impose on your reunion."

Mrs. Gardiner lifted the teapot. "It would be no imposition. As you know, we have had the pleasure of Lizzy's company quite recently." She flashed a smile at Elizabeth. "It is a treat to see her again so soon. Our two eldest nieces are particularly dear to us."

"Then it will be my pleasure to join you."

So much for Elizabeth's intentions of dining alone in her room! She was suddenly aware of the flaws in her appearance, her wrinkled and dusty travelling dress, her hair styled with the utmost simplicity, yet still slipping out of its constraints to curl upon her neck. It was not how she would have chosen to appear when meeting Mr. Darcy again. She still could not believe she was sitting in the same room as him. How she wished this opportunity had presented itself to her before Lydia's disgrace! But there was no mending it now. She had recognized too late how well they would suit one another and that she would always feel an emptiness in her heart where he might have been. Even a continuing acquaintance was dubious, present circumstances notwithstanding.

She accepted a cup of tea from her aunt, then watched as Mrs. Gardiner prepared Mr. Darcy's cup, adding sugar without asking his preferences. As he thanked her with his usual gravity, Elizabeth's mind returned to the puzzling question of what he was doing there. Clearly he had become a regular visitor in the weeks since the Gardiners had returned from Derbyshire, yet he came to call in the afternoon and without his sister. Her uncle seemed to treat him as an intimate, and he was even aware of Lydia's presence. She wished that her sister's shame could have been hidden from him, but it was too late for that once Mr. Bingley and Miss Darcy had appeared at Netherfield. It had been too much to hope that they would not tell him. At least his sister had apparently been correct when she said her brother would not deny the acquaintance, for what little comfort that might be. But it was beyond puzzling to see him pursuing the Gardiners' company now. One might almost think he sought them out because of it!

A wave of heat rushed over her as she realized that was exactly what had happened. Mr. Thomas Wickham had not in fact miraculously appeared out of nowhere and offered marriage to Lydia for an absurdly low financial remuneration. The miracle had a name and was sitting before her.

Why, oh why had he done it? Why had he chosen to involve himself in a matter that was none of his business, one which required connection to the family of the man he most justly despised, and to have done all this for a girl he could neither regard or esteem? Her heart whispered it had been for her.

A sudden hope filled her, a thought that it might still not be too late, that perhaps his admiration for her had withstood these impossible circumstances. But it was a hope shortly checked by other considerations, and she soon felt that even her vanity was insufficient, when required to depend on his affection for her—for a woman who had already refused him—as able to overcome a sentiment so natural as abhorrence against relationship with Wickham's family. Every kind of pride must revolt from the connection. She could, perhaps, believe that remaining partiality for her might assist his endeavours in a cause where her peace of mind must be materially concerned, but no more. It was painful, exceedingly painful, to know that they were under obligations to a person who could never receive a return. They owed the restoration of Lydia, her character, every thing, to him.

How heartily did she grieve over every ungracious sensation she had ever encouraged, every saucy speech she had ever directed towards him. For herself she was humbled; but she was proud of him. Proud that in a cause of compassion and honour, he had been able to get the better of himself. It was yet another proof of his worthiness and of her own grave mistake in refusing him when she had the opportunity. She found herself blinking back hot tears.

"Lizzy, are you ill? You look quite pale," her aunt said.

She struggled to regain her composure, and was able to answer with a nearly steady voice. "No, not at all. It has been a long day, that is all." No sooner had she said it than she regretted her words when she saw Mr. Darcy looking at her with deep concern. It was impossible to look away, impossible not to wish that she could gaze into his eyes forever. It was as if an invisible line connected them, one which no one but themselves could sense. She could see his breathing becoming uneven.

She needed to look away, but she could not make herself do so until her uncle cleared his throat, reminding her of their circumstances. He said, "Perhaps you should rest while Mr. Darcy and I discuss our business in my study." Was there an element of warning in his voice?

She wondered exactly what part of the 'business' they needed to discuss, but she merely nodded and sipped her cooling tea.

Chapter 15

DARCY'S ELATION AT the unexpected sight of Elizabeth - and the touch of her waist under his hands - warred with his mortification of her discovery of his part in her sister's wedding. He had not intended her to know. He did not want her to credit him for it, and most especially he did not want her gratitude. No, gratitude was not what he wanted from Elizabeth Bennet at all. What he wanted was impossible and did not merit thinking about, though it seemed to preoccupy him both day and night despite all his efforts to discipline his errant thoughts. But it was not gratitude that he wished to see in her eyes. That was only a reminder of his shame.

He placed the envelope from the solicitor on Mr. Gardiner's desk. "This is the final copy of the settlement for your perusal."

"That was quick," Mr. Gardiner observed. "I had not expected to see this until the end of the week."

"I was anxious to have it signed before either of the principals could change their minds."

Mr. Gardiner examined the paper, his finger running down the lines of text. "This seems well in order."

"I had not realized Miss Bennet knew of my involvement in these matters." Darcy could not completely keep a reproach from his voice, since he had specifically requested that the Bennets be left in ignorance of his role.

Mr. Gardiner looked up at him sharply. "I assumed you had made her aware of it."

"No." Darcy's voice was clipped.

"You appear here unexpectedly within minutes of her arrival, and I am expected to believe this was complete coincidence? I am grateful to you for all your assistance, but I am not blind, nor a fool. I assure you that, even though I said nothing, my eyes were working perfectly well when I encountered the two of you in the hall, nor was I unaware of how you watched her at Pemberley."

Darcy flushed. "If you are implying that I was aware of her presence here, I assure *you* that I was not. It was a complete surprise to me. As for the rest, Miss Bennet was startled to see me and lost her balance. I was helping to steady her." His heart had barely stopped racing from it even now, and his hands could still feel the curves of her waist.

Mr. Gardiner's eyes narrowed. "May I inquire, then, as to the nature of your intentions toward my niece?"

What had happened to his normal imperturbability? It had apparently been destroyed by breathing the scent of lavender in Elizabeth's hair. But it was useless to deny his attraction to her. Mr. Gardiner had clearly already discovered it. "In as much as Miss Bennet does not look favourably upon me, it is safe to say that it does not matter what my intentions are, since they would come to naught. But I wish her no harm." It was hard to force out the words when all he wished was to give Elizabeth everything she could desire for the rest of her life. Unfortunately for him, that meant he needed to stay away from her.

Mr. Gardiner was silent for a moment, then spoke in more understanding tone. "I had not realized that was how the land lies. My apologies."

"Accepted." He hoped they could drop the subject now.

"I admit I had thought Lizzy's judgement to be superior to that, but there is no accounting for women's tastes."

It was not a subject Darcy wished to discuss. "Speaking of which, I hope Miss Lydia has not changed her mind."

"Not at all. She is sufficiently distracted by the excitement of being married at sixteen that she seems willing to forget the circumstances, and she accepts Mr. Thomas Wickham's blandishments at face value."

Darcy could hardly believe the foolish child was Elizabeth's sister, but in this case, her credulous nature worked to his advantage. "He has continued to call?"

"Most faithfully. I have no complaints of him."

"Good." He had not precisely doubted Tom's word on these matters, but he was relieved to know he had not been deceived.

Mr. Gardiner opened his inkwell and dipped his pen in it before signing his name across the bottom of the settlement. He sanded it lightly and laid it aside to dry. "Have you any word on his future?"

"He is looking to sell his commission. He says soldiering is a young man's job, and plans to let a house. I have indicated to him that Hertfordshire should not be on his list of possibilities."

"Well, in a few days our job will be done. I cannot say I will be sorry for it."

Darcy could not feel sorry for anything at the moment. His mind was already travelling to Elizabeth's nearby presence.

TO ELIZABETH'S SURPRISE, dinner was not the strained event she had expected. Mrs. Gardiner's facility as a conversationalist, the surprisingly mature behaviour of Mr. Thomas Wickham, and Lydia's apparent awe of her future husband provided an atmosphere where there was little to embarrass Elizabeth in front of Mr. Darcy. It had felt odd to meet this new Mr. Wickham who bore a distinct resemblance to his younger brother, yet seemed to have more steel under the surface charm. Hopefully his firmness of spirit would keep Lydia's excesses under control.

Elizabeth was seated as far as possible from Mr. Darcy, which gave her an opportunity to observe his beloved face and commit the lines of it to memory, but precluded easy conversation. The occasional questions he directed toward her showed a stiffness of manner which did not characterize his interactions with her aunt and uncle.

She was torn between relief and regret when Mr. Darcy announced he must be leaving shortly after dinner ended. Mr. Gardiner went to call for his carriage followed by Mr. Wickham, and, with a smoothness that could only have been orchestrated, Mrs. Gardiner claimed she could hear the baby's cry and needed to check on her, taking Lydia with her.

Elizabeth was so unnerved by this unexpected development that she hardly knew what to say to Mr. Darcy now that they were alone.

Finally she collected herself enough to indicate that she had not expected his presence there, wishing him to know that she was not deliberately throwing herself in his way.

"Your uncle told me as much," he said gravely, but he did not offer an explanation of his own presence.

She gathered her courage and looked straight at him. "Mr. Thomas Wickham. What sort of man is he?"

He made no pretence of failing to understand her question. "He is as fond of money and good times as his brother, but does not share his willingness to pursue them at any cost. He is honest, and will make a better husband than his brother might have."

"That is hardly the greatest of commendations, under the circumstances," she responded.

"Forgive me. I did not mean to impugn his character. I believe he will treat your sister well." He fell silent, then roused himself to speech again. "Georgiana would no doubt be happy to see you while you are in Town. Were she aware of your presence, I am sure she would invite you to call upon her."

Elizabeth heard what he had carefully not said, that his sister was not to be expected to call at Gracechurch Street. The knowledge hurt, though she could not claim there was another choice. The very idea of exposing Miss Darcy to Lydia mortifying beyond measure. "If I have the opportunity, I will be sure to call on her." Even if it would mean another occasion of torturing herself with what she had lost.

"I thank you." Darcy had no opportunity to say more, as Mr. Gardiner returned with the intelligence that his carriage was waiting. Elizabeth bid him a quiet adieu, wishing she could see what was in his heart, but knowing that in the end it would make no difference. Even if he still cherished tender feelings towards her, nothing could come of it.

ELIZABETH WAS GLAD to be busy the next few days, as it was the only thing that could keep her mind off Mr. Darcy. She half-wished she had not seen him again; it had only made her more certain what a good man he was and how much she had lost in him. It was some consolation to know she was still dear enough to him that he would undergo such mortification and expense to alleviate her suffering.

She longed to ask her uncle whether Mr. Darcy would be returning, but she could not justify the inquiry. Mr. Gardiner did not mention Mr. Darcy's name; the only person who did that was Lydia, and then only to complain about what a dull fellow he was. It made Elizabeth's hand itch to slap her.

She had some opportunity to further her acquaintance with Mr. Thomas Wickham, whom she found to possess much of his brother's easy manners, but seemed rather more solid in character. It was difficult to judge his substance since he spent much of his time flattering Lydia. Elizabeth wondered whether Mr. Darcy paid him extra for that service.

Soon the morning of the wedding arrived. Elizabeth deliberately closed her ears to all of Lydia's self-satisfied comments about being the first to marry and her wonderings about whether her dear Thomas would wear his red coat or the blue for the ceremony.

Lydia's chattering then turned to worry. "I do so hope that nothing will occur to delay matters. Do you think my dear Thomas will be at St. Clement's on time? I would so hate it if he were late. I think I would go distracted! If we are beyond the hour, we cannot marry all day! Can you imagine?"

"I can imagine that if we do not hurry, we shall be the ones who are late," Elizabeth said sharply. "The carriage is at the door, and our aunt and uncle await you."

Lydia was immediately all smiles. "I am so glad you are come to London, Lizzy. I would not for all the world be married without one of my sisters to stand up with me!"

"I can indeed see that your wedding day would be far less satisfactory if you had no one to remind that you are first to marry, though you are youngest. Weddings have so little to do with actual marriage, after all." Elizabeth doubted her sister would even notice the irony.

"See, that is exactly what I mean!"

Eventually she managed to herd Lydia down to the coach where the Gardiners waited and they set off to the church. Elizabeth reflected that a less joyous wedding party would be difficult to imagine, with the exception of the bride who evidenced enough excitement for the entire

City of London.

On their arrival at the church, they discovered that the bridegroom had been timely, to Lydia's loud and oft-repeated relief. He took his place at the altar, but Elizabeth had eyes for no one but the gentleman by his side. He had come.

For a moment the world seemed to narrow down to the very spot where Mr. Darcy stood. The strained sunlight coming in the window threw his features into relief, making him look almost like a statue in a museum, and then he smiled. It was only a slight, tentative smile, but she knew it was for her. She felt her skin tingling all the way down to her toes in their tight leather half-boots.

She floated up the aisle behind Lydia and Mr. Gardiner, buoyed by that smile. She had not allowed herself to hope for this, for one more day when she could be with Mr. Darcy on an equal footing, as if none of the problems between them existed. It was a day she would keep in her memory as a treasure to be looked upon over the years. It was enough.

Elizabeth took her place beside Lydia at the altar, but for her, the bride and groom hardly existed. All her attention was focused on the man who stood opposite to her. He was making no pretence of watching the ceremony. Elizabeth heard the familiar words droned by the curate who had no doubt performed this rite hundreds of times and did not even know this particular couple. Odd, that he could be marrying Lydia and Thomas Wickham and not know the entire history of the matter, how this unlikely ending had come about from the most unpromising of beginnings.

Darcy's dark eyes were focused on her as if he was trying to read her very soul. She wondered if he could indeed know the feelings that were inside her, the affection, the longing, and the hopelessness of anything beyond this moment. Did he still blame her for her past harsh words, or had he found forgiveness in her heart for her?

She tried to focus on the ceremony as the curate droned on about the purposes of matrimony. "...To avoid fornication; that such persons as have not the gift of continency might marry, and keep themselves undefiled members of Christ's body...." It was a fine description of the true purpose of today's wedding, which was in response to carnal lusts and love of money. Not a firm foundation for a marriage, but better than some, she supposed.

Darcy's eyes bored into her as the curate continued that marriage was also ordained for mutual society, help and comfort. That was the kind of marriage she might have had with him. She knew now that he could be relied on for help and comfort, exactly those traits she had once thought he completely lacked.

What would it be like if she were the one standing before the altar, hearing the words of the vows from him, promising to love and cherish her, till death parted them? She could almost hear how the words would sound in his deep, sonorous voice, echoing through the empty church. But it would not have been empty for them. They would have married according to the normal process of affairs, with family and friends as witnesses, not this lonely mockery of a wedding between two people who hardly knew one another.

Elizabeth knew she should look away, but the connection was too intense. It was almost palpable, and she wondered in the back of her mind whether her aunt and uncle would notice anything. She would not be surprised if Mrs. Gardiner was watching them.

"Those whom God hath joined together let no man put asunder." The words swirled around her, shivering through her mind and body. Never to be put asunder - what a thought! She had never before imagined a man to whom she would long for such a connection, for something that went beyond the demands of society and the requirements of family. What would a wedding night be like with such a man, to allow him as near in body as in spirit? Her body grew taut at the thought.

So rapt was she in her thoughts that she almost missed the responses when they began. It was *his* mouth, forming the words, "Christ have mercy upon us," that reminded her of where they were. She realized how improper her behaviour must appear, and resolutely turned toward the curate for the remainder of the ceremony, concentrating on the actual bride and groom as if her thoughts of them could guarantee them a happy future. Lydia was supposed to be her focus today, not Mr. Darcy, no matter what her treacherous heart might say.

DARCY WAS BOTH moved and shaken by his experience of the wedding. There was the mockery of a marriage taking place before him, but in his heart, he was the one making the vows to Elizabeth, promising to love and cherish her, and to worship her with his body. Heaven knew his body already worshipped her; it had almost since they had first met, despite all his efforts to forget her, to transfer those feelings to another, more suitable woman. She was so deeply entwined in his heart that he was hardly aware where one began and the other ended.

He wished he knew what she was thinking. She had steadily held his gaze through most of the ceremony, but whether it was with disdain or pity he could not say. Perhaps it was nothing more than a desire to avoid watching her sister's simpering. Elizabeth had looked away from him at the end, and never looked back as the curate droned the remainder of the rite in his completely disinterested manner. Had he frightened her, or perhaps embarrassed her with the obviousness of his emotions? Surely it must be troubling on some level to have to face an unwanted suitor. Elizabeth was soft-hearted and generous; he knew that well. She would not wish to be cruel to him. But it was not her kindness he wanted.

He remained aware of her each step of the way as they filed out of the church. Lydia hugged Elizabeth and said a cool goodbye to her aunt and uncle, then climbed to join her new husband in their rented carriage, paid for by Darcy's money. Lydia enthusiastically waved an embroidered handkerchief as they drove away, leaving behind a significantly less enthusiastic audience.

Mr. Gardiner spoke first. "Well, that is done, and I am not sorry to see it over."

His wife added, "It will be so pleasantly calm and peaceful at home! Though I have a duty first. I promised to write to my sister Bennet with every detail of the wedding. Perhaps I will leave out just a *few* details, though." Her archness was almost an echo of Elizabeth's.

"I am sorry for Lydia's behaviour today," Elizabeth said to her aunt.

"It was hardly unexpected." She turned to Darcy. "Lydia dearly wanted a celebratory wedding breakfast, and we refused. It seems to me there has been quite enough celebration of an event that is unworthy of it."

"I cannot argue," he said, although for himself, he regretted the lack of a wedding breakfast. It would have been an opportunity to spend another hour in the same room with Elizabeth. Since she had not come to visit Georgiana, this might well be the last time he saw her.

He found himself stepping toward her, as if in half-involuntary protest of the possibility. She stirred at his approach, giving him a saucy smile.

"Miss Bennet," he said, his first words spoken aloud to her all day.

"Mr. Darcy," she replied. "I am a very selfish creature; and, for the sake of giving relief to my own feelings, care not how much I may be wounding yours. I can no longer help thanking you for your unexampled kindness to my poor sister. Ever since I have known it, I have been most anxious to acknowledge to you how gratefully I feel it. Were it known to the rest of my family, I should not have merely my own gratitude to express."

"I hope it has not given you any uneasiness," he said stiffly. "It was my responsibility to mend matters as well as I might. I need no gratitude for doing my duty."

"Your duty? And how precisely did it become your duty to watch over my errant sister?"

He was surprised she did not understand. "Had I revealed what I knew of Wickham sooner, the elopement could never have occurred."

"I might as well say that, had I read a certain letter, it might not have occurred, but I hope you do not consider me completely to blame."

"Of course not! You were following the proper course, and I cannot fault you for it."

"Well, regardless of your opinion, I am still grateful to you."

"I do not want your gratitude," he said, the words coming to his lips without a thought of how ungracious they might sound. "If it gave you relief, in that I am happy. But on a day such as this, when I cannot help thinking of how it might have been different, please do not speak to me of gratitude."

The teasing expression left her face, replaced by one he did not understand until he realized the sudden luminousness of her fine eyes was the result of welling tears. He watched with horror as a drop slid down her cheek, cursing himself for raising the issue of his rejected suit at one of their rare moments of harmony. But before he could say anything, she ducked away from him and put her hand through her aunt's arm.

He felt her withdrawal like a knife. He heard her voice, discussing some future plan with great animation, and felt rejection afresh. Why did he keep thinking she would somehow forgive him? It was far too late for that. He should have said nothing at all, and not allowed the depth of her eyes to draw more from him than should have been said.

There was only one thing left he could do for her, and that was to stop embarrassing her. He approached Mr. Gardiner who was settling with the curate, and informed him in a low voice that he was required to depart.

"Will you not come back to Gracechurch Street with us for some refreshment?" that gentleman asked.

"Not today, I thank you. Business calls."

"Another time, perhaps. In the meantime, please accept my thanks for your assistance in the successful settlement of this matter."

"It was my pleasure." Why could he not simply have said that to Elizabeth? "Your servant, sir." He bowed and strode away, forcing himself not to take a last look back at Elizabeth.

ELIZABETH WISHED SHE could walk out to recover her spirits; or in other words, to dwell without interruption on those subjects that must deaden them more. Mr. Darcy's behaviour astonished and vexed her.

"Why, if he did not wish my company," said she, "did he speak to me at all?"

She could settle it in no way that gave her pleasure.

"He could be still amiable, still pleasing, to my uncle and aunt; and why not to me? If he fears me, why approach me? If he no longer cares for me, why speak to me as he did? Teazing, teazing, man! I will think no more about him."

Her resolution was for a short time involuntarily kept by the approach of her aunt, who was more satisfied by the ending of the morning than Elizabeth had been. "I thought Mr. Darcy looked quite well, did you not, Lizzy?"

"I was surprised that he left without a word to us."

"Your uncle said he had urgent business."

"So urgent he could not take a minute to bid us good day?"

Her aunt gave her a keen look. "Perhaps he may have had another reason. I saw he was speaking to you immediately after the wedding."

Elizabeth's cheeks grew warm as she recalled how he had refused her thanks. He wanted nothing from her, not even that. That he still had feelings for her she did not doubt, but she was equally certain he was ashamed of them. "We exchanged a few words."

"Do you plan to call on his sister?"

Elizabeth shook her head. "I would not feel right doing so, not after what happened. If he did not want to be with us, I cannot imagine he still wishes her to be in my company. Besides, it would be most uncomfortable trying to explain my presence in London to her. She has been honest and kind to me; I do not wish to repay her with deception."

"But is she not already aware of Lydia's original elopement?"

"Yes, but I do not think her brother likely to tell her of the eventual outcome." And then there was the true reason she did not wish to call at the Darcy townhouse. It would hurt too much to see Mr. Darcy again.

Chapter 16

"WELCOME HOME, SIR," said Briggs, the footman who greeted Darcy at the door.

Darcy handed over his hat and stripped off his gloves. He had resolved today would be different from every other day in the last week. Every day when he came home, he had asked whether his sister had received any callers, eagerly at first, and then later without much expectation. If Elizabeth were planning to call on Georgiana, she would have done so by now. After he had explicitly invited her to do so, it was practically a snub. Her feelings were clear.

He slapped his gloves down on the side table. "I will be in my study," he said brusquely.

"Yes, sir."

He would not ask. He was determined. All the way home from White's he had planned it out. Briggs was no doubt already wondering why his master kept asking him about callers. He would not give him any more reason to wonder.

"Will there be anything else, sir?" Briggs asked.

"Not tonight." He forced the words out through gritted teeth. He would not ask about Elizabeth, no matter how much he longed to see her.

"Very well, sir," Briggs said to his already retreating back.

Darcy made it almost to his study before he expelled a deep breath. Defeated, he looked over his shoulder. "Briggs? Were there any callers for my sister today?"

Briggs looked up from the gloves he was folding neatly. "No, sir. Miss Darcy has spent the day practicing her music and conversing with Mrs. Annesley."

Darcy jerked his head in an abrupt nod, pretending it did not hurt, at least until he had closed the study door behind him.

BINGLEY DID NOT look happy to be receiving a caller, but he poured two glasses of port and handed one to Darcy with a stiff smile. "Cheers," he said.

Darcy nodded in acknowledgement. "I am glad to see you in good health. I was worried when you seemed never to come to White's."

His friend shifted from one foot to the other. "Darcy, I must apologize for my behaviour when we met last. I do not fully recall what I said to you that night when your sister and I returned from Netherfield." He paused for a moment as if the name were difficult to say. "But I imagine it was the usual drivel I say when I have had too much to drink. It is not something I am in the habit of."

"I am perfectly aware of that, and you said nothing inappropriate. Do not give it another thought. My only surprise was that you did not fall ill in the carriage."

Bingley, seeming relieved, took a sip of port and lounged in a tall leather chair. "There were moments when I thought I would. But the spirits were medicinal in that particular case. My sister was being unusually unpleasant about subjects I had no wish to discuss."

Darcy could imagine all too well what Miss Bingley might have had to say about the Bennet family in general and Jane Bennet in particular. "I am glad I was not there."

"I wish I had not been there either."

"Will you come to White's with me?"

Bingley thought for a moment and then shook his head. "I am not in the mood for that sort of joviality."

So Bingley was, as expected, still pining. Darcy would have to take action. "Did you happen to read this morning's newspaper?"

"There was nothing in it to interest me."

"Do you have a copy? There is something I would like to show you."

"There is one somewhere, I am sure." Bingley rang the bell and instructed the manservant to fetch the newspaper. "If it is about the Peninsular War, I am not interested."

Darcy raised an eyebrow. "You would prefer to read about the latest goings-on around Town?"

Bingley groaned. "Spare me."

The man returned, paper in hand. Darcy took it from him, holding it carefully by the edges to avoid smudging the print. He opened it to the marriage announcements and folded it back to display part of one column, then held it in front of Bingley. On the off-chance that Bingley's malaise was sufficient to keep him from reading even that much, Darcy pointed to the announcement that read, "Lately, Captain Thomas Wickham, to Miss Lydia Bennet of Longbourn, Hertfordshire."

Bingley grabbed the newspaper in apparent disbelief. "Is this true?"

"So it would seem."

"But everyone said he had abandoned her." He apparently did not notice that Captain Wickham's Christian name had changed.

"Perhaps there was a misunderstanding, or he changed his mind," Darcy prevaricated. "In any case, they are wed now."

Bingley dropped the newspaper and sank back in his chair. "Thank God for that. I have been out of my mind with worry for Jane. I will sleep easier now."

"Will you return to Netherfield?"

He sat up straighter. "I could, couldn't I?" he said with his first hint of liveliness.

"You still hold the lease to the house, so I imagine you can do whatever you please."

"So I can. I can go back. Jane loves me, I know she does. She as much as said it, that last day. She said she could not bear to harm my name. Can you imagine such a woman?"

Only one woman haunted Darcy's imagination, but he was not about to say that. "She is very honourable, then."

"Wait until I tell her...." Slowly the animation left Bingley's face. He placed his glass down carefully on a side table.

"What is it?"

"I cannot do it. I cannot marry her."

"Why not?"

"For all the reasons Jane gave me then. I am sure this marriage will help restore the family's good name to some degree, but it will not be enough. Too many people know that her sister was seduced and abandoned, even if a marriage was eventually patched up somehow. It would never have been an equal match between Jane and me. She is a gentleman's daughter, but her mother is not, and now the family name is tainted."

"I cannot believe you would let such things stop you!"

"They are the very things you once quoted to me as arguments against the marriage! If it were only me, I would not care. But there is Caroline to think of. If I were to marry Jane Bennet now, it would hurt her marital prospects substantially. She would lose the tiny bit of acceptance she has gained in the ton. I cannot condemn her to an impoverished future for my own selfish gain. Then there is the matter of any children we would have. My father wanted me to purchase an estate and become a landed gentleman of sorts, to marry advantageously, and to continue to rise in the world. He would have wanted his grandchildren to be accepted everywhere among the finest people. He spent his entire life working for that. But the children of the son of a tradesman, however well-to-do, and a poor disgraced gentlewoman would not be accepted anywhere. I cannot do it. Our situation in society is too precarious."

"Think, man," Darcy urged. "Are your father's dreams more important to you than your own? He is dead, and you are alive."

"Caroline is alive as well," Bingley said miserably. "Can you honestly say that I have the right to ruin her prospects? She has acted as my hostess for years, and took care of me before that. Is this how I should repay her? Is that the act of a gentleman?"

Darcy rubbed his hand across his brow. He had been so certain Bingley would return to Jane Bennet, but the points his friend made were difficult to contradict. It *would* hurt Bingley's standing, though perhaps not as much as he thought given the size of his fortune, but the impact on Miss Bingley, who had yet to make her fortune through marriage, would be much larger. Her dowry was not large enough to compensate for the inferior connections she would bring. But a marriage between Bingley and Jane Bennet would guarantee Elizabeth's future, at least enough so that he need never worry that she would not have a roof over her head. A year ago he had talked Bingley out of marrying Miss Bennet, mostly for his own benefit. Was he pushing Bingley into the same marriage now for his friend's benefit, or was it again his own interests speaking? "Perhaps the impact on the Bennet family name will not be as severe as you think."

"Last autumn, before the scandal, you told me it was an inappropriate marriage. It has only become worse since then."

The devilish part was that he knew Bingley was right. "You must do as you see fit, then," he said heavily. He drained his glass of port, not even tasting the fine wine as it went down his throat.

"Yes, I must." Bingley's expression was bleak. "I beg your pardon, Darcy, but I am not in a proper frame of mind for company. Perhaps we could meet again tomorrow."

Darcy stood. He had done nothing but give his friend a moment of false hope, and he had experience enough with lost hope to understand the cruelty of it. "Of course. I will wish you a good evening, then." He knew that his own evening would be spent in bitter self-recrimination.

BRIGGS ENTERED DARCY'S dim study silently, holding a silver tray bearing a card. Darcy was not unhappy to be interrupted; he could not keep his mind on the letter he was attempting to write in any case. It was hard to describe the events of the last month to his uncle without mention of any of the happenings most significant to him. In the first page he had found nothing more interesting to communicate than the weather in London and a list of acquaintances he had seen at White's. Was that all there was to be in his life now?

He picked up the card with a sigh. It was not a familiar one, so he held it in the lamplight. Mr. Edward Gardiner. His heart began to gallop. Mr. Gardiner had never called on him before; it had always been the other way around. "Is the gentleman alone?" he asked brusquely, unsure what answer he desired.

"Yes, sir."

Now that he possessed the answer, he was disappointed. "Show him in." No doubt it was nothing more than some unfinished piece of business relating Elizabeth's sister's wedding. He set his pen in its stand and put the letter to one side.

Mr. Gardiner entered, looking more the amiable gentleman he had met at Pemberley than the stressed businessman trying to secure his errant niece's future, so presumably nothing catastrophic had happened. That at least was something for which to be grateful. Darcy rose and bowed to his guest. "Mr. Gardiner, it is a pleasure to see you again."

"I hope I am not disturbing you, Mr. Darcy. If you have business to attend to, I can call another time." He gestured to the half-finished letter.

"Not at all. My mind was wandering and I am glad of the distraction. Will you sit down and join me in a glass of brandy?

"Thank you, that would be quite refreshing. This grey, chilly weather becomes tiresome after a time."

Darcy poured two snifters of brandy and handed one to his guest, then took a seat across from him. "Your health."

Mr. Gardiner sniffed the brandy appreciatively and took a sip, rolling it around in his mouth. "You have fine taste in brandy, sir."

"I am the beneficiary of my cousin in the military, who has an unusual aptitude for acquiring goods smuggled from France. He knows I have a weakness for French brandy."

"Thank you for sharing it, then."

"My pleasure."

"Mr. Darcy, you have no doubt guessed that this is slightly more than a social call. I was hoping to ask your advice on certain matter."

Darcy experienced a moment of unpleasant surprise. In his experience, a statement such as that was usually the preliminary to request for financial assistance. He had thought better of Mr. Gardiner. "I am at your service."

"You had excellent insight and better luck than I in persuading my niece Lydia into a marriage when she was refusing to consider such a thing. Now I find myself facing another young woman in difficulties regarding matters of the heart, and could benefit from any thoughts you might have on the matter."

Darcy blinked in surprise. "I am hardly an expert on the

emotions of women. They are a mystery to me." He was tempted to tell him to ask Elizabeth just how inexpert he was, but he was trying to forswear bitterness.

"As they are to us all! If I could make sense of them, this would be much simpler. But the ladies do not tell us their mysteries, do they? Of course, gentlemen can be equally mysterious on matters of the heart. In this case, I am baffled by both. The young lady is obvious in her interest in the gentleman, at least to those who know her well, but tells my wife that he wishes nothing whatsoever to do with her. This does not seem in keeping with the behaviour of gentleman in question, who is clearly overflowing with admiration for the young lady, yet does not speak."

"If you are speaking of my friend Mr. Bingley, I am afraid I have no assistance to offer. I have already spoken with him at length about Miss Bennet, but despite his heart, he is constrained by other measures."

Mr. Gardiner raised an eyebrow. "I am sorry to hear that, but it is not in fact my niece Jane of whom I am speaking. This is a more peculiar case, wherein the gentleman claims that the young lady dislikes him. Both the lady and gentleman are usually rational and insightful people, but in this particular instance, each seems almost willfully blind to the other's sentiments, yet each is suffering. I am at a loss as to how I might assist them, if at all."

Darcy could not see how he could possibly be of any help in such a matter, but for the sake of politeness, did his best. "Have you spoken with both of them?"

"My wife has spoken with the young lady, who still appears inclined to put the worst reading on the matter. Although I have great respect for the gentleman in question, I do not know him sufficiently well to raise such an intimate matter, at least not directly."

"Have you tried addressing it indirectly?"

Mr. Gardiner gave him a significant look. "You might say so, but I do not believe he understood me properly. He seems equally inclined to believe the matter to be hopeless."

"It sounds as if you have done all that is in your power, and if an answer is to come, it must come from the principals."

Mr. Gardiner shook his head sadly as he swirled his brandy. "You are no doubt correct, no matter how difficult it may be to watch my dear Lizzy crying her pretty eyes out."

Darcy stiffened. "Elizabeth is in love?" Emotions warred within him. He would kill any man who hurt Elizabeth, but he would also happily kill any other man who looked at her. It was one thing to forswear her when she did not want him; it was something else entirely to think of her with someone else.

"Forgive me, I should not have mentioned her name. Please forget that you heard it."

Only reflexive manners allowed Darcy to nod in response. How could any man fortunate enough to win Elizabeth's affections be so foolish as to let her go? Even if he thought she did not care for him, would he not at least try to convince her otherwise? He would do anything for her sake!

Then it hit him with the force of a galloping horse. The room seemed to swim before him until it dissolved into the image of Mr. Gardiner's probing eyes. "I see," he managed to say in a strangled voice.

"Do you?" the older gentleman remarked mildly.

"But... perhaps the gentleman is correct in his view of her sentiments."

"I am sure he believes himself correct; but I am equally certain he is not. My niece is a direct woman, and if she were set irrevocably against a man, she would not hide it from me or anyone else. In this case, she seems unable to believe anything but the best of him, yet looks away whenever he is mentioned, and seems sadder each day in his absence. Sad enough, in fact, that we determined it was best to send her home to recover her spirits. But my wife and I both regret that two such pleasant and insightful young people should suffer so owing to a misapprehension of each other's intentions."

"I see." He did not in fact see. "I invited Miss Elizabeth to call on my sister while she was in London."

"Yes, I recall that. Later she seemed to be of the opinion that she would no longer be welcome to do so. I am not certain why that might be, but she seemed quite firm in her impression."

As if Elizabeth could ever be unwelcome! Darcy was certain Mr. Gardiner must be overstating Elizabeth's feelings for him, but was it possible that she was no longer irrevocably set against him? He did not deserve such a softening of her regard, but if it existed, perhaps it could be deepened with time. She had not seemed unhappy to see him at the wedding until the very end, when she turned away from him in tears, but perhaps he had misinterpreted that. Women often cried at weddings, did they not? Maybe it was nothing more than the emotions of the moment.

If it was true, he could show her there was more to him than she had seen in the past. If it was true.

Chapter 17

AFTER A WEEK back at Longbourn, Elizabeth decided that nothing in the world could please her. In London, she had constantly thought about Mr. Darcy, hoped against hope to see him, and regretted all her lost opportunities, to the point that she was glad to return home. Indeed, Longbourn was a pleasanter place than it had been when she left. Many, though not all, of their neighbours were now acknowledging the Bennets again, and they began to receive the occasional invitation. Whispers no longer followed them on the streets. Kitty had regained her spirits once Lydia's marriage was announced; much like her mother, she could not see any reason that this was not cause for celebration. Jane's usual equanimity was more in evidence now, though from time to time Elizabeth would catch her looking off into the distance with a sad expression, and with strong suspicions that her sister was thinking about her former suitor. Jane displayed no interest in discussing Mr. Bingley, although when pressed, she would say only that he was the most amiable man of her acquaintance, but nothing more than that. Given the circumstances, Elizabeth refrained to the best of her ability from teasing. But still, her mind was filled with nothing but Mr. Darcy.

Mrs. Bennet demanded her least favourite daughter's company more often than had been her wont, requiring Elizabeth to provide detailed reports of Lydia's wedding to all of her friends. It was not clear what they made of the substitution of one Mr. Wickham for the other, and whether any credence was placed in the reasoning that it had been a natural error to assume that Lydia had run off with the Mr. Wickham that they knew, rather than with the brother to whom he had presumably introduced her. When Elizabeth described Mr. Thomas Wickham to her family, her father announced his great pride in a new son-in-law who knew how to make love to everyone. Privately Mr. Bennet questioned her further about the arrangements, but she pleaded ignorance and referred him to her uncle. She did not reveal her knowledge of Mr. Darcy's role in the affair, nor that she had seen him in London.

Elizabeth felt overall that the outcome was as positive as could be hoped under the circumstances, but nonetheless she often found herself noticing a new emptiness in her life. It was not difficult for her to guess the reason for this change. She was determined to forget her feelings for Mr. Darcy and to think of him merely as a generous friend, and on occasion was even successful at this for several minutes at a stretch.

One afternoon she and Kitty paid a visit to Mariah Lucas at Lucas Lodge. Mariah had received a letter from Charlotte and was excitedly recounting all their adventures at Rosings. She only mentioned Mr. Darcy's name twice, but each time, Elizabeth felt as if a pit were opening deep within her, and that everyone must have noticed her reaction. All her memories of Kent were now deeply entwined with the figure who remained all too clear in her inner vision.

On their return to Longbourn, Hill informed her that her father was asking for her, and even then Mr. Bennet emerged from his library, closing the door behind him. "Ah, Lizzy, you are quite the person I have been hoping to see," he announced with a certain glee.

Elizabeth was certain that some major teasing was to follow, and resigned herself to whatever embarrassment her father might raise on this occasion. "I am at your service, sir."

"There is a *person* who has requested a private word with you. I assume you are at leisure to see him?" Mr. Bennet rubbed his hands together.

Elizabeth's eyes widened. "Not Mr. White? Please, you may give him my answer, which you know quite well." She was not in the mood for a repeat performance of Mr. Collins' proposal, no matter how much it might entertain her father.

"And miss all the fun? Certainly not, Lizzy. I expect you to speak for yourself."

She sighed and gave a resigned look. "Very well."

"Do let me know if there is bloodshed; I can send to town for the surgeon."

Elizabeth glared at him as she laid her hand on the knob, then she took a deep breath and let herself inside, immediately closing the door in her father's face. She opened her mouth for a few pre-emptive words, then was struck dumb when she realized the gentleman peering out the window before her was too tall to be the portly, balding Mr. White. It was Mr. Darcy.

Her mind went blank. She grabbed the back of the chair nearest her for support.

He turned to face her, his countenance at first severe, then lightening into a slight smile. "Miss Bennet."

Attempting to recover her composure, Elizabeth approached him and held out her hand. "Mr. Darcy, this is indeed a surprise."

He took her hand and bowed over it, then, after a slight hesitation, gently touched his lips to the back of it. Elizabeth almost jumped from the sudden sensation that ran down her arm and deep inside of her. She had forgotten she was not wearing gloves, and the softness of his lips against her tender skin seemed to burn like a brand. Her heart began to flutter as her eyes locked with his well-remembered dark gaze.

He did not release her hand immediately. "I hope not a completely unpleasant one, though from your expression, perhaps it is."

"Not at all. I was expecting someone else, and was startled, but it need not follow that the shock is unpleasant."

His smile faded as he dropped her hand. "You were expecting someone else?" It was practically an accusation.

"Not actually expecting, but when my father told me... well, suffice to say my thoughts ran to someone with whom I do not at *all* wish to have private conversation, hence my surprise."

He seemed to relax a little. "Will you not have a seat, Miss Bennet?"

Sensing this was not the moment to tease, she declined to point out that he need not offer her a seat in her own house. His tension reminded her of something, but she could not place it, not when her body was tingling from his presence. She forced herself to recall that he could not offer her what she most wished for, but it made her proud that he had sought her out for any reason.

He did not sit, but instead leaned an arm against the mantelpiece. "I asked your father for permission to speak to you…" He hesitated, as if trying to make a decision. "To speak to you about a rather complex matter. If I may?"

"I am all ears," she said. "I assume it must be a matter of some import to bring you such a distance."

"It is to me. Your opinion of the matter remains to be determined." He chewed on his lower lip for a moment. "I have spent the last several days in the company of my friend Bingley. He is severely out of spirits, and I am concerned for his well-being."

She had not known what to expect from him, but it was certainly not this. "I am sorry to hear it, sir."

"He has been distressed since his return to London. It is a matter of the heart, as I am sure you understand. I had hoped that once your youngest sister was married, he might return to Netherfield with a certain intention in mind, but it was not to be. Although he is greatly desirous of such an outcome, he believes it will never be possible because of the recent scandal. I pray you forgive me for my bluntness; I mean no disrespect to you or your family. Bingley's position in society is precarious. He is valued for his wealth, but despised for his background. He does not feel he can choose a bride who is touched by scandal without endangering his position and that of his entire family."

Had he come all this way to tell her that Bingley would not return to Jane? If so, he had wasted a trip. It had never occurred to her that there was any reason to hope for such a thing. "I understand."

"Have I offended you, Miss Bennet?" he asked almost tentatively.

"Not at all. I am aware of the facts of the matter." The taste was bitter in her mouth.

"I have tried to find some solution to this dilemma. In the past Bingley has fallen in and out of love quickly, but it seems his feelings for your sister are deeper and more durable. I would like to see my friend happy, and I hope I am right in assuming your sister would be made happy by such a development as well."

"I cannot violate any sisterly confidences, but I will not contradict you."

He nodded his thanks. "I have found only one possible solution, one way of raising your family's status sufficiently to overcome the gossip. I do not know if it will please you, but I have decided to make the effort nonetheless."

Elizabeth's pulses quickened even further. For a moment she thought it was possible that he intended to make her an offer after all, but that would hardly be displeasing to her. What could he mean?

"If you, Miss Bennet, were to find it in your heart to accept an offer of marriage from me, such an alliance would elevate your sister's status enough to overcome Bingley's worries. The sister of Mrs. Darcy of Pemberley would be considered eminently eligible for him. I know that you once felt I was the last man in the world you could be prevailed upon to marry, but this circumstance, in combination with my hope that I have risen at least a small amount in your estimation since then, suggested to me that you might be prevailed upon to offer a different answer now." He paced back and forth, his hands behind his back, not looking at her.

"Mr. Darcy, I ..."

He held up his hand. "Please, Miss Bennet, allow me to speak my piece before you offer a response. I wish to address some of the concerns you might have over such a union. Regardless of your current feelings, it would be my hope that with further experience of me, you might come to feel some sort of affection for me, but I realize that may not be the case. I would, however, do whatever I could to make your life as happy as it may be." Perspiration began to appear on his brow. "I cannot promise to make no demands of you. Not only does Pemberley need an heir, but, as you are well aware, I am subject to ardent feelings toward you which I doubt I would be able to ignore indefinitely, and I will not disguise it. However, I am willing to try to keep my demands on you to a minimum."

By this point Elizabeth was biting her lip in an effort to keep from laughter. She rose to her feet. "Mr. Darcy, this is quite unnecessary. I..."

"I will not ask you for a response now, but rather that you give the matter some consideration. It is, after all, a major decision." He did not look at her.

"May *I* ask a question of *you*?"

"Of course."

"Is Mr. Bingley aware of your intention to sacrifice your own marital prospects for his benefit?"

If possible, he flushed deeper. "I have not told him. I did not wish to give him hope that might be once again disappointed. But in any case, it is no sacrifice for me. As you know, I have long desired to make you my wife, so I would also be a beneficiary. The truth is that you are the only one being asked to sacrifice yourself for the happiness of your sister and Bingley. I can only promise to do my best to repay your sacrifice in our life together."

"Would you be asking this of me if it were not for Mr. Bingley and Jane?"

He looked down at his boots. "Not at this point."

Elizabeth wanted to close her eyes as hope was replaced by sinking pain. If only she could flee the room! But he would still demand her answer, and now she did not know what it should be. At least he was being truthful with her. She would rather have died than discover after they were married that it had not, in fact, been his wish. She lifted her chin. "So it is for your friend that you are making this offer?" She was pleased that her voice did not tremble.

"At this time? Yes, I would have preferred it to be different, that it could be a matter of making both of us happy, but I owe Bingley this much."

"Your loyalty to your friend is admirable." Elizabeth's throat was tight.

He took a step forward, looking pained. "I *am* loyal. My sentiments do not alter easily. My presence here should tell you that much."

She wondered if he was speaking of her as well as of Bingley. Perhaps he did still cherish tender sentiments towards her, and that sweetened the sacrifice for him, but could it be enough? Or would she one day discover that he resented her for the degradation she would bring to his family name? No, he would not do that; he was too honourable to blame her for his own decision.

He was a good man, an honest man, he would treat her well, and she loved him. Could that be enough, when what she longed for was to hear that he desired above all things to marry her?

Her indecision must have shown in her eyes, for he drew closer to her, and said, "I *will* do anything within my power to ensure your happiness, I promise you that."

His endearing tentativeness gave her the strength to claim her own wishes. It was enough. Even if he had reservations, he wished to marry her, and they had a better ground for affection than many couples. "Then our happiness is assured, since I intend to make you happy as well," she said firmly.

He blinked. "You do?"

She was tempted for a moment to tease, to ask if he would prefer that she make him miserable, but it was not the proper moment. "Yes, Mr. Darcy, I do."

"Does that mean… that you will make me the happiest of men?"

She laughed to see the look of delight dawning in his eyes. "Yes, I will marry you, though I must make one small confession."

His shoulders tightened. "What is it?"

"That I am not doing this for the benefit of either my dearest Jane or Mr. Bingley, but on my own behalf, and that you would have received the same response if you had not mentioned them."

An expression of utter astonishment came over his face, but was quickly overtaken by a look of heartfelt delight which created an answering acute pleasure in her. "Do you truly mean that?"

"Although I may on occasion espouse opinions that are not my own, I assure you that in this case I am not doing so. It gives me the greatest of pleasure to accept you."

He stepped toward her, stopping mere inches away, and raised his hands to touch her cheeks with the lightest of caresses. "My dearest, loveliest Elizabeth." He seemed almost to be tasting the syllables of her name.

She shivered with the intimacy of it, overtaken by an unexpected desire to fling herself into his arms. Her entire being seemed concentrated at the point where she felt his consuming touch. She had not known there could be such pleasure, and she longed for more of it. Almost without thought, she lifted her finger to trace the curve of his lip.

His sharply indrawn breath told her he was far from indifferent. His hands moved to cup her face in a gentle hold, and with agonizing slowness, his eyes never leaving hers, he moved the last few inches until their lips met.

It was an astonishing discovery for Elizabeth, as if her very being was reaching out to his. She did not think she could bear to have this moment end.

His lips drew away just far enough to whisper, "I have dreamed of this, but not dared to hope." Then his arms were around her, crushing her to him. "Forgive me, but I cannot believe this is true."

Elizabeth laughed happily, then raised her face to him again. "I assure you I am quite real." She brushed her lips against his, glorying in her daring.

He returned the kiss with interest, and his gentleness began to move into something new. Elizabeth shivered as sensations previously unknown began to rush through her. For the first time in her life, she understood what it meant to be weak at the knees. How could the mere touch of lips create such a flood of longing within her?

Elizabeth became suddenly aware of the strength of the body pressed against her softness. A warmth deep inside her seemed to spring into life. Mr. Darcy made a sound deep in his throat, then began to scatter kisses across Elizabeth's face, moving down to the exquisitely tender skin of her neck, creating a new, unexpected source of pleasure, intense enough to make her pull away in shock. Her voice trembled as she said, "Sir, my father will be wondering what has happened to us."

Mr. Bennet's voice sounded behind her. "He most certainly will," he said with a steely edge.

Mortified, Elizabeth resorted to pure instinct. She buried her face in Mr. Darcy's shoulder, and was grateful as the warm support of his arm came around her.

"Your daughter has done me the very great honour of agreeing to be my wife."

"Under the circumstances, I suppose I am glad to hear that, but for the moment, I must ask you to be so kind as to allow me some time alone with Lizzy."

Darcy's arm around Elizabeth's waist slackened as if to release her, but she caught hold of the lapel of his coat with one hand and his arm with the other and shook her head fiercely.

Darcy hesitated. "Elizabeth seems to prefer that I stay."

"Does she now? Well, young man, if you choose to stay, do not expect me to mince my words to protect that pride of yours." He pulled out the chair behind his desk and sat heavily. "Lizzy, are you out of your senses, to be accepting this man? Have not you always hated him?"

Elizabeth straightened and glared at her father, feeling Darcy's tension beside her. "I do not hate him. Once I did not like him as well as I do now, but I assure you I am very attached to him, and have been for quite some time. I want nothing more than to be his wife." The look of joyous pride she received from Darcy made her feel half-intoxicated.

"Or, in other words, you are determined to have him. He is rich, to be sure, and you may have many fine clothes and fine carriages. But will they make you happy?"

"Have you any other objection," said Elizabeth, "than your belief of my indifference?"

"None at all. We all know him to be a proud sort of man; but this would be nothing if you really liked him." He shot a cold look in Darcy's direction as if proclaiming such a thing to be impossible.

"I do, I do like him," she replied, with tears in her eyes, "I love him. Indeed he has no improper pride. He is perfectly amiable. You do not know what he really is; then pray do not pain me by speaking of him in such terms."

"Lizzy," said her father, "I have given him my consent. He is the kind of man, indeed, to whom I should never dare refuse any thing, which he condescended to ask. I now give it to you, if you are resolved on having him. But let me advise you to think better of it. I know your disposition, Lizzy. I know that you could be neither happy nor respectable, unless you truly esteemed your husband; unless you looked up to him as a superior. Your lively talents would place you in the greatest danger in an unequal marriage. You could scarcely escape discredit and misery. My child, let me not have the grief of seeing you unable to respect your partner in life. You know not what you are about."

By her side Darcy stiffened. "Mr. Bennet, I must ask you not speak to Elizabeth in this manner."

"I am her father, and I will say what I like! I told you I would not mince my words. My daughter is too precious to be wasted on a man with nothing but wealth to commend him."

"But he is far more than that!" Elizabeth cried. "He is honourable, trustworthy, generous, and the best of men. I speak not from a brief acquaintance. My estimation of him is not the work of a day, but has grown over many months and stood the test of long suspense, and I am certain he is the best possible husband for me, and the only man in the world who could make me happy."

"Well, my dear," said Mr. Bennet, "I have no more to say. If this be the case, and I can only hope that it is, then perhaps he deserves you, despite his most recent behaviour." He glared at Darcy over his glasses. "In my own library, no less!"

"If my word in support of him is not enough for you, Father, I beg of you to seek the opinion of my uncle Gardiner. Mr. Darcy is the one who arranged Lydia's marriage, restored her reputation, and our good name." To Elizabeth's amusement, Darcy frowned and looked fixedly away.

"Is this true, Mr. Darcy?" Mr. Bennet demanded, rising to his feet.

"I have nothing to say on the subject," said Darcy in his haughtiest manner.

"You must tell me how much you spent to bring the match about, and I will repay you."

Mr. Darcy drew himself to his full height. "I will not accept a penny of your money. All I did was done for the love of your daughter, and that is the end of the matter."

Elizabeth was tempted to laugh at the sight of the two men most dear to her squabbling like cocks in a henhouse, but she doubted that either of them were in full possession of their usual sense of humour. "Come, Father, will you not shake Mr. Darcy's hand for my sake?"

Mr. Bennet gave her an indulgent smile before proffering his hand. "There is no arguing with a young lover, so I will not even try."

Darcy shook his hand. "You may be certain that I will do everything within my power to make your daughter happy."

"I am glad to hear it, though I doubt there are many young men who tell their future father-in-law that they intend to mistreat their bride. You still face your greatest challenge, which will be informing Mrs. Bennet."

Elizabeth laughed. "I hope you will allow me a few minutes to accustom myself to the idea before entering the lion's den! Perhaps I could show Mr. Darcy the gardens." And perhaps there he might kiss her once more.

Mr. Bennet cleared his throat. "I think not, Lizzy. If you wish to speak privately with your, ahem, intended, I believe the bench under the willow would do admirably - the bench, I might add, that is in full view of this window." Settling himself behind his desk, he removed his glasses and stared pointedly at their clasped hands.

Darcy's lips tightened momentarily, then he inclined his head. He did not, however release Elizabeth's hand, and after a minute Mr. Bennet picked up a leather-bound book and, with one last significant glance at his daughter, began to read.

"Come," Elizabeth said softly, drawing Darcy out of the library. She knew that she was getting off lightly given the scene her father had interrupted. There was so much she wished to say to Darcy, and they were lucky to be allowed this much privacy. It was hard, though, when she longed for so much more than a handclasp.

She was grateful that they did not encounter anyone on their way outside. She was not yet ready to share him with anyone else. When they reached the old willow tree, she sat deliberately with her back to the house.

She had spent many a day curled up with a book in that very bench and it had always felt spacious, but now, as she sat there with Mr. Darcy, she felt all the heat of his proximity, as if some source of power was transferring itself between them through the narrow conduit of their hands. Elizabeth hardly knew what to say or to do, but she needed to break the spell over her. Speaking scarcely above a whisper, she said, "I apologize for my father."

He leaned toward her, careful to maintain a few inches distance. "There is no need," he breathed softly. "He is within his rights. It would take more than that to cast a shadow on my happiness today, knowing that someday it will be *my* right to be alone with you whenever I choose."

Elizabeth was sure her cheeks were now flaming scarlet. It was one thing to accept his proposal, and another to move into imagining their marital relationship, but the intensity and warmth of his gaze told her that his thoughts were far beyond taking an undisturbed walk together. An odd, not entirely unpleasant ache churned in her stomach, and seemed to settle in the private place between her legs. "If I survive breaking the news to my mother, that is."

A smile lit up his eyes. "It will be my business to make certain that you do. I do not intend to lose you now."

The tension in the air between them was almost palpable. She lowered her voice again. "And your family? Are they aware that you planned to make me an offer?"

He shook his head. "Although your uncle had given me reason to hope, I was not certain enough of whether you would even receive me, much less accept me, to tell anyone of my intention."

She looked up. "My uncle? What did he say?"

"He told me that you would be pleased to hear from me. Since I had given you so much reason to dislike me, I interpreted this to mean that I had redeemed myself sufficiently in your eyes that you might be willing to give me chance to convince you I had attended to your reproofs, and that perhaps I could eventually win your affection. I began to lay my plans, but I should have believed him in the first place."

"Then why did you come to me speaking only of Bingley and Jane, and not for yourself? Was it simply an excuse?"

"In part, yes. I hoped you would accept me on my own merits, but when you seemed displeased as you came in to see me, I feared you would refuse me out of hand. I knew you were not indifferent to me, and so I hoped Bingley's dilemma would be enough for you to give me the opportunity to woo you over time."

"All of which was delightfully unnecessary! How fortunate for you that I should prove so reasonable as to love you on my own."

Darcy's heart faltered at the words he had never expected to hear from Elizabeth. "You do me an honour I do not deserve."

"I fail to see any reason why I should not love you!"

"Apart from my insulting behaviour and words throughout our acquaintance, my anger at Hunsford, and the appalling way I treated you at Pemberley? Is that not some cause for doubt?"

"We shall not argue for who had the greatest share of the blame for that evening in Hunsford, since there is more than enough to go around. As for Pemberley, you may have been intemperate, but I had given you what must have seemed like inhuman provocation. I am still horrified by how my words must have injured your poor sister, all through my pride in refusing to read your letter. I hope you were not too shocked when, after that, I risked everything by writing to you."

"Not shocked at all, but touched, and worried about your obvious distress. I wish I had known then what had happened. I would have done anything in my power to assist you."

"Whereas I thought you must be furious with me for my foolishness! I could not have been more surprised when I received your response. I had by no means expected you would encourage Mr. Bingley to seek out Jane once more, but I was proud of your generosity."

"I am almost afraid of asking what you thought of me, when we met again at your uncle's house in London," he said.

"I felt nothing but surprise. And embarrassment, I might add, when I managed to lose my footing!"

"You can have no idea how many times I have replayed that moment in my mind. I had longed for you so much, and to have you appear in front of me, and to have an honourable reason to touch you and to stand near you was nothing but a sheer delight. Your fragrance was lavender, as it is today. I will never forget it."

"Yet you looked so stern. I was afraid you were angered with me, or thought I had deliberately thrown myself in your way."

"Had I known that, I would have dropped to my knees in an instant and begged you to deliver me from my suffering! Your poor uncle thought I had engineered the entire thing."

"It seems my uncle has been very busy as a matchmaker." "We are indeed indebted to your uncle for our current good understanding."

"He will be very pleased to hear it, and no doubt insufferably smug."

"I cannot believe that. We must invite them to Pemberley for Christmas."

She grew still, looking down at their entwined fingers. "Pemberley. I still cannot quite conceive of living there."

"Whereas I have spent many months imagining you living there, so it seems perfectly natural to me."

She gave him a serious look. "What of the others in my family? I cannot imagine you would wish to receive my sister Lydia and her husband at Pemberley."

"I would not object, though I would need to speak to Georgiana first. I do not know how she would feel about seeing George Wickham's brother. She does not particularly recollect him, as he took up his commission when she was still in the nursery."

"Do *you* object to seeing him?"

"I have already given that some consideration, and as long as he treats your sister well, I have no objection. We have had our disagreements in the past, but they were the conflicts of an older boy attempting to control the younger ones. I am willing to start anew. He has not the taste for mischief that his brother does."

"You are very generous."

He stood beside the hay bale. "I would do far more than that to ensure your happiness."

"I still do not understand why you still believed I disliked you, despite my letter."

He looked searchingly into her eyes. "I invited you to call on my sister, but you never came. I thought it must be out of a desire to avoid me."

"I did not call upon your sister because it hurt too much to even think of you. I thought you had quite given up on me, and it would only pain me to face the reminder of you. And I do not know what I would have told her if she asked me about my family. I did not wish to distress her as I did at Pemberley."

"Distress her? Of course not. She was quite taken with you in Derbyshire."

"Until I spoke of Mr. Wickham, at least. I was surprised she gave me another chance in Hertfordshire."

"She wanted to see you. She knew I loved you, and that you spoke out of lack of knowledge, not out of malice."

Something in Elizabeth melted at his words. It was an odd relief to hear him claim his affection for her in such a matter of fact way.

He continued, "I will return to Town tonight to tell her the happy news. She will be delighted to hear it."

"Tonight? Must you go so soon?"

"While I would like nothing else in the world as well as to stay by your side, I think it best that I return tonight. I also intend to make application to Bingley for the use of Netherfield for the next few weeks, which will also provide me with an opportunity to inform him of these new developments."

"Do you truly think he will come for Jane?"

"I believe he will. He cares deeply for her, and it is only his sense of duty to his family that has kept him away."

"I hope so for my own sake, as it will otherwise be necessary for me to restrain my current happiness in her presence."

Darcy's face sobered. "Are you truly happy?"

"Can you not tell?"

"I know you are a kind person, and that you feel a debt to me for what I did for your sister."

"You over-estimate my dramatic ability, sir! And must you leave today?"

"There is a certain pressure of time. Bingley, having decided a future with your sister was impossible, has reacted in his usual impulsive way. He is preparing to make an offer for another lady. Once that happens, there would be no going back, so I must forestall him."

"He is in love with another woman already? If he is that fickle, perhaps Jane is well rid of him!"

"He is not at all in love with her. He decided that if he could not have the woman he loved, it did not matter whom he married. It mattered so little, in fact, that he allowed his sisters to choose his prospective bride. I am acquainted with her. She is reasonably well-born, reasonably well-dowered, reasonably well-connected, reasonably well-featured, and otherwise not at all reasonable or pleasant. She would make Bingley's life a socially acceptable misery. So I decided to gamble that you might accept me and allow me to woo you afterwards."

If the delightful feelings he was generating in her now were what she could expect from his wooing, she would look forward to it. "A fine gamble, since the wooing proved unnecessary."

"I will woo you every day of my life. And I will never forget your generosity in allowing me the opportunity to do so."

"How long will you stay in Town?"

His grip on her hand tightened. "Will you miss me, then?"

"I have done without you for weeks, so I imagine I will once again survive," Elizabeth teased. Then, seeing his quickly hid disappointment at her response, she added, "Naturally I will look forward to your return."

He raised first one hand to his lips, then the other. "If I can see Bingley tomorrow, and I do not know why that would be difficult, I will return the next day. I do not think I could stand to be away any longer. I have waited so long for you that I am impatient about every minute we must spend apart."

"A far better answer than mine! I shall have to study to flatter you better."

"Do not change a thing about yourself." Darcy reached out a finger and touched a curl of her hair that lay on her face. "You are perfection already."

Chapter 18

IN THE END, it was determined between them that Elizabeth would apply for her mother's consent alone that evening. Elizabeth could not imagine how her mother would take it; sometimes doubting whether all his wealth and grandeur would be enough to overcome her abhorrence of the man. But whether she were violently set against the match, or violently delighted with it, it was certain that her manner would be equally ill adapted to do credit to her sense; and she could no more bear that Mr. Darcy should hear the first raptures of her joy, than the first vehemence of her disapprobation. Hopefully, by the time of his return, the worst of the storm would have passed.

First, though, there was the parting to be endured, as Elizabeth's new happiness warred with the emptiness she felt when he departed. She laughingly chided herself for missing something she had not had until a few hours earlier, but still felt warm tears in her eyes.

She sought out Jane in the still room to open her heart to her. Though suspicion was very far from Jane's general habits, she was absolutely incredulous here.

"You are joking, Lizzy. This cannot be! Engaged to Mr. Darcy! No, no, you shall not deceive me. I know it to be impossible."

"This is a wretched beginning indeed! My sole dependence was on you; and I am sure nobody else will believe me, if you do not. Yet, indeed, I am in earnest. I speak nothing but the truth. He still loves me, and we are engaged."

Jane looked at her doubtingly. "Oh, Lizzy! it cannot be. I know how much you dislike him."

"You know nothing of the matter. That is all to be forgot. Perhaps I did not always love him so well as I do now. But in such cases as these, a good memory is unpardonable. This is the last time I shall ever remember it myself."

Jane still looked all amazement. Elizabeth again and more seriously assured her of its truth.

"Good Heaven! can it be really so! Yet now I must believe you," cried Jane. "My dear, dear Lizzy, I would—I do congratulate you—but are you certain? Forgive the question. Are you quite certain that you can be happy with him?"

"There can be no doubt of that. It is settled between us already, that we are to be the happiest couple in the world. But are you pleased, Jane? Shall you like to have such a brother?"

"Very much. I have always had a value for him, and his great love for you speaks volumes to his worth." Jane turned away as she spoke, then fell silent.

"What is the matter? Are you ill?"

"No, dearest Lizzy. I am very happy for you, and I beg you to disregard it if I should have my own moments of sadness. I am glad Mr. Darcy has the courage to marry you in adversity."

Elizabeth longed to tell her that Mr. Bingley might yet return, but dared not raise hopes that might again be disappointed. She prayed Mr. Darcy was correct in his assessment. It would be a cruel blow to Jane if she discovered Mr. Bingley was courting another so very soon. "He is fortunate to have the resources to ignore our recent difficulties. Not all gentlemen could afford to do so."

"You are quite right, Lizzy," said Jane bravely. "I could not have borne to have caused distress in Mr. Bingley's family. It is for the best that it happened as it did."

"As very little has ever happened which you did not say was for the best, you will forgive me if I do not completely agree," Lizzy teased.

"When will Mr. Darcy return here?" Jane said with forced cheerfulness.

"In two days. He had business in London which required his personal attention."

"Then we have two days to celebrate his good fortune in acquiring so exemplary a bride."

MR. DARCY RETURNED AT the earliest possible moment on the given day, and Elizabeth was delighted to discover he had not come alone. She had been watching for him, and felt a flare of delight watching his tall form exit the closed carriage, then turn back to offer his hand to Miss Darcy. She waited at the window for a moment, hoping to see a third figure emerge, but apparently it was just the two of them. Perhaps Mr. Bingley could not leave London on a day's notice. She was glad she had not mentioned her hopes to Jane.

The dizzying rush of pleasure she felt when he entered the room and their eyes met almost overrode her anxiety at coming face to face with Georgiana. Georgiana appeared paler than she had been at their last meeting, and there was a look of strain on her face. Elizabeth's heart sank. They had been on such good terms during her visit to Netherfield, but then Elizabeth had been merely her brother's friend, not the sister of Mrs. Wickham. For all Georgiana's willingness to befriend her during their disgrace, the idea that her brother would be marrying into a family that included the Wickhams could not but be distasteful and perhaps mortifying to her.

Elizabeth, sensible of her position as the girl's elder, smiled and reached out both hands. "Miss Darcy, it is delightful to see you again."

"The pleasure is mine," Georgiana said in a quiet voice. "May I express my delight that you will soon be my sister?"

"It cannot possibly exceed my own," Elizabeth assured her, but then there was no time for further individual conversation as Mrs. Bennet, Kitty and Mary converged on Georgiana, loudly exclaiming over her fine travelling dress.

Elizabeth took the opportunity to lock gazes with Mr. Darcy. She had not realized her heart would pound so at the mere sight of him, and such was her delight at his arrival that it was a moment before she realized his slight smile did not quite reach his eyes. She sidled closer to him and said, "I hope your journey was not overly taxing."

"Not at all."

She lowered her voice so no one else could hear. "Was your business in London successful?"

"No, it was not." His interest seemed engaged by his sister's interactions with the Bennets.

"I am sorry to hear that." Elizabeth was growing puzzled. Mr. Darcy seemed a different man from the ardent lover of two days earlier. He did not even seem particularly pleased to see her. Had his aunt managed to convince him he had made a mistake? But no, he would hardly have brought his sister if he wished to break off the engagement. Could he feel it had been a mistake, but felt honour bound to keep his word to her?

The very thought made her stomach clench, but she was not prepared to suffer in silence. If something were the matter, she would rather know it at once. "Mr. Darcy, perhaps you would like to see our little wilderness?"

His brows drew together. "Will your father allow it?"

"I do not see him here; do you?"

"But…"

She raised an arch eyebrow with a teasing smile. "Sir, are you avoiding my company?"

To her immense relief, his expression lightened. "Never, my dearest. Nothing could give me greater pleasure." He held out his arm to her.

At first it was enough merely to take his arm and walk by his side in silence as they left the house. There was nothing unusual about that; he had always been a man of few words. When they passed the artfully ruined stone wall that marked the entrance to the wilderness, he asked, "Will your father not be angered if he discovers you are here with me?"

She shrugged, untroubled by the prospect. "No doubt, but that will pass, and I need to be with you."

He halted unexpectedly. Taking both her hands in his, he pressed them to his lips. "Dearest Elizabeth, you cannot imagine how sweet those words sound upon your tongue."

For a moment she did not understand, then she realized how her words must have sounded, and flushed with embarrassment. "In that case, I shall strive to say them more often. But in truth, I was concerned about you. You were so quiet and distant earlier."

With a deep sigh, he dropped her hands. Her heart sank to see the expression on his face. Perhaps he was indeed happy to have her company, but he might have realized that marriage went far beyond that.

Finally he said, "It has been a difficult few days, and I have dreaded what I must tell you."

"You regret proposing to me." Elizabeth's mouth was dry.

He avoided her eyes. "That is perhaps not the best way to put it."

She felt as if she were a long distance away, buried in a cave somewhere. Distantly she said, "You need not fear that I will force you into a marriage you no longer desire. If you wish for freedom, it is yours."

He turned to her and abruptly gripped her arms, hard enough that she had to hide a wince. "Elizabeth, do not say such a thing! Of course I wish to marry you. I have always wished to marry you. Nothing has changed."

Her pain began to edge into anger. "You cannot have it both ways, sir. If you truly wished to marry me, you would not regret proposing to me. I had not realized you would be so easily influenced by the opinions of others."

"By the opinions of others? What on earth do you mean?"

She raised her chin in the air. "I assume that your family has convinced you that our engagement is a degradation, as you once thought it would be."

"No! That is not the case." He seemed to suddenly realize that his hands were imprisoning her, and he relaxed his grip carefully. "It does not matter to me what they think. While I have some regrets, my wishes have not altered in any way. I regret that you agreed to marry me under false pretenses, and now I have trapped you by announcing our engagement. My regrets are *for* you, not *about* you."

"False pretenses? What do you mean?"

"I did not know it at the time, but the very day that you did me the honour of agreeing to marry me, Bingley was making an offer of his own, which was in turn accepted. He is an engaged man. It is too late for him to return to your sister."

Elizabeth closed her eyes, struggling to control her breathing. "I am sorry to hear it. I had hoped he and Jane would find happiness. But that was not why I agreed to marry you, as I said at the time. Perhaps you missed that part."

"I know you are very kind-hearted, and that given the choice, you would put a good face on your acceptance even if it was only for the sake of your sister."

"You have seen enough of my frankness to know better!" she teased, though in her heart she admitted it was likely true that she would have said something similar even if she did not mean it. But she *had* meant it. "You persist in doubting my regard for you?"

"It seems I must, though it is not out of a lack of faith in you, but from the certainty of knowing I have not pleased you in the past."

"Perhaps that was once the case, but my feelings are now so widely different from what they were then, that every unpleasant circumstance attending it ought to be forgotten. You must learn some of my philosophy. Think only of the past as its remembrance gives you pleasure."

"I cannot give you credit for any philosophy of the kind. Your retrospections must be so totally void of reproach, that the contentment arising from them is not of philosophy, but, what is much better, of innocence."

"But surely you must have known the truth of my sentiments when...."

"When?"

"What we did... in the library." They had reached the narrow wooden bridge that crossed the brook, and she looked down at it as if it might suddenly open into a yawning chasm.

"I see," he said quietly. "I should no doubt apologize for my loss of control then."

"Please do not! In case you did not notice, I made no complaint about it. Boldly she stroked the sleeve of his coat, the strength of his arm apparent even through the fine fabric. "Although I am reminded that I have one other question regarding your proposal."

"And that would be?" He sounded cautious.

"Whether you are firmly committed to the idea of keeping your demands of me to a minimum. I should find it very disappointing if you did." She gave him an arch smile.

His eyes flared, and he made a visible attempt to control himself. Just when Elizabeth thought she had perhaps gone too far, he said in a voice so level he might have been making a response in church, "You say the most astonishing things, Miss Bennet."

She raised a mischievous eyebrow. "Shall I stop? I was of the impression that you enjoyed my impertinence."

"You would be wise not to trust too far the restraint of a man violently in love! Otherwise you might find yourself facing a repeat of the scene in the library." His slight smile softened his words.

Elizabeth's spirits soared. "Your warning has been noted, but as I have told you on a previous occasion, sir, my courage always rises with every attempt to intimidate me."

"Then I shall ask in return, how soon do you wish to be married? Very soon indeed?"

She laughed. "Very well, sir, I shall refrain from tormenting you."

His reply was low. "Elizabeth, you have tormented me almost since the first time we met. By day, by night, awake, asleep - it does not matter, you haunt me."

"Yet you have kept your silence until now, which is why I wonder whether you have regrets."

His look turned serious. "My only regret is that we did not reach this understanding long ago. At your sister's wedding, I felt almost as if it were our wedding day, as I had imagined it so often. My tongue may have been silent, but in my heart I was repeating those same vows to you. I was already bound to you, regardless of whether you cared for me or not."

"But that day you spoke to me so coldly when you told me you did not want my thanks! I was sure you wanted nothing more to do with me."

"Never that! But after imagining binding our souls together in eternity, it was bitter to be given your gratitude. I wanted your love, till death us do part, not thanks in the name of your family for doing nothing more than my duty."

"Nothing more than your duty? You have a very broad idea of duty, then! I suppose *I* had nothing to do with your actions then?"

"That the wish of giving happiness to you might add force to the other inducements which led me on, I shall not attempt to deny. But your family owe me nothing. Much as I respect them, I believe I thought only of you."

His words produced a flood of tenderness in Elizabeth. Impulsively she stood on her toes and kissed him. His look of astonished delight was all the reward she could desire.

"If that is how you will thank me, I will devote my life to earning your gratitude," he said in a voice that was slightly unsteady.

Her eyes danced. "How fortunate for you, then, that I am happy to do it!"

Darcy's eyes darkened. He wondered if she had any idea of how much she tempted him. Her kiss had only whetted his barely controlled desire for her, and he did not wish to frighten her. "Elizabeth, may I kiss you?"

She turned a limpid gaze on him. "Do you intend always to ask my permission?"

He whispered her name, and as if by instinct she slid her arms around his neck. He caught her to him, astonished by the sensation of her light, pleasing body pressed against his own. Every inch of him that touched her seemed to be reborn in fire, and his need for her flared uncontrollably. Still he struggled to contain himself, nibbling gently at her tender, innocent lips, teaching her the art of kissing. He could feel her process of discovery and the unmistakable moment when her flirtation turned into passion. His hands of their own volition slid down to the curves of her hip and pressed her tightly against him, her yielding softness meeting his aching need.

She moaned softly as his lips began to travel down her neck, desiring to taste as much of her as she would allow. She gave a little gasp when he reached the base of her neck, arching herself to give him better access.

He had always seen Elizabeth as a woman of passion, so her awakening did not so much surprise him as overpower him like a tidal wave. His lips sought to gain ever closer access to her neckline and the points he desired almost unbearably, and she did not deny him. But reason fought through the fog of desire that encompassed him, and he managed to pull himself away from temptation.

She laughed unsteadily. "I fear I have quite disarranged your cravat."

Darcy's cravat was the least of his worries. "Elizabeth, you must always feel free to stop me. You intoxicate me beyond the point of reason."

And now she was giving him that arch smile that he always ached to kiss. Self-denial suddenly lost its last shred of appeal, and he drew her back to him, gently opening her lips to him and finally tasting the delights he had longed for. Her sweetness was the finest of wines, yet full of joy. Drunk on it, he let his hand steal to the curve of her breast. The softness there fitted his hand as if made for it.

She drew in a sharp breath and he could feel her withdrawal. He rested his forehead against hers. "I should take you back to the house while I can still call myself a gentleman," he said.

"Must we?"

Her pleading look was almost his undoing, but in the nick of time, remembered that it should be enough that she wished to be with him. With that knowledge, perhaps he could restrain his baser impulses. "Your wish is my command, my love."

He expected her to pull away from him then, but instead she leaned her head against his shoulder with a contented sigh. He tightened his arms around her, so that at least he could have the pleasure of feeling her body against his. He still could not believe that she had finally agreed to marry him. If he had his way, she would stay in his arms forever.

A feline yowl, followed by a loud hiss, interrupted his reverie, and he regretfully released Elizabeth. "What in the world was that?"

Her bewitching smile was back. "If I am not mistaken, there is a green-eyed monster in the woods." She crouched down and snapped her fingers. "Tully! All is well. He was not hurting me."

A small nose appeared from under a bush, followed by the rest of a large ginger cat. He stalked over to Elizabeth and rubbed against her hand. She glanced up as she scratched under the cat's ears, sending him into paroxysms of pleasure. "This is Tully, who has apparently appointed himself as my chaperone."

"So this is the famous cat that Georgiana was so enchanted by?"

"Oh, yes, he took quite a shine to Georgiana. He loved sitting on her lap. He will be glad to see her again." She stroked the cat's fur one last time and then rose to her feet. "Speaking of Georgiana, we have probably left her alone with my family for long enough."

Darcy took her hand, entwining his fingers with hers. "Do you suppose your father would permit me to take you to Netherfield tomorrow? There is something I would very much like to show you there."

MR. BENNET'S PERMISSION having been duly sought and given, Darcy collected Elizabeth shortly after breakfast the following day. If it happened that Darcy's sense of direction was such that the curricle took a remarkably indirect route back to Netherfield, Elizabeth made no complaints.

Georgiana met them on their eventual arrival at Netherfield. Elizabeth had hoped to find her back to her usual spirits after a night's rest, but the girl remained quiet and withdrawn. Elizabeth wondered if she tended to be more restrained in her brother's presence, or whether she might be less than pleased over their engagement.

Elizabeth attempted to draw her into conversation, but with limited success. Finally she turned to Darcy. "Did you not tell me there was something you wished to show me here?"

He smiled. "Yes, but we will have to go outside for it. Georgiana, would you care to join us?"

The girl demurred, pleading a need to practice her music. Darcy seemed perfectly happy to have his intended to himself as they went outside.

Elizabeth seized the private moment to ask a question. "Is anything troubling Georgiana? She does not seem particularly glad to see me on this trip, but perhaps she is just tired from travelling yesterday."

Darcy frowned. "In truth, I do not know. She seemed genuinely delighted when I told her of our engagement, and spoke with great enthusiasm of having you as her sister. But the next day, she became unusually quiet, almost withdrawn. I am concerned for her, but I do not think it has anything to do with you. She had just gone out with one of her friends from school. Perhaps they quarreled."

"I will try to find some time with her alone. Perhaps I can

discover what is troubling her. I know your family must disapprove of the match, and it would be dreadful if she felt that way as well."

"If you can convince her to talk to you, I would be very much in your debt. And here is our destination."

"The stables?" Elizabeth hesitated just outside the door. "I should warn you that I am not particularly partial to horses."

He raised a surprised eyebrow. "Indeed? Fortunately, it is not a horse which I wish to show you."

A smile illuminated her face. "Then I will be happy to see it."

The smell of hay and horses suffused the half-lit stable. Elizabeth followed him to one of the stalls where he squatted next to a pile of wiggling fur. A sharp bark identified it as a dog even before her eyes adjusted to the darkness. But it was not just a dog, but a springer spaniel and pile of sleeping puppies.

Darcy looked up at her with a smile. "I hope you do not dislike dogs."

She shook her head, leaning closer. A tiny brown nose poked its way out from the pile of puppies. She reached out a finger, then laughed as it was promptly cleaned by a rough puppy tongue.

Darcy ruffled his fingers in the dog's fur. "This is Lycisce. I raised her from a pup, and her sire before her."

"Lycisce? Is that not the name of one of Actaeon's hounds?"

" 'Lycisce with her brother Cyprius,' yes. My own Cyprius is at Pemberley still, but Lycisce does not like to be far from me when she is whelping. She would rather travel in a carriage surrounded by whimpering puppies than be left behind."

Seeing his obvious affection for the dog, Elizabeth wondered with amusement to what degree Darcy also disliked being separated from her. "My father used to tell us stories from Ovid. I remember the tale of the hounds well."

Darcy extricated a small bundle of black and white fur from the pile. "Would you like to hold one? They are almost six weeks old."

Elizabeth took it gingerly, then cradled the warm puppy against her chest, perching herself on a low bale of hay. The puppy stretched, then butted her hand with its nose. "Do they have names?"

"Not yet. I have not decided whether I will keep one."

"I do not know how you could bear to give them up! What will happen to the others?"

"They will go to various families. The line is well-known for their hunting abilities. Georgiana had planned to take one, but decided on a cat instead after making friends with yours."

"Tully? I am not surprised."

"Tully is an odd name for a cat."

Elizabeth blushed. "It is short for Catullus. Another classical reference, but for far less dignified reasons, as you can imagine." She stroked the puppy's soft fur. He seemed determined to explore; his tongue reached out to her cheek. A warm feeling spread through her as she held him close.

Darcy watched her in silence, transfixed by her softened expression. Elizabeth's fine eyes had shown so many moods over the course of their acquaintance – teasing, lively, infuriated, restrained, contemptuous, tearful, and more recently full of desire – but he had never seen this look before. What would it be like to have that unguarded and adoring gaze turned on him, as if Elizabeth trusted him with her very soul? Someday it would happen, he hoped, when they had spent more time together and there was less uncertainty, perhaps when they had children of their own. The idea of Elizabeth, her body rounded with his child within her, was enough to set his blood racing with desire to make his vision into reality.

Lycisce gave a low growl. Darcy shushed her, then said, "I believe she has had enough company for now. She is very protective of her pups."

Elizabeth was oddly reluctant to give up the snuggling puppy. Impulsively she said, "Could I have this one when he is old enough?"

Darcy's face lit up. "Of course. You may have anything your heart desires."

She kissed the puppy's head, then placed him carefully next to his mother, her hand lingering for a moment on his head. Then she took Darcy's hands. "Thank you."

"You need not thank me."

"I meant for showing me the puppies. They are precious."

"Not as precious as you, my love." His lips brushed against hers.

"My sweetest, loveliest Elizabeth."

Without a thought she moved into his arms. It was risky enough being alone in the stable without adding an illicit embrace to her sins, but she longed for the comfort of him and the sense of his strength flowing around her and into her.

He nuzzled her forehead until she raised her face to him, then he kissed her eyes and her cheeks before reaching his mouth. Enveloped by his scent of musk and leather, she felt the tip of his tongue tracing her lips, sending tingles of excitement plummeting through her. Her lips parted, allowing him to deepen the kiss and send her into a blissful world of sensation.

His hands stroked her back, so lightly that it caused a frisson of sensation, drawing all her attention to the points in her body where he touched her, creating a longing for more. He made a guttural sound as his hands slid down to the curves of her waist, then further down until he pulled her hips firmly against his thighs. Now it was her turn to gasp at the swell of desire from her private places as he rubbed against her. The sensation was almost too much, threatening to make her forget everything beyond this moment. If she did not stop now, she might not find the strength to do so later.

Reluctantly she pushed against his shoulders, first tentatively, as if she hoped he would disregard her scruples, then more firmly.

He released her immediately, though with a sigh. "My dearest Elizabeth, I hope at least you are in no doubt as to how ardently I adore you."

She gave an arch smile which was only a bit shaky. "I am beginning to understand that, yes."

"However, you may be certain that if visiting puppies always leads to such delightful diversions, there will be puppies all over Pemberley."

She laughed, as he had intended, and they returned to the house without further incident.

Chapter 19

IT WAS TWO days before Elizabeth found the opportunity to speak to Georgiana, who still seemed disinclined to talk. Finally, after having several conversational gambits meet with little more than polite silence, Elizabeth said, "I have long wanted to apologize to you for my unfortunate words at Pemberley. In addition to being under a misapprehension about Mr. Wickham's character, I had no idea that a mention of his name would be hurtful to you, or I never would have said such a thing."

Georgiana seemed unusually interested in the pattern on her teacup. "You need not apologize. It was nothing. I should not have reacted as I did."

Elizabeth reached over and laced her hand with the girl's. "Georgiana, I hope that when we are sisters, you will feel able to confide in me. I am used to having sisters to share my sensibilities and my secrets, and you will be as dear to me as any of them."

Georgiana blinked hard. "I would like that, too. I will tell you the truth, then. I know that you are fond of Mr. Wickham. You need not worry about me. I will not make a fuss."

Elizabeth frowned. "You are under a misapprehension, then. I was once fooled by Mr. Wickham's charm, I admit, but I now know him to be a blackguard of the worst sort."

It was clear that Georgiana did not believe her. "That is not what he told me a few days ago."

"I beg your pardon?" Elizabeth was sure she must have misunderstood the girl.

"He said he is a great favourite of yours, and he has high hopes that once you and Fitzwilliam are married, you will be able to convince my brother to allow him to return to Pemberley." Her voice trailed away to a whisper at the end.

Elizabeth hardly knew what to say. "Georgiana, Mr. Wickham is aboard a ship to Canada, if he has not arrived there already," she said gently.

A tear dropped from the girl's face. "I do not know who told you that, but he is in London. I saw him."

"Are you certain?" Elizabeth's first thought was that Darcy would be furious.

"Of course I am certain. I am hardly likely to make a mistake of that sort, am I?"

"Does your brother know?"

"I did not tell him. He has been so happy about your engagement, and I did not want to spoil that for him. You need not worry. I can tolerate Mr. Wickham's company." The tears welling in her eyes belied her brave words.

"Well, *I* cannot! I do not understand how this has come to pass, but what he told you is not true. He may believe it himself, though I cannot imagine how. I have not seen him since before I first met you, and I have been very happy in thinking that our paths would never cross again. Even if your brother were to allow him to return, which I cannot imagine under any circumstances, *I* would not."

Georgiana buried her face in her hands, her shoulders shaking silently. Wordlessly Elizabeth brought out her handkerchief and slipped it into the girl's hand. At first she could do nothing but to wait and watch compassionately, but as Georgiana dabbed at her eyes and began to regain her composure, Elizabeth put her arm around her.

Georgiana said in a trembling voice, "Please forgive me, Elizabeth; I am so sorry to be behaving like a child. I never know who to believe, it seems."

"You have done nothing wrong," Elizabeth reassured her. "But your brother needs to know of this."

"No!" cried Georgiana. "Please, do not tell him. He will be so angry!"

"He will be angry, yes," Elizabeth said gently, "but not at you. He needs to be aware of this."

"I cannot bear it when they fight!"

For a moment Elizabeth was unsure of her meaning, then she understood. "Your brother and Mr. Wickham?"

The words began to tumble out of Georgiana's mouth. "I do not understand why Fitzwilliam hates him so much, and cannot see his good features. And once they begin to quarrel, then George says the most outrageous things and it is as if he is a different person entirely. Why can't they just talk to one another? They used to be best of friends."

This was an unexpected complication. Elizabeth had assumed that Georgiana would share her poor opinion of Mr. Wickham. "I am of your brother's mind on this," she said very gently. "After all, he is the man who ruined my sister Lydia."

Georgiana dashed tears from her eyes. "I know that, but I also know *him*. He was always very kind to me. He would never have done such a thing had he not been driven to extremities of poverty. Oh, I understand why my brother could not allow me to marry a steward's son, and that George was more interested in my dowry than in me." Her voice shook, and she was silent for a moment. "But even poor men must have something to live on, you know. I cannot blame him for that."

Elizabeth opened her mouth to contradict her, but then recalled saying something similar herself on hearing of Wickham's engagement to Mary King. How easy it was to fall into a web of half-truths! And Georgiana was very young. "I cannot put as kind an interpretation on it, but regardless, he will not be welcome at Pemberley or anywhere else I might be. You may rest assured of that."

Georgiana pressed the handkerchief over her eyes. "Thank you. I do not believe him a bad man, but when I see him, it brings back all the horrible mistakes I made and how foolish I was."

"Of course," Elizabeth said soothingly.

DARCY SCOWLED AT the newspaper in front of him, not seeing a word of it. It wasn't that he begrudged the time Elizabeth was spending with Georgiana; he was grateful that she was taking on part of his burden of discovering what was lowering his sister's spirits. He did not doubt that Elizabeth would like to see him as well, and he certainly was not jealous of his own sister. It was just that it was damned difficult to concentrate on anything knowing that Elizabeth was only a few rooms away from him and not *with* him - not, of course, that he would be concentrating on anything *but* Elizabeth if she were there.

He missed her with a longing that went beyond the purely physical, though it was indubitably physical as well. Her passionate response to his kisses was both a delight and a torment. Having finally won her consent, he wanted to be married to her *now*, or at the very least, to indulge in the greater permissivity a more sophisticated lady might permit during engagement. He had heard often enough of such things at his club, but Elizabeth had not been raised among the *ton* and was unlikely to share those sentiments, and he had no intention of asking her for more than she was willing to give. He was too grateful that she was giving him anything at all.

Still, when he thought of the months they had wasted and how they could have been married by now, he could not help wanting more of her. Even now that they were formally engaged, he still had moments of being uncertain of her regard and fearing that some other impediment might come between them. And it certainly did not help that she was with Georgiana instead of him, and thus denying him even the modest relief he could find in her kisses.

As if conjured by his thoughts, at that moment Elizabeth herself slipped inside the room. The latch clicked audibly as she shut the door behind her. Darcy spared no more than a second on hoping that his sister was not aware that they were alone together behind a closed door. Those sentiments were too rapidly overcome by his imagination flying to how best to enjoy these moments of privacy with Elizabeth.

His body was already making its own assessments, and Darcy had reason to be grateful for the loose fit of his trousers as he stood and walked over to take her hands, careful to keep a safe distance between him and her tempting body. He gave her a gentle but lingering kiss — well, he had *intended* it to be gentle and lingering, at least, but as Elizabeth responded by moving closer to him and sliding her arms around his neck, it turned into something completely different. Without conscious decision, he found himself joining his mouth to hers with the greatest of abandon, asking for and receiving the reassurance he needed that she felt some degree of the same need that he did.

As her soft form fitted itself so naturally to his body, his hands, seemingly of their own volition, slid downward to press her tightly against that insatiable part of him that wanted her most. By God, she was a fast learner! Just two days earlier, Elizabeth had stiffened in shock when he had done the very same thing, yet today she moved against him eagerly. If there was much more of this, his resolve not to push for more of her was going to be history. His baser instincts had already taken notice of the fainting couch in the corner of the dressing room that served as his study. Dressing room – he had best not think of dressing or undressing at the moment.

He forced himself to loosen his grip on her and to turn his attention to dusting her face with light kisses. After a minute, he was able to release her entirely, though the look in her eyes, dark with desire, almost undermined his determination. "This is a delightful surprise," he said, pleased that his voice was close to its normal evenness.

To his satisfaction, she was still breathless as she said, "I need to discuss something important with you."

"Of course. What is the matter?"

Instead of replying, she crossed to the sideboard, poured a glass of brandy from the decanter, and brought it to him.

He took it from her with raised eyebrows. "Am I likely to need this?"

"Quite possibly."

He took a sip of it, reluctant to have more. He needed all of his wits about him to maintain his resolve. "As long as you tell me you love me, nothing can be that bad." He leaned back against the edge of the desk, creating a little more safe distance between them.

"I do love you. Very much, in fact." She took a deep breath. "George Wickham is in London."

He straightened abruptly. He had expected anything but this. "Damn him," he said savagely. "I knew it was too good to be true. I do beg your pardon, Elizabeth."

"Unfortunately, that is not all of it. He spoke with Georgiana…"

"He did *what?*" He slammed the brandy snifter down on the desk, heedless of the delicacy of the glass. "And she *allowed* it?"

"I do not believe she had much choice. She was out with a friend - Annabelle, I believe was the name she mentioned - and her mother having ices at Gunter's. Mr. Wickham approached them and asked Georgiana to introduce him to her friends. She was afraid of causing a scene, so she did as he asked. Annabelle's mother asked him to join them."

"To *join* them? I had thought Mrs. Mason a sensible lady, but it seems my trust was misplaced."

Elizabeth tactfully decided not to challenge his assertion that the unknown Mrs. Mason should have rejected a presumably presentable acquaintance of Georgiana's. "It seems he has discovered our engagement, and is hoping to find some benefit for himself in it. He told Georgiana that he was a favourite of mine and that I would persuade you to allow him to return to Pemberley. Is there no limit to his impudence? Do you suppose he thinks I will forgive him for what he did to Lydia?"

His fury was such that he dared not respond for fear of what he might say. Instead, he strode to the window and stared out as if he might find answers there, his fists clenched at his sides.

After a minute of silence, Elizabeth said in a small voice, "I hope you know that I want nothing to do with him."

Darcy released a harsh sigh, then turned to her. He could not allow his anger to affect Elizabeth. "Of course not, but I did not need this, not now." He took her hands in his and kissed first one, then the other. Then he took her hand and drew her down onto his lap and into his arms. "*This* is what I need most." He kissed her just below her ear, but did not attempt to capture her lips. To do so would be unwise, as he had chosen the only place he could sit and hold her the way he wished, which was the dangerous fainting couch.

"I am happy to provide comfort, then."

He refused to think about what comfort she might provide. He had to concentrate on dealing with Wickham, not with his own physical desires. "Still, I must put an end to this. I had thought my dealings with him were done. I will have to return to London."

"So soon?" Elizabeth's hand tightened on his arm.

"Today. The longer he thinks he has escaped my notice, the harder it will be. Believe me, dearest Elizabeth, I would far rather remain here with you, but I cannot allow him to approach Georgiana without consequences, or he will be forever appearing in our lives."

"Of course. It is just that you have been here such a short time." Despite her words, Elizabeth now seemed unperturbed by the prospect of the separation. "I must hope for a speedy resolution of this matter, then."

He traced her cheekbone with his finger, wondering what she was truly thinking. Was he being a fool to believe she cared for him as he did for her? "Tell me once again, Elizabeth," he said, his voice rough, "Tell me that you will wait for me."

"How could I not? Even if I had such a strange wish, we are betrothed, and nothing can change that."

"Nothing but a parson's words, and that day cannot come soon enough for me. I have lost you so often that I never cease to worry that something will come between us again. That is why I am impatient to have my ring on your finger." He followed the words with action, his fingers encircling her finger like a living ring. "Till death us do part," he murmured. "Tell me you wish for it, too."

Seeming caught in the intensity of his gaze, she whispered, "I want nothing more than to be your wife. I wish I were yours this very moment, and nothing would ever separate us again." She tightened her arms around his neck, pressing herself closer to him, as if trying to make herself part of his very essence.

If he could not in fact make her his, hearing that she wished for it was the next best thing. As she trembled slightly in his arms, his body ached for her, but he remained in control until the moment that her lips sought out his.

Darcy made a strangled sound deep in his throat, trying to hold back and to keep the kiss gentle. But Elizabeth apparently felt no such restraint, or perhaps she merely had too much faith in his self-control, for she boldly slipped her tongue between his lips, emulating what he had done to her previously. It was more than a man could be expected to bear.

Elizabeth was not thinking about self-control as he crushed her to him, exploring her mouth demandingly and with a thoroughness that left her both breathless and needing more. His hand rose to cup her breast, and she arched into it. Unexpectedly she felt his thumb caress her nipple, first gently, then rolling it between his fingers, sending acute stabs of desire deep within her. As she moaned her pleasure and he once again claimed her mouth, Elizabeth stopped thinking at all. There was nothing but her body and his, the pleasure and the longing that consumed her.

His hand abandoned her breast, leaving her bereft. How could he stop, when he had just awakened these amazing sensations in her? Then she felt a new intimacy and warmth as his fingers crept under the neckline of her dress, the roughness of his skin starting fires on her tender flesh as his fingers began to play with her peak. It was pleasure; it was torture; and she needed more. Much more. Involuntarily she moved against him, the heat of her secret places rubbing fiercely against his hardness, and she felt a returning pressure that excited her in ways she did not understand. Engulfed by the fierce pleasure he was giving her, she was barely aware of her sleeves sliding down her arms until she felt the cool air on her tender breasts.

Darcy's breath caught, and Elizabeth opened her eyes to see his gaze fixed on her newly exposed flesh. He dipped his head, kissing her neck, her collarbone, and further down. "Elizabeth," he whispered reverently, then he tasted the tip of her breast and drew it into his mouth.

She gasped as ever more intense pleasure lanced through her, stabbing straight to her womb. The sensation became even stronger as pressure grew against her thighs. It was his hand, she realized dimly, and she writhed against it, seeking more and more stimulation, her entire body consumed by need for him. Then the pressure changed, and she felt the heat of his hand directly over the juncture between her legs. It did not even occur to her to protest; her only fear was that he might cease, leaving her adrft in a sea of desire.

From his first sight of Elizabeth's ivory breasts, Darcy had given up any effort at resistance. If Elizabeth had shown even the slightest sign of discomfort or concern, he could have rallied himself, but even he could not make a case for stopping when her fingers were woven through his hair to keep his mouth at her breast and her hips undulated against his hand as if seeking more. She even gave a whimper of distress and tightened her hands on his head when he withdrew his hand, and seemed unsatisfied until that hand began exploring its way beneath her skirt. No, he could not resist any longer. What little sanity remaining to him was reserved for making certain that Elizabeth was hurt no more than physically necessary in the process of satisfying both of them.

The skin of her thighs was astonishingly silky. He noted absently that he wanted to kiss every inch of them someday, but his goal lay higher yet. And she seemed just as eager, her cry of pleasure as his fingertips began roam her wetness turning into a gasp as he discovered her nub.

Elizabeth succumbed to sheer sensation as he touched her. His mouth still tugged at her breast, and she moaned her pleasure. Time seemed suspended within the rhythm he established, sucking and stroking in cadence, sending rushes of exquisite pleasure through her body. Then, just as she thought she might die of pleasure and need, his finger stilled and he lifted his head. "Dearest God, Elizabeth, I love you," he whispered.

His eyes were almost black, and she found herself falling into them. How could anything that felt so right be wrong? This was how it should be, how it needed to be. His finger still in intimate connection with her, she pressed her lips against his passionately, using the motion of her hips to urge him on. When he still seemed to hesitate, leaving her in an agony of need, she whispered, "Please, Fitzwilliam."

"Elizabeth," he breathed, and then his finger started to move again, circling faster as he suffused her with sensation until she could not remember anything else. Then a fountain of pleasure erupted from the spot he touched her, sending ecstasy through every part of her, wave after wave of it, cresting in a shimmering burst of bliss that took over her very soul and rendered her half-mindless.

His arms tightened around her, and somehow she was lying back on the fainting couch, her body still throbbing in the last spasms of satisfaction. Her skirts were up around her hips, and she did not care. She did not care about anything but him.

Darcy's voice was rough as he spoke in her ear. "Elizabeth, my own sweet temptress, I will stop now if you wish it, but I cannot hold back much longer."

Elizabeth wanted nothing more that to remain in intimacy with him, to forget that he had to leave her once again and that any impediment existed. Sometime in the last few minutes, she had left behind the last fragments of her reserve, and nothing mattered anymore but that she was a woman in love. She kissed him fiercely and said, "Don't stop."

Darcy no longer doubted his actions. Nothing could possibly feel more right. They were engaged to be married, Elizabeth wanted it, and he desired her with an unimaginable urgency. He drew away only long enough to deal with the waistband of his trousers, then returned to her arms and the exhilarating sensation of his need pressing against her most sensitive flesh. He rocked against her, making her twist against him with pleasure and glorying in his ability to do so, but even that was not enough. He pressed against her opening, feeling the resistance as he began to move. Then, in a moment he would never forget, suddenly it was no more and he was deep inside her, possessing his Elizabeth at long last.

At her fleeting cry of pain, he managed to still himself and to kiss her tenderly. He wanted her to remember their joining with the same happiness he would. "My Elizabeth," he whispered. "My beloved. My very own." Then she began to strain against him, seeking to pull him even further in. His last restraint disappeared with the delight of feeling her legs twining around his, urging him deeper, faster, harder with the passion he had always sensed within her. He lost himself in the rhythm of her, as pleasure and triumph ran riot in his body. Through it all he somehow sensed her tension rising until at last her body spasmed around him, sending him over the edge to the final moment when he spilled his seed within her. He collapsed against her, a sheen of sweat on his brow.

As Elizabeth gradually came back to herself, she knew she ought to be shocked at what had so suddenly occurred, but instead she felt a rush of tenderness for him, holding him close and stroking his thick hair. Nothing could mar the sweetness of the moment.

After a few minutes, Darcy raised his head, his face questioning. A lock of dark hair had fallen into his eyes, and Elizabeth gently moved it away. She sensed he was struggling for words, and she could see the beginnings of guilt in his expression. She touched his lips with her fingertip and said, "I have discovered something today. Your sister, exemplary as she is in so many ways, is *not* a good chaperone."

A smile tugged at the corners of his mouth. "I suppose not, though I am hardly in a position to complain. Still, I did not intend that to happen, Elizabeth. Please believe me."

"I know that. Neither of us intended it, but it was beautiful. I absolutely insist that you have no regrets."

He shook his head. "Any regrets I have are for your sake only. I would not have hurt you for anything, and I fear that I may have. But this — this is the assurance I need, although I could never have admitted it even to myself. Now I am yours and you are mine, and nothing can change that."

"Nothing can ever change that," she agreed. She tightened her arms around him, wishing she never had to let him go.

Chapter 20

MRS. BENNET DID not take the news well that her future son-in-law had departed precipitously. "What did you say to him, Lizzy? I hope your impertinence has not driven him away. You are not married yet, after all. Oh, you have no pity on my poor nerves!"

While Elizabeth was accustomed to the litany of her mother's nervous complaints, her words about not being married yet made her cheeks hot. Even if the slight soreness between her legs did not remind her at every step of what had occurred at Netherfield, she had the odd sensation that the change must be apparent in her face and with every breath she took. There might be no external evidence, but still it seemed beyond belief that even Jane had not noticed any difference in her. An odd mixture of embarrassment, shame, and a sort of pride overflowed in her, but first and foremost, she felt that everything had changed, and nothing would ever be the same again.

Jane's voice interrupted her reverie. "Lizzy, are you well?"

"Quite well," she said automatically.

Kitty snickered. "She is already pining for him, can't you tell?"

Elizabeth decided to ignore her, especially as there was a certain truth in her words. "I am perhaps a little fatigued, that is all." Her lips quirked as she imagined what their response would be should she have told them the truth of why she was distracted.

Mrs. Bennet fanned herself with her hand. "You must try to please him in all things, Lizzy! Just look at you. Your hair is mussed and your dress wrinkled. And you must wear your stays tighter and your neckline lower. That is how to keep a gentleman interested and happy."

Elizabeth wondered half-hysterically what her mother would say if she told her that Darcy was responsible for her disarray and that he found her neckline quite tempting enough. Jane put a hand on her arm.

"Mother, you are embarrassing her. Come, Lizzy, you must rest."

ELIZABETH WAS RELIEVED when Jane left her to return downstairs. She had asked Jane to loosen her stays, but had been reluctant to disrobe with her sister present. Now that she was alone, she stripped off her clothes. She hung her dress in the wardrobe until such a time as Hill could help her put it on again, and sat on the bed to examine the shift she had just removed. As she suspected, it carried damning evidence in the form of small bloodstains and a residue of sticky fluid. She held it in her hands for a minute, taking in the truth of what she had done with a sinking feeling at the pit of her stomach. An image flashed before her of Mr. Darcy as he must be at this moment, riding toward London, and she wondered what he must be thinking of her. He had not seemed distressed at her behaviour, but it was possible that might have changed on reflection.

She would not think of that. Instead, she found a fresh shift to wear and took the incriminating one to her vanity. Fortunately, the ewer was full, and she poured half of its contents into the basin. The soiled section of her shift followed, and she began to dab at the stains, rubbing the cloth firmly against itself. She could not possibly send it to be laundered with such evidence on it . The laundry maids would recognize it for what it was, and discretion was too much to be expected from them. And while it might be common enough among the circles Mr. Darcy frequented in London for an engaged couple to anticipate their wedding vows, Meryton was a small town, and its inhabitants always in need of fresh gossip. She had no wish to be fodder for them.

She checked the fabric again. Better, but telltale splotches still remained. She scrubbed at it more vigorously, wishing she had some of the strong soap used in the laundry.

The door clicked open behind her. Startled, Elizabeth jerked her head around to see the intruder. It was Jane, bearing a tea tray. "Lizzy, I thought you might like some tea." She set the tray on a side table, then looked over Elizabeth's shoulder at the blood-stained shift. "Did your courses come early, then? No wonder you are so tired."

Elizabeth bent her head but said nothing. She and Jane knew

each other's cycles well, and it would not take Jane long to realize that her courses could not possibly be *this* early.

"Here, I will take care of that. You should have told me you needed help." Jane took the wet shift from Elizabeth's hands. "You should rest."

Fighting the urge to snatch the shift away from Jane, Elizabeth quietly sat on the bed, feeling terribly exposed. Jane hummed softly as she wrung the fabric through the water. Elizabeth could not decide whether she hoped her sister would guess the truth or not. It suddenly seemed a terrible sin to try to disguise the truth. She said in a low voice, "I am not having my courses."

"Did you injure yourself, then?"

"No."

Finally Jane looked over her shoulder with a puzzled air. "I do not understand."

Elizabeth essayed a teasing smile, though she suspected it did not quite reach her eyes. "I was alone with Mr. Darcy in his study for some time."

It was a moment before Jane's eyes grew wide. "Do you mean that... oh, my dearest Lizzy!" Her cheeks reddened and she looked away, scrubbing ferociously at the shift as if trying to wash out her new knowledge.

"I am afraid so," Elizabeth said lightly. "Will you ever forgive me?"

Jane's hands stilled. "Of course. There is nothing for me to forgive, is there?"

"It was not something either of us had planned."

"You need not explain to me. After all, you are engaged to be married."

"Dearest Jane, you are far too good, but I appreciate your efforts to think well of me despite the circumstances."

"Is this why he left?"

Elizabeth shook her head. "No, he truly had urgent business to attend to. He did not wish to go. That is how it began – we were both unhappy to be parted, and one thing led to another."

"Does it distress you?"

Elizabeth knew her sister was not speaking of Darcy's departure any longer. "Yes, and at the same time no. It is strange. I am both shocked and astonished, and yet I cannot help thinking that perhaps it was better this way. Now my wedding night holds no fear for me. Had we waited, my nerves might have been as bad as our mother's by the time we were married!"

"It is not so terrible, then?"

"Not terrible at all, I am happy to report."

Jane looked up with a weak smile. "Well, then, it must have been for the best."

DARCY WAS IN no mood to sit in a carriage, so he rode ahead on Bucephalus while his valet followed with his luggage. On a clear stretch of road, he spurred his horse to a canter, despite the risk if he suddenly overtook a vehicle. Bucephalus would be able to stay clear in any case; Darcy had trained the stallion himself. The wind rushed past him as Bucephalus half-flew down the road.

He ought to be feeling shame for seducing Elizabeth. He ought, at the very least, to be devastated by their separation, though he supposed at some level that he was disturbed by it. He certainly ought to be filled with rage and outrage toward George Wickham for approaching Georgiana, but instead he felt elated, almost exhilarated.

The long months of loneliness, rejection, and uncertainty were over. Elizabeth had committed herself to him in the most basic way possible, and there could be no going back. No more concern about whether she might change her mind, or that she might wish to have nothing to do with him, or agonizing late into the night about whether he had forced her into an engagement she did not wish for. No, by God, she had shown that she cared for him, and if she did not feel the deep and passionate love he did for her, perhaps that might yet come. Regardless, she was finally his, as he had been hers for more than a year. All would finally be well.

No pricks of conscience disturbed him. They were engaged, after all, and would be married in a month. She had been willing and seemed untroubled by the event. She knew he would never abandon her to her fate, as some men had been known to do, so there was no cause for alarm. Indeed, he could not bring himself to have the least regrets. Elizabeth was well and happy, it made no difference to their future, and now he was spared weeks of worry about what might come between them. He felt on top of the world, all powerful, unconquerable.

Soon he would have to put his mind to how he would locate George Wickham, but there would be time for that when he reached London. For now he would simply glory in the knowledge that Elizabeth was his forever.

DINNER AT LONGBOURN seemed to last forever to Elizabeth. Although there was no sign of anything amiss apart from Jane's occasional worried glances, she felt as if she must have a brand on her forehead signifying her guilty action. What would the rest of her family think if they knew?

She wondered with an odd amusement if her mother would scold her for foolishness or praise her for making every effort to secure Mr. Darcy. Surely she had no reason to worry that Mr. Darcy would call off the engagement now that he had enjoyed her without the price of a wedding ring. After all, the announcement had been in the papers, and it would disgrace him to go back on his word. Not as much as it would disgrace her, but she knew he would avoid shame to his family name at all costs. And he had been loyal to her for so long, through trials and tribulations most men would never endure.

No, Mr. Darcy loved her, that was certain, and he would never abandon her. That was foolish thinking. But she could not help wondering if his opinion of her might have changed. She had made no effort to stop him, as he might rightfully expect a lady to do, nor even chided him after the fact for his lack of control, which would hardly have been fair in any case as she had not objected. Would it make him question her moral character? It had seemed for a moment as if he had expected her to be angry with him, and her only thought had been to reassure him, rather than to preserve what bits of modesty she still retained. But what must he think of her now? Certainly he had doubts about her family's character already, and Lydia's behaviour had not helped in that regard. Would he think her like Lydia? Did he now regret offering to make her his wife, or worry about her potential influence over his sister?

Her other concern was for Jane. She had not yet found the courage to reveal to her sister what she had learned about Mr. Bingley's engagement, but Jane was bound to hear of it sooner or later. It would no doubt be in the papers soon, and at least Elizabeth could choose to break the news in privacy rather than have Jane discover it in public. So the following day, with a heavy heart and armed with extra handkerchiefs, she asked Jane to walk with her in the little wilderness, well shielded from public view.

She was trying to find the courage to begin when Jane said, "Lizzy, what is the matter? You have been out of spirits ever since Mr. Darcy's departure. Did you quarrel after, umm, when you met last?"

Elizabeth almost laughed at her sister's unexpected interpretation of her desire to speak privately, but the subject hardly lent itself to humour, especially when she recalled all the months Jane had grieved over Mr. Bingley. "No, all is well between us. But he did give me a certain intelligence that I was not happy to hear, and I suspect you will be even less pleased by it." She paused to take a deep breath.

Jane's countenance grew pale. "Has something happened to Mr. Bingley? Is he injured, or ill?"

Elizabeth bit her lip. "No, to the best of my knowledge, he is well, but he is... engaged to be married." She hurried through the last few words, then looked down at the ground to allow Jane time to recover.

"I see," said Jane, her voice colourless. "It is not a surprise; I had assumed he would not wait long to take a wife."

They walked in silence for a few minutes, then Elizabeth said, "Mr. Darcy believes that Mr. Bingley does not care for the lady, but rather that he accepted the choice of his sisters, since he could not follow his own heart."

Jane gave an odd half-cough which Elizabeth strongly suspected covered a muffled sob. She handed Jane her handkerchief. "I am very sorry to be the bearer of ill tidings, Jane."

"There is nothing ill about these tidings," Jane said in a voice that might have sounded calm enough had it not been undermined by a slight trembling. "I am happy for Mr. Bingley. He needs a wife and I have no doubt that he has chosen wisely. He is such an amiable gentleman that if affection does not already exist between the two of them, it soon will."

"Jane, you are more generous than any other woman in your position would be," Elizabeth said ruefully, realizing that her sister did not want sympathy.

"It is not generosity," said Jane with a slight sniffle. "He offered me his heart and his hand and I refused him. Why would I not wish him to be happy with someone else?"

Elizabeth decided that it would not be the better part of wisdom to point out that her sister had not wanted to refuse him, so she kept her silence on that point. "You are very good."

"What I *cannot* bear is how people will look at me when they hear the news." Jane's voice held an unusual sharpness. "Full of pity and derision for the spurned woman, and all the talk about how I should have tried harder to have won him, and now I will be an old spinster. If only I could tell them that he loved me, but that could never be. I wish I never had to see any of them again, but I will have to see them, day after day, just as it was after he left the first time. I *hate* it."

"I wish he had been a stronger man, one who would listen to his heart instead of the advice of others, and then none of this would have happened," Elizabeth said, realizing for the first time that it was the truth. She had blamed Mr. Darcy for Mr. Bingley's first departure from Netherfield, but that had been just another evidence of her prejudice against him. No matter what Mr. Darcy had said, the fault lay with Mr. Bingley for allowing himself to be swayed. She was suddenly grateful to be marrying a man who made his own decisions without regard to the opinions of others.

Chapter 21

ELIZABETH'S LAST MEETING with Mr. Darcy might not have troubled her much at the time, but she soon found that what had happened between them hung over her, even as she told herself again and again that it was a private matter between the two of them. Whenever she sat down to write a letter to Mr. Darcy, her pen froze after a few words. She did not know what to say to him without discussing the subject most on her mind, and she did not want to dissemble by writing a falsely cheerful letter.

Her anxiety grew as she received no word from him. Perhaps he also did not know what to say, but her worry about when he might return and what he might be thinking was near to driving her mad. In an attempt to lay her worries to rest, she finally forced herself to pen a note reporting that she had called on Georgiana at Netherfield and that her spirits seemed improved. To her delight, a response came the very next day.

> *My dearest Elizabeth,*
>
> *How odd it seems to write to you without fear of discovery or scandal. Since I cannot be in your presence, I must content myself with this. I had hoped to return to Netherfield by now, but my business has taken longer than expected. London seems very lonely when you are far away. Dare I hope that you are missing me as well?*
>
> *I paid a call to Mr. & Mrs. Thomas Wickham two days ago, and I am glad to report that your sister is in good health and seems happy in her present circumstances. Her husband is looking forward to leaving his regiment next month and has begun investigating possibilities for a permanent home for them. Your sister expressed a wish to live in*

Town, but he is set on finding a modest house in Derbyshire.

Thank you for checking on Georgiana. It is a relief to know that you are there for her.

In closing, I will say only that I treasure the memory of the recent times we spent together at Netherfield. I am forever grateful to have finally earned your good opinion, and I would not risk that for anything. Please know that I hold you in my heart every minute of the day, and that I can hardly wait for the moment when we will be together once more.

Forever yours,
Fitzwilliam Darcy

Tears of sweet relief came to Elizabeth's eyes as she read his final words, understanding the underlying reassurance about their last meeting. She told herself sternly that she had known all along that his sentiments towards her would be unchanged, but she held the letter to her heart for several long minutes, finding solace in the knowledge that his hands had touched it. For the first time since Darcy's departure, a real smile came to her lips. She read it again until she was near to knowing the words from memory.

She wished she could share his news of Lydia with her family, since Lydia was a poor correspondent and they had heard little from her since her wedding, but it would have been difficult to explain why Mr. Darcy would have found himself in Gravesend when he was supposed to be in London. Presumably he had thought that Thomas Wickham might have some ideas where his miscreant younger brother might be hiding. She hoped his assessment of Lydia's happiness was correct, and that Thomas was treating her well. It was perhaps just as well that they would settle in Derbyshire where she could keep a watchful eye over her sister.

THOMAS WICKHAM WRINKLED his nose at the odor emanating from the alley. He checked the piece of paper that bore the address in hopes he had been mistaken, but he was not. Folding the paper and dropping it back in his pocket, he began to make his way down the alley, stepping gingerly to avoid the rotting trash that littered the street. He shook off a young bit of muslin that tried to take his arm, though he could understand her mistake. Why else would a gentleman come into such a place?

The alley opened into a small court. The cobblestones were slippery, and Thomas did not even want to think about why that might be. The boarding house was obvious by the cracked sign that hung in the window. He was not looking forward to this.

A rap at the door summoned a slatternly wench who eyed him hopefully. "What can I do for you, good sir?"

"George Wickham. Is he here?"

"I think so, in his room, most likely. Probably not in his cups yet, either, lucky for you." She pointed up the stairway.

The stairs squeaked underfoot as he ascended. He pounded on the door the girl had indicated. George had damned well better be there. He was tired of this quest.

He expected his brother to be as disheveled as everything else in this place, but the dapper man who opened the door had taken obvious care with his appearance and looked ready for a day at his club. He should have known; George would never allow his looks to suffer. His looks and charm were his bread and butter.

"Thomas, old chap! What brings you here? Not that I'm not delighted to see you, of course." With the same quicksilver smile he had always used to forestall trouble, George shook his hand heartily.

Thomas steeled himself not to give in to that smile. "I'm here to talk about your future."

"My future? I'm a bit down on my luck at the moment, but I just learned of a marvelous opportunity to…"

"Don't bother, George. I've heard it all before."

George stepped back with a hurt look. "What's the matter? Are you angry at me?"

"I'm here to tell you it's time for you to move on. Leave the country."

"What? You appear here after, what, three years, and tell me to leave the country? Come along, Thomas, what sort of joke is this?"

"The most serious kind. Darcy bought up your debts, more than enough to put you in debtors prison. He's willing to settle for you leaving the country. Canada or India, whichever you prefer."

"Darcy? I should have known. But it doesn't matter. He won't do anything to me now. He's getting married, have you heard? And his future wife has a soft spot for me. It's going to be a whole new day. Darcy will do as I ask."

"If his future wife ever had a fondness for you, it disappeared after you seduced and abandoned her sister."

"If that's all it is, I'll marry the girl. She's a silly little slut, but no matter."

Thomas felt no emotion, which made it all the more strange when he saw his fist connecting with his brother's jaw. He watched with clinical detachment as George crumpled to the floor, his head striking against the bedstead with a satisfying thunk.

George blinked several times, then propped himself up on one elbow, his free hand rubbing his chin gingerly. "What the devil was that for?"

"Insulting my wife, who, despite your influence, is a good enough girl, when managed correctly."

George cautiously put his head down on the floor. "I must be dreaming. I haven't had enough to drink to be seeing things yet."

"You aren't dreaming, and yes, I married the girl you ruined, and have done quite well with her. If you had not abandoned her, perhaps *you* would be the one receiving a generous allowance from Darcy and with a pretty little wife to boot."

"Damn Darcy! So he is paying you to betray your own brother, is he?"

"No, I am behaving just as you would do, by acting in my own best interest, no matter who may be hurt by it." Thomas hardened his voice. "When Darcy marries, he will be my brother as well, and he has far more to give than do you. He wants you out of the way; therefore, I do as well. So is it to be Canada, India, or debtor's prison?"

"There is no need for this," George said in his charming voice. "Tell Darcy I have left England forever. I will go to the continent and seek my fortune, and when he forgets about all this, I can return, perhaps with a wealthy wife of my own. Surely you would not send your own brother into exile half way across the world?"

"It will be debtor's prison, then. I will inform the constable."

"No, wait!" George struggled to his feet, holding onto the bedpost for balance. "If I must, I will go to India. There are fortunes to be made there. But I must speak to Darcy first."

Thomas seriously doubted George would ever put in the labour necessary to earn his keep, much less a fortune, and he was certain that he meant no good by asking for Darcy. Still, it was to be expected. "I will arrange for it," he said coolly.

"A LETTER FOR you, Lizzy," said Mary, dropping a folded envelope in her sister's waiting hand.

"More love notes?" Kitty teased. "Can he not survive a few days without your company?"

This time the handwriting was not Darcy's. It was in a hand unfamiliar to Elizabeth, who raised her eyebrows at the seal on the back. "A coat of arms," she said mildly. She broke the seal and perused the contents.

"Well, Lizzy, what is it?" demanded Mrs. Bennet.

Elizabeth smoothed the fine paper in her lap. "It is an invitation to dine with the Earl and Countess of Matlock."

Jane's mouth formed a silent O. "When?"

"Next week, in London."

Mrs. Bennet fanned herself vigourously. "A personal invitation from a peer? Oh, Lizzy, how grand you will be! You must have a new dress for the occasion; yes, you absolutely must. Just wait until I tell my sister Phillips that you will be dining with an earl!"

Elizabeth could not admit the truth of the matter, which was that she was less excited about meeting the Matlocks than by the guarantee that she would see Darcy again even if he had not resolved the matter of Mr. Wickham. It already seemed as if they had been apart forever. She stroked the invitation with a slight smile.

MR. DARCY'S NEXT brief note arrived several days later, and to Elizabeth's disappointment, it included the news that he did not anticipate returning to Netherfield before Elizabeth herself was to travel to London, having apparently heard of her invitation from his uncle. By reading between the lines, she could tell that the delay stemmed from difficulties in the search for Mr. Wickham, but her heart complained slightly that she wished her betrothed would have found time somehow to return to her, however briefly, or at least to write a longer letter.

But she was not by nature one to blame others for things that could not be changed, so she mustered her spirits and instead focused on finishing her gown. Jane was assisting her in sewing it, since the milliner in Meryton had not been able to promise to prepare it on time. But Elizabeth was pleased with how the lovely blue silk was taking shape. She had sketched a copy of one of the latest designs from Ackermann's Repository for her pattern, since the fashions in Meryton were several seasons behind those in Town. She would appear enough of a country cousin to Darcy's aunt and uncle who were accustomed to the finest London society could offer simply because of her lack of Town polish, so it was important to her to appear her best and not to put Mr. Darcy to shame. Since her father's pocketbook could not extend to the finest in lace or jewels, she would have to rely on the cut of her dress for style.

It was a large undertaking involving many fittings, alterations, and late nights stitching by candlelight, interposed by frequent complaints from Kitty about how she also needed a fine new dress and teasing from Mr. Bennet about fripperies, but it did serve to keep Elizabeth's mind off Mr. Darcy's absence.

On the day before she was due to leave, she packed it carefully in her trunk, caressing the silk sleeves and smiling at the thought of Mr. Darcy's expression when he would see her in it. The only time he had ever seen her dressed at her best was at the Netherfield Ball, and even that had been a dress two seasons old. She had a sudden longing to feel the warmth and safety of his arms around her once again, though the thought reminded her of their last meeting and brought a blush to her cheeks.

She travelled by public stage, grateful that there were only two other passengers, both older ladies. Shortly after they left Meryton, a steady rain began to fall, which at first pleased Elizabeth since it kept down the dust from the road and freshened the air. The sky grew dark as the rain became heavier, and one of the ladies had a fit of the vapours when a bolt of lightning struck not far from the road with a resounding boom of thunder that shook the carriage. Although Elizabeth had always been partial to the drama of storms, she did not think the road the best place to be during one, especially as she began to hear the horses' hooves slapping through the mud and making it splash up against the coach. But she was not particularly nervous until the coach took a mild slip sideways and ground to a halt.

The coachman cursed loudly as he dismounted. He circled the coach, complaining under his breath the whole time, then knocked on the side of the coach to inform them that one wheel was stuck in the mud. A steady stream of foul language assaulted their ears as he began to dig it out. Finally he seemed satisfied with the job he had done, and he asked the ladies to step outside the coach to lighten the load while he coaxed the horses to pull it out. Elizabeth was none too happy to be standing in the pouring rain with only a bonnet protecting her, but she stood it with forbearance since the poor coachman had been sitting outside in it all along.

He nickered at the horses and pulled at the bridle of one of the lead horses. They strained against the load, tossing their heads as their hooves slipped on the muddy road. Elizabeth shivered with the cold and wrapped her arms around herself in an attempt to stay warm, silently urging the team on. Finally the stuck wheel began to spin, and with a sucking sound it pulled free. The coachman's triumph lasted only a minute, though, before the wheel once again was mired deep.

The road was otherwise untraveled since all sensible people would be staying indoors in the storm, so the travelers were helpless to do anything but stand beside the road until the evening post coach passed, by which time Elizabeth was soaked through, cold and miserable. Her teeth chattered for most of the hour it took to reach the post house in London, where she fervently hoped that someone from the Gardiner household would have stayed all these hours to meet her.

As they approached their destination, Elizabeth could make out a familiar form standing in front of it, peering into the gloomy rain, and for the first time in what seemed like days, a smile came to her face.

Darcy was already beside the coach ready to hand her out by the time the coachman opened the door. As soon as he touched her icy hands – she had removed her sodden gloves some time since, lest they shrink around her fingers – he said with visible concern, "Elizabeth, you are half-frozen!"

She stepped down past him, eager to reach the shelter of the post house. "I cannot argue the point, but I am very glad to see you. Thank you for waiting for me."

"How could I have done otherwise? I was close to sending out search parties for you."

She was grateful that he had not pointed out the obvious, that he had asked to send his carriage for her and she had refused, not wanting to make a show of her journey. Once again, he had been proven correct.

He snapped his fingers at a lad idling by the door. "Have my carriage brought round immediately, and hot bricks for the lady. Immediately, I say!"

A few minutes later, but not too soon for Elizabeth, she was ensconced in the Darcy carriage, Darcy's greatcoat wrapped around her, and hot bricks at her hands and feet. The greatest warmth, though, seemed to come from Darcy's arm around her shoulders, holding her close to him, and his lips pressed to her temple. She had not realized how badly she had missed the reality of him until he was there at her side.

When they arrived at the Gardiners, her aunt bustled them inside to sit by the welcoming fire in the sitting room, but Mr. Darcy stayed only a few minutes. "It is more important to find some dry clothes for you, and I will not put your health before my own pleasure in your company. After all, I will see you tomorrow evening."

"In the evening?" Elizabeth said. She had hoped to spend part of the day with him.

Darcy made a face which indicated his agreement with her. "Unfortunately, there are matters which require my attention during the day, but after tomorrow, I will be completely at your disposal."

Elizabeth looked closely at him. The darkness at the posting house and in the carriage had disguised the fact that his face was drawn and grey with fatigue, more than waiting several hours for her could account for. She wondered how hard he might have been working in an effort to be able to return to her, and what the outcome of his labors had been. She did not want to be one more task on his agenda, so she would learn to be patient.

Chapter 22

MRS. GARDINER'S MAID arranged the loose curls on Elizabeth's face. "There you go, miss. My, but you do look fine!"

Elizabeth had to agree. The blue silk set off her fair skin and dark hair, and Mrs. Gardiner had brought out her precious string of pearls - a wedding gift from her husband - to go around her neck. Her hair was decorated with tiny white flowers which looked like stars among her curls. If it was not as lavish as jewels would have been, it was more elegant than her usual ribbons. It was quite a good presentation for a country gentleman's daughter, which would be enough to let her hold her head up high among the aristocrats.

It was not the prospect of meeting Darcy's powerful relatives, though, that made her wish she could pace the room instead of sitting stock-still with a hot curling rod in her hair. That particular urge sprang from her anticipation of seeing Darcy again for long enough to have a real conversation. They had been apart for over a fortnight, far more time than they had spent together since his businesslike proposal. It was natural, she decided, to have some concern given the changes in their relationship and Darcy's undoubted annoyance at having to spend so much time dealing with the question of George Wickham. For at least the thousandth time, she wondered whether Darcy had found him yet or not, and what had passed between them if he had. It even occurred to her fertile imagination that Darcy's absence from Longbourn might be related to an injury from a duel, a thought which made her feel vaguely ill. Surely he would not fight Wickham, would he? Was not Wickham's social status such as to make that outcome unlikely? But perhaps Wickham trained with Darcy in their childhood and learned skills with the pistol and rapier not usually acquired by a steward's son.

Elizabeth clenched her hands together. It was not like her to fret unnecessarily; as a rule, she found it best to take each moment as it came, but for some reason, that had never worked when she tried to apply it to Mr. Darcy. She half-smiled. He would be happy to know that she cared for him enough to worry so, but she would prefer to have her old carefree self back. But not, of course, if it meant losing Mr. Darcy! She hoped he would arrive early to collect her, if for no other reason than to put an end to her musings.

Her wishes were destined to be disappointed. Darcy had not yet arrived when she came downstairs. Her appearance was suitably complimented by her aunt and uncle, and with some amusement Elizabeth was made to promise to loan her silk dress to their youngest daughter when she was old enough to wear it, which the little girl seemed to assume would be by the impossibly ancient age of fourteen.

Half an hour passed as her aunt kept her company in the sitting room, then an hour. Elizabeth, attempting to remain as still as possible so as not to disturb her carefully set hair, more than once had to remind herself to still her impatiently tapping foot. She looked up eagerly each time at the sound of wheels on cobblestones, but as Gracechurch Street was well-trafficked, there were many false alarms.

Finally she saw a fine carriage pulling to a halt in front of the house. She rose from her seat in a ladylike manner, even though her heart wanted her to jump up and run to the door like an impatient child. To her shock, the gentleman who entered the sitting room was not Mr. Darcy. It took her a moment to recognize that the elegantly dressed gentleman as Colonel Fitzwilliam.

He must have seen her dismay, since he did not wait beyond the brief moment of a formal bow to speak his piece. "Miss Bennet, it is a pleasure to see you again, although I suspect the feeling may not be mutual when I tell you that I am here in place of my cousin. He has been unavoidably delayed, and sent a note asking me to accompany you to my parents' house, where he will meet us."

Unavoidably delayed? When she had been counting the minutes until she could see him again? Her throat choked up, and it was a minute before her good breeding returned to the fore and she was able to say, "On the contrary, Colonel, I am delighted that we will have the opportunity to renew our acquaintance en route."

He smiled amiably. "If I were not loathe to question the veracity of a lovely lady, I would suspect you of polite fiction, but since I am quite happy to have your company to myself, I will not do so. You must, however, allow me to tell you that my cousin will no doubt be rendered speechless tonight by your beauty, though I dare not praise it myself lest I incur his jealousy."

The colonel inquired after her health, then asked for an introduction to Mrs. Gardiner, whom he assured that there was a maid in the coach to serve as a chaperone, and that he would safeguard Elizabeth as if she were his own sister. "I do this not only for your sake, madam, since my cousin would run me through if I allowed any harm to touch one hair on her head, which would be a tragedy indeed since her appearance is perfection itself."

Elizabeth laughed, as he clearly had intended her to do, and took the arm he offered her. The carriage, as she had expected, was finer than any she had ridden in before, though the colonel seemed to take its luxurious sprung seats and gilt paint for granted.

Once they were en route to Matlock House, Elizabeth remembered her manners enough to thank him for taking the trouble to collect her himself, rather than merely sending a carriage.

He laughed. "By doing so, Miss Bennet, I gave myself the pleasure of enjoying your smiles rather than enduring my father's scowls. He is, I fear, in a temper. He does not countenance tardiness in anyone except himself, and Darcy was out of his favor even before this. But do not worry; his mood will have passed by the time we arrive."

Elizabeth decided to risk an extremely frank question. "Does his displeasure by chance stem from Mr. Darcy's engagement to me?"

Colonel Fitzwilliam smiled amiably. "Never fear, Miss Bennet. He will be charmed by you when you meet, but it is true that my aunt, Lady Catherine, has already had her say with him. She is suffering from bitter disappointment that Darcy will not marry her daughter, not that such a thing would have come to pass even had he never met you. But she finds it easier to have someone else to blame, and as a result, my father has heard that you entrapped my cousin by your arts and allurements. He will see soon enough that his worries are groundless."

Elizabeth suspected that Lord Matlock had expressed a stronger opinion of her than an accusation of using arts and allurements to catch his nephew. "I hope so. And Mr. Darcy, is he well? I hope it is nothing serious that has delayed him."

Colonel Fitzwilliam's attention seemed to be caught by something outside the window. "He did not offer an explanation in his note."

She noticed the colonel's careful avoidance. It did not signify, though, since Darcy himself would be able to explain himself soon enough.

ELIZABETH WAS GLAD that the colonel had prepared her for her arrival at Matlock House. She had assumed they would be dining only with Lord and Lady Matlock, but as it happened, several other family members had been invited, including the colonel's eldest brother, Viscount Kenilworth, and his wife; two sisters and their husbands, and Darcy's great-uncle, Judge Fitzwilliam. There was no sign of Darcy, but Colonel Fitzwilliam led her through the receiving line of his relations. Lord Matlock was gruff, but appeared to have recovered from his fit of temper, though his ruddy face suggested a choleric temperament. Lady Matlock was graciousness itself. Elizabeth discovered quickly why Colonel Fitzwilliam was Darcy's particular friend in the family, as the Viscount's slurred speech indicated he had already made a close acquaintance with spirits that day. His two sisters spoke cordially enough, but their faintly incredulous looks reminded Elizabeth of the Bingley sisters, and their conversation revolved solely around events of the Season which they must have known could mean nothing to Elizabeth.

They spent over an hour in stilted discussion in the sitting room, with no one daring to raise the question of the absent bridegroom. The butler came in twice to inform Lady Matlock that dinner was ready, but each time she waved him away. Elizabeth smiled graciously, but underneath her spirits were troubled. What could possibly have delayed Darcy this long? Did he have no appreciation of the uncomfortable position he had placed her in?

Lord Matlock's countenance became sterner as time wore on,

and finally he barked, "Where is that damned boy? I will not be kept waiting any longer for my dinner."

Lady Matlock, no doubt with the ease of long practice, appeared not to have heard her husband, and continued in her conversation with one of her daughters while making a subtle signal to one of the footmen. The butler reappeared a minute later, and this time Lady Matlock rose and announced that dinner was served.

Elizabeth suspected her colour was high as the colonel escorted her into dinner and took the seat which had obviously been intended for Darcy. He continued to chat amiably with her as if nothing was amiss, but she noticed that he tapped his fingers restlessly on the arm of his chair.

The elegant array of dishes presented before them was far beyond what Elizabeth had ever seen at a family dinner, but she did not have to feign a fashionable disinterest in food since her appetite seemed to have fled. She concentrated on keeping her chin high and a smile on her lips, as if she had not noticed anything was amiss in Mr. Darcy's absence, nor that Lord Matlock complained loudly about each dish and threatened to dismiss the cook no less than three times.

The first remove was already in place when a footman delivered a folded paper to Colonel Fitzwilliam. He opened it and scanned it quickly, then folded it and returned it to the servant. "From Darcy," he announced unnecessarily, since the entire table had gone silent and was looking in his direction. "The matter that delayed him is more serious than it initially appeared, and he is uncertain if he will be able to leave it at all today."

"That damned puppy!" the Earl growled. "Where is he, anyway, that is more important than his own family?"

"I do not know, but he mentions calling a surgeon for someone, so apparently there is some sort of emergency. Miss Bennet, he sends his most particular apologies to you, and says he will contact you in the morning."

"Thank you, Colonel," Elizabeth said calmly, though inside she felt much less certain. She had caught a glimpse of the note while he was reading it, not enough to make out more than a word or two, but she was sure the handwriting had not been Darcy's.

The meal seemed interminable after that. Elizabeth did a respectable job of presenting her usual lively self, but it was nothing more than an act. When Lady Matlock stood, indicating that it was time for the ladies to withdraw, Elizabeth felt she could stand it no longer, and she whispered softly in the Colonel's ear.

He nodded understandingly, then said, "I fear that Miss Bennet is much troubled by a headache, and hopes she might be excused from the remainder of the evening."

Lady Matlock, showing her good breeding, turned to her guest with an expression of concern as if she believed the patently weak story. "My poor dear! Of course you must go home at once. A cold compress over one's eyes is a sovereign remedy for a headache, and it has saved me more than once. You must promise me to try it yourself. I cannot bear the thought of anyone suffering from a headache for a moment longer than is absolutely necessary."

Colonel Fitzwilliam volunteered to see her home, refusing her offer to take a hackney cab. "Darcy would never forgive me if I did otherwise!" he said.

"Damned boy," grumbled Lord Matlock to nobody in particular, leaving his wife to receive Elizabeth's thanks for the invitation.

By the time she was in the carriage, Elizabeth could no longer maintain her bright smile. It was like a bad dream, being abandoned by Darcy and subjected to his uncle's ill temper and the supercilious looks of the younger members of the family. If Colonel Fitzwilliam had not inherited his mother's good manners, it would have been completely unbearable.

The colonel made no pretense of idle chatter this time. "I do not know what could have happened to Darcy. It is quite unlike him, I promise you, to fail to appear, and I know he was most anxious to see you. I am certain there must be a good reason that will be revealed to us in time."

"Is it possible he has been injured? Or Miss Darcy? You mentioned a surgeon."

"I cannot see how he could have sustained a serious injury tonight. He said that Lord Regenfield had sent for a surgeon; perhaps it was for his lordship."

Elizabeth rubbed her chilled hands together. "Perhaps whatever delayed him in the first place simply took longer than he expected." She tried to keep her tone brisk.

"Perhaps. I cannot say." The colonel's firm tones told Elizabeth that he knew what had originally delayed Darcy, but that he had no intention of sharing it with her.

After a mostly silent ride, they arrived at Gracechurch Street. Colonel Fitzwilliam walked her to the door. When Mrs. Gardiner came to greet them, her bright smile faded when she realized it was not Mr. Darcy who stood beside her niece. The colonel briefly paid her his respects, then bowed and departed.

Mrs. Gardiner frowned in concern. "Lizzy, you do not look well. Where is Mr. Darcy?"

Elizabeth pulled off her gloves and tossed them aside. "I do not know. He failed to make an appearance."

"He did not attend? Oh, my poor Lizzy! What reason did he give?"

"He sent a note about some sort of emergency."

Mrs. Gardiner closed her eyes briefly, then put her arms around Elizabeth. "There must be a good reason. Mr. Darcy is not the sort to ignore his responsibilities, and yesterday he was so anxious to see you."

"Perhaps he will prove to have a very good reason. If you will excuse me, aunt, I would like retire now."

Her aunt reluctantly let her go, saying, "I am certain he will be here first thing in the morning to explain himself." Elizabeth did not respond.

Chapter 23

ELIZABETH'S NIGHT WAS mostly sleepless. Lying alone in the dark, her imagination would not be bounded, and in it she had seen Darcy lying in a pool of blood or drowned in the river. What could possibly have kept him from her, if not some terrible accident? Her cheeks burned with mortification at the recollection of her dinner at Lord Matlock's house. It would have been a disaster if it were not for the good breeding evinced by Lady Matlock. If Elizabeth could feel gratitude for anything about that endless evening, it was to her.

She did not know what she would do if there was no word from Mr. Darcy this morning. The fear delayed her from making an appearance at breakfast, as if somehow waiting longer would increase the chances that she would find happy intelligence there on her arrival. He could not have changed his mind about marrying her, could he? The engagement had already been announced, and surely his honour if nothing else would demand that he follow through on it, or so she hoped. She would not have believed it possible that she could doubt him so, but she would have equally disbelieved that he would strand her with his uncle and aunt.

When she finally descended, Mrs. Gardiner was waiting for her, a smudged newspaper sitting before her. One glance at her aunt's face was enough to convince Elizabeth that her fears were justified. Her stomach twisted.

"Lizzy, my dear." Mrs. Gardiner took her elbow and led her to the table, going so far as to pull out Elizabeth's chair for her.

Numbly Elizabeth obeyed her and reached for the newspaper, quite out of keeping with her normal manners. She scanned the headlines, but they were all about the Peninsular War or the doings at

St. James Palace. Her eyes jumped from article to article, scanning for Darcy's name.

Mrs. Gardiner pointed to a paragraph in the society column. "I am so very sorry, my dear. I would never have thought it of him. We have been sadly misled."

One must be led to wonder whether young people today understand the meaning of betrothal. It is with great shock that we report an unfortunate disturbance at Lady R's soiree yesterday when Mr. D of Derbyshire, whose engagement was noted in these pages only a fortnight ago, was discovered in a tender moment with Miss S, late of Somerset, who is also betrothed, but unfortunately not to the gentleman in question. One can only offer one's deepest sympathies to Miss F's intended who found himself in the embarrassing position of discovering the twosome, though it might perhaps be noted that he has had a most fortunate escape. We can only hope for the continuing good health of the two gentlemen (if such a term can be applied to one of them) this morning, as rumour has it that a dawn engagement between the two was discussed.

Her eyes blurring, Elizabeth read it a second time in the vain hope that she had misinterpreted it the first time, but the words swimming before her refused to change. Surely it must be some sort of mistake, a matter of a misplaced letter when it might have been a Mr. E, not Mr. D, but how many gentlemen of Derbyshire could have announced engagements a fortnight ago? Or perhaps it was just gossip, an attempt to smear his name in revenge for some imagined slight, but he had been inexplicably absent at dinner. It could not be true. He was not the sort to dangle after one lady when engaged to another. But how well did she in fact know him? Was it anything beyond her own desire to believe him honourable that made him seem so? Or had slaking his lust for her rendered her of little interest to him? No, that she could not believe, recalling his tenderness toward her the night of her arrival.

She had so often thought the worst of him, and always been proved wrong. This time it would be different. They were engaged, and she would stand by him. She blinked back her tears of pain and anger.

Now was not the time for them. "It could be nothing more than gossip," she said with greater calm than she felt. "I will not rush to judgement on him before I know the facts of the matter."

"That is a most sensible attitude, Lizzy. We should allow him to defend himself, although if it proves to be true..."

"Should it prove to be true, I will know what to do." Elizabeth kept her voice steady with an effort. It was hard to know what to believe, but Darcy had always been truthful with her. She would ask him about it directly, and trust him not to create a scene.

They did not have to wait long, although it seemed that each minute lasted days. It was still before midday when Mr. Darcy was announced by the servant. Elizabeth tossed her embroidery aside without her usual care as she rose to her feet.

He did not look happy to be there. In fact, Elizabeth wondered if it might be the last place he would want to be, as his expression lent credence to the tale in the newspaper. He came straight to her, though, reaching to take her hands in his.

"Elizabeth, I must apologize for my failure to join you last evening. I hope you know that I wanted more than anything to be with you, and nothing but matters of the gravest urgency could have kept me away from your side. I am beyond sorry to have left you to face my relatives by yourself. My cousin tells me you acquitted yourself admirably, but I can guess how difficult it must have been for you, and it is all my fault. My behavior was inexcusable, and I humbly beg your forgiveness for it."

Although his words were appropriate, Elizabeth noted that he gave no word of explanation, and that he looked pained rather than overjoyed to be in her presence. A terrifying coldness settled itself around her heart. She carefully extricated her hands from his and folded them behind her back. "Whether or not it is inexcusable remains to be seen when I am unaware of the nature of this urgent matter."

He grew yet more pale, something she would not have thought possible. "It was a series of events, difficult to explain except that each delay led to another one. I cannot blame you for being angry with me. I have behaved unforgivably."

215

"May I ask you one question?"

"Of course."

She took a deep, shaky breath, glancing at her aunt for courage. "Were you, or were you not, discovered in an intimate moment with another lady last evening?"

He swore, then said. "I was, but it was not what you think. Believe me, Elizabeth, I would never…."

Her heart sank at his words. Somewhere she had kept the hope alive that it might be untrue, but now even that hope was gone. "Then we have nothing further to say to each other."

"Elizabeth…"

"Nothing at all."

He looked at her an expression of mingled incredulity and anger. "Surely you cannot believe that I would so much as look at another woman!"

"I would not have believed that you would fail me last night, either. Clearly my judgement leaves much to be desired."

"If you will allow me to explain…"

"Please do."

"I received an urgent message regarding a friend – Bingley, in fact - who was in some danger. I thought I could deal with the matter quickly, but when I found him, he was unwilling to leave his present situation."

Elizabeth found herself growing more angry every moment. "Are soirees in London often dangerous?"

"When one begins to combine heavy drink and expert duelists, they can be."

"And Bingley could not be trusted to handle these matters for himself without you to rescue him, yet you still found time to be caught in a compromising situation with another woman. Yes, I see it quite clearly now. Thank you for your explanation."

"And this is your estimation of me?" he bit out. "This is how little I am to be trusted!"

Mrs. Gardiner swept between them, holding up a hand toward each of them. "That is quite enough, I think. I will remind you there are young

216

children in this house. This can be discussed without raised voices and accusations. Come, Lizzy, I would have you sit down and hold that sharp tongue of yours for a few minutes. Mr. Darcy, as a guest in this house, you are not subject to my authority, but I cannot allow you to speak to my niece in that manner. If you cannot be civil, I must ask you to leave."

Elizabeth, too hurt and angry to respond, turned her back on both of them and wrapped her arms around herself, tears of mortification filling her eyes.

In a voice of forced calmness, Darcy said, "You are quite right, madam. We have played this scene before, and the outcome was not a pleasant one. Forgive me for taking up so much of your time." With these words he hastily left the room, and Elizabeth heard him the next moment open the front door and quit the house.

Elizabeth collapsed into a chair, her legs suddenly unwilling to hold her up. She barely noticed her aunt's arm around her shoulder and could not hear the gentle words she spoke for the painfully great tumult in her mind.

How could she have been so foolish as to believe in his love? All her life she had heard that men wanted only one thing from women, and once they had it, they lost interest. She had not believed it, and even if she had, she would have sworn on her hope of heaven that Darcy was not such a one, that he truly loved her. But it was true. She had given herself to him - oh, such foolhardiness! - and now she was nothing more than an obligation to him. To the rest of the world, she would be nothing but a disreputable woman because of a broken engagement to a fickle man.

Her eyes widened as she realized she might not even be that fortunate. Behavior such as she had engaged in with Mr. Darcy might have consequences; that much she knew, but she had thought it of little import since they would be married soon. Now that was no longer the case, and if she proved to indeed be increasing, she would be ruined beyond a hope of redemption. Her hand stole over her abdomen. Was there still something of him within her?

But at that moment, the future hardly mattered to her. She had lost him, and the years ahead yawned emptily before her. How could she have been so foolish as to have believed him? How could he have betrayed her so?

Her aunt placed a cup of tea in her hand. "Here, Lizzy, you must drink a little," she said in a soothing voice. "Take a deep breath – that's right. And now just a sip of tea. Good. It is a terrible shock, I know, but you are strong and will survive this. Once you are calm, perhaps things will look a little different."

"How could they possibly look different?"

Mrs. Gardiner sighed. "I do not know, but I do believe this much, that he cares about you and is also suffering."

"His suffering may be great, but he admitted to being with another woman!"

"He also mentioned heavy drink, and he would not be the first newly engaged young man to make one terrible mistake. Men can be very weak creatures, my dear. If he is truly repentant, it may be in your best interest to listen to him."

"I cannot. I cannot!"

"What, then, will you do?"

How could she think about the future when she was being ripped in two? "I will go home to Longbourn, I suppose. Tomorrow morning, since it would be too late today." And there she would learn to face life again without him.

"I think it is best for you to stay here, my dear. Going home would cause talk, and it would be better to allow some time to pass."

A knock sounded on the front door, and Elizabeth knew instantly who it must be. "Please do not make me talk to him! I could not bear it, not now."

"I will take care of it." Mrs. Gardiner left the room, and could be heard giving instructions to the manservant that Miss Bennet would not see Mr. Darcy today.

She returned a few minutes later with a fresh cup of tea which she exchanged for the full one Elizabeth still held. "Here, this will warm you," Mrs. Gardiner said. "Now drink up, there's a good girl."

Because it was easier than arguing, Elizabeth drank, even though the tea was sugared more than she liked. It still tasted bitter to her. She wondered vaguely what Darcy would be doing now, and why he had tried to see her again. How would she ever explain this to her parents? Her father would tell her that Darcy was a foolish fellow who was not worth her time, and her mother would counsel her to look the other direction in response to his indiscretions.

At her aunt's urging, she finished her tea, staring blankly at the wall opposite her. It was better to think of nothing at all.

"Come, my dear, let me take you upstairs. You will feel better after a rest."

As if she could possibly sleep now! But for lack of anything better to do, Elizabeth agreed. In her room, she allowed her aunt to unbutton her dress and settle her into bed as if she were still a child.

Finally Mrs. Gardiner left, and the tears Elizabeth had barely held at bay began to fall, first slowly, then in a torrent of sobs that faded only when sleep unexpectedly overtook her.

THERE WERE MANY wakeful souls that night at Darcy House. Darcy's valet and his butler were standing a short distance from his study - just far enough so the master could not quite see them if he emerged, as he had told them emphatically and repeatedly to go to bed and to leave him alone, an option which they had given at least five seconds' consideration before dismissing as ridiculous. A yawning footmen in the gallery leaned back against the wall, his ears alert for the sound of the butler's footsteps lest he be discovered in such dereliction of his duty. A second footman had a more fortunate position below stairs where he took it upon himself to entertain the kitchen maid, who could not retire lest the master have a moment of hunger, but who was more than happy to entertain herself with the footman as well.

The cause of it all, oblivious to the activity around him, had uncharacteristically slammed the study door shut and turned the key. That left him no outlet for his rage apart from pacing like a caged tiger. He had spent the afternoon enduring a brutal set down from Lord Matlock and exhausting two horses. It still had not been enough to take the edge off the helpless anguish that filled him, so he had taken the unusual step of going to a gaming hell, where he discovered that even a combination of strong drink and high stakes could not distract him. He had snarled at a few acquaintances before one friend took him by the arm and told him in no uncertain terms that whatever was bothering him, he should go home and stop inflicting it on others. So here he was, all alone with his thoughts.

Solely to have something to do with his hands, he poured himself a glass of port which he then proceeded to ignore in favor of leaning an arm against the mantelpiece and staring into the fire. The flames were high, since only a few minutes previously he had been savagely poking at the logs. What in God's name was he supposed to do now?

He could still see Elizabeth's cold, angry face in his mind. He had been desperately anxious to see her; it had been so long since he had heard her laugh, since he had held her in his arms, and she had occupied almost his every thought and longing. He had dealt with Wickham and other unpleasantness almost without concern, for all his energy had been taken up in missing Elizabeth. Her delayed arrival had seemed an eternity, but at least he had the opportunity to spend a few minutes with her, even if she had been soaked and miserable. Today he had hurried to Gracechurch Street at the earliest decent hour, needing her so badly he could feel it eating at his insides. It had not even occurred to him that she would not be pleased to see him. Annoyed about the previous evening, perhaps, but she would understand – not refuse to allow him even to explain.

He had left before his fury made him say too much, and after half an hour's walk to calm himself, he had returned to the Gardiner house to try once more. This time, though, the manservant refused to admit him, nor would he bear a message to Mr. or Mrs. Gardiner, much less Miss Bennet. Furious, Darcy had no choice but to depart. He had made enough of a spectacle of himself as it was.

How could she believe him faithless? His loyalty to her had remained untouched through many months; did she think it could change so quickly? Then again, after that nonsense in the morning paper, it would be hard to think otherwise. By God, if he had read in the newspaper that Elizabeth had been found in another man's arms, he would have been ready to commit murder.

He would not stand for it. Elizabeth might hate him right now, but eventually she could be brought to see reason. He had the upper hand here; if all else failed, he could ride to Longbourn and inform Mr.

Bennet that he had already taken Elizabeth's virtue. She would not deny it - she was too honest for that - and she would have no choice but to marry him. But by God, that was not how he wanted to win her! Not after the sweetness of how she had come into his arms, or the sensual pleasure of exploring her body, nor the joy she had given him which had kept him going these last terrible weeks.

He slammed his left fist into the marble mantelpiece. The pain of it was almost a relief. He cradled his throbbing hand to his chest. He needed Elizabeth. That was all there was to it.

This was even worse than that horrible night at Rosings after she had refused him. Now he knew better what he was losing. He had thought then that he could reach her by writing a letter, and only discovered later how wrong he had been. But after that experience, after losing the warning against Wickham that made her unable to protect her sister, surely she could not refuse a letter from him now?

It might not work, but there was nothing else he could do.

Chapter 24

ELIZABETH WAS THE first one awake at the house on Gracechurch Street. In truth, she had hardly slept at all, and had been awoken by a nightmare where she was being devoured alive by a monster with Mr. Darcy's face. There was no point in trying to fall asleep again after that. She doubted that even her aunt's doctored tea would work.

She wandered down to the kitchen where the maid was just building up the fire to heat water. There were several of the cook's delicate pastries remaining from the previous day, but Elizabeth found she had no appetite, so she repaired to the sitting room where she endeavoured to the best of her ability to keep her mind completely blank. She was sufficiently successful at this that her eyes were only slightly reddened by the time the family appeared for breakfast.

Her aunt and uncle spoke to her with an almost painful gentleness, as if they expected her to shatter like a porcelain figurine at any moment. Elizabeth half-wished she was in fact a porcelain shepherdess; porcelain could feel no pain. She ate breakfast because it was expected of her, though she could not remember afterwards what she had eaten, only that it sat like a lead weight in her stomach. When Mrs. Gardiner suggested that her niece might accompany her and the older children a walk, Elizabeth weighed the advantages of distraction against the pressure of having to keep up appearances, but the deciding factor was that if she went out, she might, by some unlikely chance, see Mr. Darcy, and that would be more than she could bear. She elected to remain at home, claiming she wished to finish reading her novel. Mrs. Gardiner looked unconvinced, but did not argue.

When the family had departed, save the youngest children in the nursery with their nurse, the house was as quiet as a house in London ever was in the daytime, with the sound of horses and carts, the cries of street vendors, and the clanking of dishes from the kitchen. Elizabeth could not settle to any activity, and moved from embroidery to a failed attempt to read a book and then to mending, which had the virtue of being useful and therefore important.

She heard a knock at the door and froze for a moment, wondering if it might be Mr. Darcy and what she would do if it was. But it was still too early for callers, so it must be a delivery or business of some sort. She heard the manservant shuffling down the corridor and the squeak of the front door opening and closing, and relaxed only when no further sound came her way.

Some minutes later the manservant appeared in the sitting room with an apologetic look. "I'm sorry to disturb you, Miss Bennet, but the gentleman told me to give you this letter and asked that you do him the honour of reading it." He held out a folded envelope.

Nausea rose in her. Elizabeth closed her eyes as if she could make it disappear. She did not have to ask who the gentleman was; she had half expected this. After all, it was what he had done at Hunsford - the letter she should have read and had not. She licked her dry lips. She might wish to refuse it, but there really was no choice. She opened her eyes and held out her hand for the letter.

She waited until she was alone again, then opened the envelope with shaking hands to find several pages in the familiar close-written hand and began to read.

My dearest Elizabeth, if you will forgive me for speaking so of you, once again I find myself putting pen to paper to attempt to explain that which must seem inexplicable. There is no apology that I can make which is sufficient to justify my absence last night. Until the very last moment, I expected to be with you, but events overtook me.

As you have no doubt already heard, I was in attendance at Lady Regenfield's soiree. This was not planned; I had sent my regrets long ago, but I received an urgent request from Mrs. Hurst for my immediate assistance there with regard to her brother. This is not the first time I have received such a summons in the last few weeks. Bingley, although normally the most temperate of individuals, has an unfortunate tendency to become belligerent when he is deep in his cups, something which has occurred on more than one occasion owing to his recent state of mind. Previous to this, I have only had to go to him and convince him to leave the public event, and I assumed that would be the case yesterday as well and that I would be able to meet you at dinner. In hindsight, it was a mistake to do so, but I erred in thinking I could deal with the problem quickly as I had in the past.

When I arrived at the soiree, Mrs. Hurst informed me that Bingley and his betrothed were with Mr. G., a previous suitor of Miss Sinclair, who had been refused by her father for the excellent reason that he is a notable rake. Apparently he bears a grudge toward Bingley for succeeding where he himself failed. Mr. G was also in his cups and in a resentful frame of mind, such that he was continually leveling insults at Bingley in a transparent attempt to provoke Bingley into challenging him. Mr. G, who is known to be an excellent marksman and a secret duelist, would not let the matter lie, and I judged he was near success at that point. Miss Sinclair, I am sorry to say, seemed to find the situation more flattering than anything else, and did nothing to discourage Mr. G. She would not agree to leave, and Bingley refused to depart without her. Since I was due to meet you, I sought the assistance of Lord Regenfield, a gentleman of excellent breeding and manners, in separating the two gentlemen.

Once that was accomplished, Bingley agreed to leave, but Miss Sinclair was nowhere to be found. That is when I would have left, save for a set of unfortunate circumstances. Shortly after I arrived in London, I was clumsy enough to sustain a trifling injury to my arm, which I had not seen fit to mention lest it worry you. It had been healing nicely, but apparently not as well as I thought, for it re-opened at the soiree. With the aid of Lord Regenfield, I retired to a private sitting room where a servant rebandaged my arm. Naturally, this involved removing certain items of my attire. The servant took my coat to clean the worst of the blood from the inside, since I did not wish it to soak through at dinner, and returning to Darcy House for fresh clothes would have made me intolerably late. He was also to bring me a shirt, since mine was ruined. Feeling somewhat the worse for wear, I reclined on the sofa and closed my eyes. When I heard the door open, I assumed it was a servant returning with the shirt, but it was instead Miss Sinclair and Mr. G, who were apparently seeking some privacy of their own. On discovering my presence, Mr. G immediately departed the scene. Miss Sinclair, however, noticed my bandaged wound and inquired about it. I requested that she leave, but she refused.

There were several lines thoroughly crossed out at that point, then the letter continued.

I am sorry, Elizabeth, but I find that I cannot describe to you the next occurrences, except to say that Miss Sinclair's intentions were not to offer me assistance. Suffice to say that several minutes later, when Mr. G returned, unfortunately accompanied this time by Bingley, I was still half-dressed and Miss Sinclair was sitting beside me. Mr. G., no doubt for some malicious reason of his own, loudly proclaimed that I had asked Miss Sinclair to accompany me to the room. I did not dignify his charge with a response, since I thought it unlikely that anyone would believe him, and expecting that Miss Sinclair would deny the accusation. It appears I was wrong in that regard. Mr. Bingley, being as I have mentioned none too sober, issued a challenge to me in such physical terms as were not beneficial to my wounded arm. Fortunately, Lord Regenfield was later able to assure Bingley that I had been alone earlier, after which Bingley thankfully regained his wits and withdrew his challenge, but only after a protracted scene in Lord Regenfield's private sitting room where Bingley received a blistering set down from that gentleman. Miss Sinclair's father also made an appearance which was unpleasant to all concerned. All in all, it was quite late by the time matters were settled, and unfortunately my physical state was such that any travel would have been inadvisable, forcing me to remain at that house for the night, attended by Lord Regenfield's doctor.

I can produce no witness to my innocence during the time I was alone with Miss Sinclair. I can only appeal to your sense of justice. If you think it likely that I would fail not only you, but also my aunt and uncle, in order to behave inappropriately with another woman, one whom you know does not have my good opinion, and was moreover engaged to my good friend, there is nothing I can say to reassure you. As for the rest, this is a true accounting of everything that occurred, and if you doubt my word, I encourage you to ask Bingley about the matter, as I anticipate you may be seeing him in the near future. His engagement to Miss Sinclair is at an end, and he is unaware of your recent dismissal of me. I will leave it to you to decide whether and when you will end our engagement, since it is possible that Bingley and your sister may yet have a chance at happiness if he is not immediately disillusioned about our prospects. It hardly requires saying that it may be wisest to wait on another account, since circumstances may prove such that you have little choice in the matter. I would ask only that you send word via a servant that you have read this letter, as I do not wish to spend the rest of my life wondering if you have done so. I will remain outside your uncle's house for some time in hopes of receiving that message.

My sentiments toward you, of which you are well aware, remain unchanged, but to spare us both further embarrassment, I will not repeat them here. I am beyond hoping that any further expression of them will make a difference. If you should at any point change your mind, I can be reached at Darcy House on Brook Street. I will only add, God bless you.

Fitzwilliam Darcy

Elizabeth put her hand over her mouth, blinking back hot tears. She did not know what to believe. He had been wrong, certainly, in abandoning her at his uncle's dinner; yet, if his story was to be credited, his intentions had been good, but he had been delayed time and again without any sense of when it was reasonable to leave until it was too late. His loyalty to Bingley was admirable, but what of his loyalty to her?

And then his offer to delay ending their engagement! It was generous in as much as it would be a gift to Bingley and Jane, yet at the same time, it served his own interest by protecting him from further gossip. She hardly needed the reminder that she might still have no choice but to marry him if she proved to be with child; that thought had kept her awake half the night, uncertain whether she wished for such a fate or to avoid it.

The manservant cleared his throat. "Mr. Darcy also left something which he said is yours, with instructions to give it to you after you had read his letter." He motioned outside the door, and the kitchen maid stepped in, cradling a squirming bundle of black and white fur.

"Here you go, miss." The girl held out the puppy to her. "Oh, he's a sweet one, he is."

Elizabeth took the puppy in trembling hands. He cuddled against her chest and looked up at her with hopeful dark eyes, just as he had that day in the barn at Netherfield when Darcy had been by her side. She buried her face in his fluffy fur, no longer able to hold back a sob.

A warm, scratchy tongue tickled her fingers. She laughed shakily through her tears, and the puppy's wet nose nuzzled into her neck. "Oh, what am I to do with you?" she asked. The puppy licked her face.

"Will there be any response for Mr. Darcy?" the manservant asked.

Elizabeth hugged the puppy closely, her arms trembling. "Tell Mr. Darcy I will see him."

Chapter 25

DARCY STOOD OUTSIDE the iron railing in front of the Gardiners' house, watching the passers-by as if it were his normal custom to loiter on the streets of Cheapside. He silently damned Elizabeth for putting him in this humiliating situation, but almost immediately turned his anger on himself. How could he have been such a fool? Bingley was a grown man and responsible for himself. If his foolishness had cost him Elizabeth, he would never forgive himself, both for losing her and for the impossible situation in which he had placed her by his loss of self-control that day at Netherfield. He did not want Elizabeth forced to marry him because of his behaviour, but at this point he would accept even that if only it meant she would give him another chance. And if she did, he would never allow anything to separate them, not Wickham or Bingley or anyone else. He had learned his lesson, and by God it was a painful one. But if Elizabeth were resolutely set against him, there was nothing he could do. Nothing except to live with the pain of having known her love for only those brief few days, and to spend the rest of his life knowing what he had lost.

He pulled his watch out of his pocket and inspected it. Only five minutes had passed since he had last checked it, but it felt more like hours. She must have finished his letter by now, if she indeed had been willing to read it at all, but the door to the house stayed stubbornly shut. He would wait for half an hour more, he decided. If she sent no message in that time, it was hopeless. He kicked his heel back against the railing, uncaring of the scuff mark on his boot that would no doubt bring down his valet's wrath later on.

Open, damn you, he told the door silently. *Open.*

As if in response to his silent order, the door opened and the old man who had taken his letter reappeared. Darcy had to force himself to walk to the stoop at a dignified pace. Hurrying would not change the answer. He tapped his cane against the step and said, "Well?"

The man's broad smile displayed several missing teeth. "Miss Bennet will see you now."

Darcy, his heart pounding, handed him his hat and cane, then followed him to the sitting room he remembered so well. The last time he had seen Elizabeth in that sitting room, he had held hope in his heart. Now he barely dared to hope at all.

Her eyes reddened, Elizabeth clutched the puppy, who was making a valiant attempt to lick her entire face. Belatedly she rose to her feet, but Darcy did not know how to read her expression. She was distressed, that was certain, but was she prepared to forgive him? He felt a stab of irrational jealousy of the ball of fur she cradled so close to her.

His mouth was dry. "Thank you for seeing me."

A tear trickled down her cheek. "I do not know what to say."

He could not bear it. In three strides he crossed the room and enfolded her in his arms, puppy and all, ignoring the discomfort in his arm. "Tell me you still care for me, and that is all I need. I will do whatever I must to resolve this."

Her shoulders shook and she buried her head against his shoulder. The puppy, now trapped between them, began to yap.

"Hush," he told it sternly, to absolutely no avail. The puppy continued to yap as if he had discovered some fine new game to play with these humans.

Elizabeth laughed shakily and kissed the puppy's head. "Of course I still love you," she said, her voice barely loud enough to hear through the racket. "That never changed, only my belief in our future. If you truly still want me, I am yours."

"I will never cease to want you." Darcy paused to disentangle the puppy from Elizabeth and set him on the floor, then pulled Elizabeth into a tight embrace. He could not find words enough to express his need for her, so he kissed her instead, the way a man dying of thirst drinks water. The stabbing pain in his arm was nothing compared to the joy he felt.

It was, however, enough to remind him that this should go no farther than kisses. He released her, but grasped her hands tightly in his, trying to find the courage to speak his piece. "Elizabeth, I cannot bear to be parted from you again. Marry me today, and stay with me always. I have a license and ring, and all we would need to do is to secure a man of the cloth to perform the ceremony."

"Today?" Elizabeth laughed at the idea, clearly not taking it seriously. "I grant you it is a pleasing idea, but my family might not agree."

"Please, Elizabeth," he urged, his eyes fixed on her. "This is important to me, and it will protect both of our reputations in light of the current gossip."

"I will not allow a little gossip to determine my behaviour," she said. "I agree it is difficult to wait, but I do wish to have my family around me at our wedding."

The manservant appeared in the doorway and cleared his throat. "Colonel Fitzwilliam is here to see Miss Bennet. He apologizes for the hour, but says it is a matter of some urgency. Are you at home, Miss?"

Elizabeth gave Darcy a concerned glance. "Please show him in."

Richard's appearance, normally impeccable, indicated he had not taken his usual time to attend to his attire. "Darcy, you deuced idiot! I thought you might be here. What in God's name were you thinking?" He added in a perfunctory manner, "Begging your pardon, Miss Bennet."

Darcy placed his left hand over his eyes. "Richard, this is neither the time nor the place…."

"You are the one who chose this time and place. What did you expect me to do when I discovered you were not only out of bed, but had left the house, and without even a sling on your arm? Sit down, damn you, before you fall."

To Elizabeth's astonishment, Darcy sat. Only then did she notice the pallor of his face was far beyond that of a sleepless night. "What is the matter?" she demanded.

When Darcy did not respond, Colonel Fitzwilliam said, "What is the matter? The matter is that Darcy is under strict doctor's orders to remain in bed and under no circumstances to use his arm, but the damned fool refuses to listen."

Horrified, Elizabeth turned to Darcy. "Is this true?"

Darcy did not meet her eyes. "My cousin is prone to exaggeration. As I told you, the injury is but trifling."

"Balderdash," snapped the colonel.

Elizabeth said evenly, "Colonel Fitzwilliam, perhaps you can tell me about this *trifling* injury of which I knew nothing until this morning."

"*He* did not tell you? That damned George Wickham winged him. It would probably be half-healed by now if he didn't keep pretending nothing happened and using the arm. We had to send for the doctor for him again yesterday."

"Richard, that is quite enough!" Darcy snapped.

Elizabeth rounded on him. "You fought Wickham?"

He nodded shamefacedly. "Do not worry. He came out of it worse than I."

Elizabeth looked questioningly at Colonel Fitzwilliam, who was clearly a better source of information than Darcy.

"Darcy hit him in the hip. He was not shooting to kill, though God alone knows why not. Wickham was, but he was as incompetent at that as everything else he sets his hand to. At least he will never walk on that leg again."

She shivered at the idea of how close death had come to the man she loved, longing for the comfort of being in his arms. "Mr. Darcy, please, I hope you will rest, for my sake if for nothing else. Is there anything I can do for your comfort?"

Darcy glared at his cousin. "Apart from certain troublesome relatives, I am perfectly comfortable."

The clatter of quick footsteps and children's voices in the hall announced the return of the family. Mrs. Gardiner appeared in the doorway, a concerned expression on her face as she looked from Elizabeth to Darcy and back again. "Lizzy, I had not realized you were expecting company."

Elizabeth flushed. "Mr. Darcy has explained himself to my satisfaction and we are reconciled. Colonel Fitzwilliam just arrived." She noticed that Darcy had risen to his feet, but was holding onto the back of his chair with his left hand.

The colonel must have noticed the same thing, since he bowed gracefully to Mrs. Gardiner and said, "Madam, I am already imposing abominably on your hospitality by appearing without an invitation, but I must compound my ill manners by asking even more of your generosity. My over-proud cousin is injured and is *supposed* to be resting with his arm immobilized. Might I impose so far as to ask if you have a room where he might rest?"

"Richard, that is completely unnecessary!" Darcy snapped.

Mrs. Gardiner exchanged a glance with Elizabeth. Mrs. Gardiner said, "Of course. I will make arrangements immediately. Would it be of assistance if I located some linen for a sling?"

The colonel's agreement drowned out Darcy's dissent. "Madam, I see you are a lady after my own heart. Darcy, do stop being a fool. Your bride-to-be deserves better."

Elizabeth laid her hand over Darcy's. "Whether it is necessary or not, it would ease *my* mind if you would rest. Will you do it for my sake?"

Darcy's glower subsided at the sight of her concerned face. "As long as you marry me, I will do anything you request."

Colonel Fitzwilliam depressed one eyelid in a slow wink at Elizabeth, who tactfully failed to notice.

Mrs. Gardiner led Darcy out of the room. Once their footsteps had faded away, Elizabeth remembered the puppy. It was nowhere to be seen. Hurriedly she looked about, and found it curled up asleep in her aunt's favourite armchair. She breathed a sigh of relief that it had done no apparent damage.

Colonel Fitzwilliam cleared his throat. "Forgive me, Miss Bennet. I am not normally an intemperate man, but convincing my cousin that he needs to take care would drive a saint mad."

"So I see! He is not, I take it, accustomed to being ruled by others."

The colonel laughed. "Not in the least. Under usual circumstances, this is not an issue, since he has the means to do whatever he likes, but it is difficult to convince him that he cannot simply *tell* his arm to heal, and that he must follow doctor's orders."

"And you are the one appointed to ensure that he does so?"

"I am one of the few people he will listen to, so nursemaid duty falls to me. In fact, his butler asked my assistance yesterday since he felt Darcy was endangering his health by going out. I had thought he would do better if I stayed with him at Darcy House, but obviously I underestimated him. I am starting to think that I should post an armed guard at his door!"

"How serious is his injury?"

"It is not dangerous to his health as of yet, but if he continues to ignore it, that may change."

Taken aback, Elizabeth said, "Whatever possessed him to fight Mr. Wickham?"

"An excellent question, and one that I asked as well. Dueling a steward's son, who deserves no such respect! What was he thinking? Darcy wanted Wickham to leave the country, but Wickham refused. Darcy thought that he would change his tune when looking down the barrel of a pistol. Wickham thought Darcy would never dare shoot him, and that he would have an easy target. Both were wrong. Wickham did not back down, and once he had hit Darcy, my cousin's restraint was at an end."

"Where is Mr. Wickham now?"

"He is convalescing and soon to board a ship to India, since he is no longer in a condition to refuse to do anything."

A thought crossed Elizabeth's mind. "Is Mr. Darcy permitted to write?"

"No, but that has not been a problem, since he has a perfectly competent secretary."

"He has been writing to me, and not through his secretary." All those letters whose brevity had worried her, and now the missive he had given her today. She hated to think of the pain it must have cost him.

The colonel sighed. "Perhaps I should move that armed guard to his bedside."

"Or..." Elizabeth paused. Was she truly prepared to do this? "Am I the reason he goes out?"

"Apart from that idiotic attempt to rescue Bingley, I believe so."

Elizabeth stood and wandered to the mantelpiece. She took down the porcelain shepherdess and turned it in her hands. She had been fascinated by the details of it when she was a young girl, and had spend hours examining it and trying to ascertain how such a thing might have been made. The shepherdess had seemed the epitome of beauty and adulthood. Now she was grown, and adulthood was not as simple as she had thought it would be. She carefully set the shepherdess down again, adjusting it so that the figure seemed to be gazing out at the room.

Chapter 26

OVER THE NEXT few hours, Darcy discovered that Mrs. Gardiner's gentle exterior hid a will of steel. In short order he found himself reclining in bed, his coat removed and his sleeve rolled up nearly to the shoulder. She clucked her tongue when she unwrapped the bandage to reveal the angry wound, and called for a basin of hot water.

"What *is* that ridiculous plaster smeared everywhere?"

"My doctor says it will draw out the infection. He trained in Paris."

"Paris? That would explain it. The French are full of foolish ideas. Most likely it is making matters worse. No wonder he is worried for your health."

"You agree with him?"

"I will have to clean it before I can give you my opinion."

Darcy frowned. Perhaps it was worse than he had believed. "I have told Elizabeth that I would like to marry her as quickly as possible."

Mrs. Gardiner raised her eyebrows at the apparent non-sequiter. "Did she agree to that?"

Darcy gritted his teeth as she probed the skin around his wound. "No, she did not."

"Neither my husband nor her father are likely to favor you on that if she is against it."

"Yes, well, I would prefer not to trouble Elizabeth with my true reasoning. She thinks I am merely impatient. My doctor thinks I will most likely make a good recovery, but he has suggested that, in the unlikely case that he is incorrect, I should make sure my affairs are in order. This is one of them."

"I certainly hope you are acting only out of an excess of caution, but even were that the case, Lizzy might prefer not to be a widow as soon as she is a bride."

"Perhaps, but her financial situation would be more secure, and, well, there are other reasons that make it important. Her reputation, and other things." Darcy vaguely realized he must be in rather worse condition than he had thought to have said even that much to Mrs. Gardiner.

Mrs. Gardiner narrowed her eyes, then shook her head sadly. "You were foolish, then. Beyond foolish."

Darcy's cheeks grew hot at her unexpectedly direct response. "That much is obvious even to me. The fact remains that I wish to marry Elizabeth now."

"That does put another complexion on the matter. Perhaps it would be simplest for you to explain matters to Elizabeth."

"And worry her further after what she has been through the past two days? Not unless I am forced to do so."

The maid appeared with a bowl of steaming water. She set it beside Mrs. Gardiner, who rolled a dry cloth into a tight twist and handed it to him before soaking a rag in the hot water. "You may want to bite down on this." Without further ado, she proceeded to thoroughly clean the wound.

By the time she finished, Darcy wished he had taken her advice about biting the cloth. His jaw ached from being clenched so tightly, and his arm burned as if she had poured salt into it. He accepted a sizeable glass of brandy which she offered him. "Thank you. This is not quite how I hoped to spend my day."

Mrs. Gardiner paused to smile at him. She gently wiped his forehead as if he were one of her children. "No, indeed, but I have no intention of allowing my niece to become a widow. You did not have to watch her pain yesterday; I did."

Darcy was oddly relieved to hear it. "Was she very distressed?"

"Near inconsolable," she said briskly.

"So was I." He was astonished to hear the words come out of his mouth.

"Then you should be very happy together." Mrs. Gardiner gently laid a fresh hot cloth over his wound. "There, that will ease the pain a little. The wound itself is shallow and has already begun to knit. It would have given you no difficulties if there were not an abscess preventing healing. It must be lanced if the wound is to heal cleanly, but perhaps you would prefer to have your *doctor* do that rather than me."

For some reason, he felt safer in her care than he ever had with London's finest physicians. "I would be just as glad to have it over as soon as possible."

She spared him a keen glance, and he had no doubt she saw straight through him. "Very well. I will need a sharp knife. Shall I bring Mr. Gardiner to hold your arm during the lancing?"

"I can manage," he said stiffly.

She shook her head with a smile. "Men are all the same."

ELIZABETH TOOK ADVANTAGE of her aunt's absence to disregard her orders to leave Mr. Darcy alone. She slipped into the room quietly. His eyes were closed, but he opened them when she sat in the bedside chair.

"Elizabeth, you should not be here," he said.

"If you are here, then I should be here," she said firmly.

He did not seem inclined to fight. "Your aunt would have made a fine sergeant-at-arms."

"She does not tolerate disobedience?" Elizabeth teased.

"Not a bit of it." He reached out his left hand to her, and she grasped it. "Elizabeth, I am sorry. I truly do not mean to be troublesome. I had hoped you need never know about what happened that day."

"I had worked that much out on my own," she said archly. "But I am glad to know. I dislike secrets, and it explains a great deal. I had wondered about the brevity of the letters I received from you."

He had the grace to look guilty. "I wanted to pour out my heart to you in those letters, but it was all I could do to write a few sentences."

Mrs. Gardiner bustled in with a basket of linens and implements. She stopped short at the sight of Elizabeth. "You are not supposed to be here."

"Because the sight of Mr. Darcy without his coat might give me a fit of the vapors? That would be unfortunate, given that we are to be married."

"You may prefer not to be present for the next part."

Elizabeth glanced at Darcy. "Do you wish me to stay or to go?"

His face reflected indecision. "I would not wish you to stay if you had rather not."

She decided to ignore his gentlemanly nonsense. "I will stay."

Mrs. Gardiner shrugged lightly, as if to say no one should blame her for the outcome. She raised the wet cloth covering his wound and probed lightly around it, causing the gentleman to wince. "Are you ready for the lancing?" she said gently.

"Yes," Darcy said tersely, his eyes fixed on Elizabeth.

"Hold still." Mrs. Gardiner took a deep breath and made a small incision with the knife.

Darcy held Elizabeth's hand so tightly that she wondered if she would have any sensation in it when he was done, but no sound escaped his whitened lips.

"That is all," Mrs. Gardiner said. "It is draining nicely." She swabbed at his arm with a damp cloth. A foul odor, like that of a long dead animal, filled the room. "Ah, yes, it is good that we did this now."

Darcy stiffly turned his head toward Mrs. Gardiner. "The pain is less," he said with an air of surprise.

Mrs. Gardiner opened a window onto the garden. "That is because the pressure is relieved. It should heal more easily now." She bundled up the soiled linens. "Do not move your arm. It needs to continue to drain. I will return shortly to check it." She smiled at them both before departing, leaving the door open.

"My poor love," Elizabeth said.

"I do not know whether to be grateful that your aunt is allowing us some time together or annoyed that she thinks me so disabled that there is no danger in leaving us alone in a bedroom," Darcy grumbled.

Elizabeth laughed. "Perhaps she trusts me to prevent you from injuring yourself further. It *is* in my best interest for your arm to heal quickly, you know." She pressed a kiss on his good hand, noting an odd bruise over the knuckles.

"She seems knowledgeable about healing."

"Her father was an apothecary and her mother a midwife. She learned from assisting them, and we are the beneficiaries." She watched his face closely to see how he would react to these details of Mrs. Gardiner's low connections.

"I am in good hands, then." He closed his eyes.

A few minutes later his breathing became deep and even. It made Elizabeth realize how truly exhausted he must be, and she felt a pang of guilt for having quarreled with him in that state. Of course, she had not known his true condition then. She smiled, taking the opportunity to gently brush a stray lock of hair from his damp forehead, pausing to caress his cheek. He turned his head to nuzzle against her hand, and she held her breath for fear she had awakened him. Apparently she had not; it must have been instinct that caused his response. Her heart almost ached with love for him, and tears burned the corners of her eyes at the thought of how close she had come to ending their engagement.

Elizabeth could have sat there and watched him sleep all day, but after half an hour Colonel Fitzwilliam joined her. "Asleep, is he? Good, he needs it," he said softly. "Apparently he was awake most of the night." There was a question in his voice.

"It has been a difficult time," she said.

"If it is not impertinent to ask, have you set a date yet for your wedding?"

Elizabeth bit her lip, recalling Darcy's earlier request. "We had planned it for about a month from now. We have only been engaged for three weeks, after all. He would prefer it to be sooner, so perhaps a fortnight might be better."

"Mrs. Gardiner says he must stay here tonight. At least that will obviate the necessity for him to sneak past me and travel across town to see you."

"I did *not* sneak," Darcy said. "I simply walked out the door as I always do."

"The sleeper has awakened, and just in time," the colonel said. "I have been questioning your lovely intended regarding when you will be wed."

Mr. Gardiner's voice came from the doorway. "An interesting question. My wife tells me that Mr. Darcy would like to marry as soon as possible in case his arm worsens."

Elizabeth turned accusing eyes on Darcy. He shrugged guiltily. "It seemed wise," he said.

Mrs. Gardiner followed her husband into the room. "I am not worried about his arm, but they have such a talent for misunderstanding each other that I would be happy to see them wed before they can do so again." She blithely ignored her niece's glare.

Mr. Gardiner crossed his arms. "Whereas I believe it would be a good idea because it would counteract much of the current gossip. It is not in his best interest, or yours, to have any attention drawn to his current state of health. So far, very few people are aware of his injury, and it would be best to keep it that way. Dueling is, after all, illegal."

"Not to mention foolish," said Elizabeth tartly.

Her aunt failed to hide a smile. "That, too, though I doubt we women will ever manage to convince men of that. But the fact remains that the best way to preserve the secrecy of the matter is to take away the cause of the gossip. If you and he are married, there will be much less interest in the matter, and with the added advantage that no one will be surprised that a newlywed couple prefers to keep to themselves and avoid society."

Colonel Fitzwilliam laughed. "I am far more selfish. I want them to marry right away because if Elizabeth is living at Darcy House, Darcy might actually *stay* there as he is supposed to."

Mrs. Gardiner cleared her throat. "Gentlemen, I suppose this is when I should mention that Lizzy does *not* like to be told what to do."

"She and Darcy will get on famously in that case," said the colonel acidly. "He *never* listens to reason."

"Richard," said Darcy with a warning in his voice.

Elizabeth leaned down to speak softly in Darcy's ear. "I think we should ignore them all and marry immediately for no reason other than because we *want* to do so."

Darcy promptly demonstrated that there was nothing at all amiss with his left arm by using it to pull her close enough to him to deliver a tender kiss. "I like that idea," he murmured.

The colonel threw his hands up. "I have changed my mind. It does not signify whether Elizabeth is living at Darcy House, but they had best marry before they drive the rest of us to Bedlam."

Mr. Gardiner rubbed his hands together. "Since we are all in agreement, we have some arrangements to make. We will need a clergyman, a license, and a ring."

Darcy pointed to his coat hanging over a chair. "If you look in the pocket, you will find a license and my mother's wedding band. It was always intended for my bride." He glanced at Elizabeth with the slightest of smiles.

Mr. Gardiner raised an eyebrow. "You are prepared, I see."

"I have been prepared, as you say, since the day after Miss Elizabeth honored me with her acceptance of my hand."

Elizabeth's uncle donned his spectacles and examined the paper. "A special license, I see. That makes it simpler. I suggest that we hold the ceremony here, since we have that option. I will undertake finding someone to perform it."

Darcy raised himself on his good arm. "You need not trouble yourself, sir. I will take that upon myself."

Colonel Fitzwilliam strode to the bed, his eyes narrowed. "*You* are going to stay exactly where you are without moving a muscle. *I* will find a minister."

"I do not need *you* to tell me what I am capable of!"

The colonel leaned over his cousin, resting one hand on each side of him and spoke very slowly and clearly. "Darcy, you are fortunate that we are in the presence of ladies, or I would tell you precisely what I think you are capable of. You will tell me what you wish to be done, and *I* will do it. That is *not* a suggestion, in case you were wondering."

"I did not wonder at all," muttered Darcy darkly.

Mrs. Gardiner favored them all with an amused smile. "While we are making *suggestions,* Mr. Darcy, I would *request* that you remain here tonight where I can keep an eye on your arm."

"I will be happy to follow *your* advice, Mrs. Gardiner," said Darcy.

"Then we will leave you to rest," she said, gesturing to her husband to accompany her.

Elizabeth chose to believe that this suggestion did not apply to her and resumed her seat beside the bed. "Is there anything I can get you for your comfort?" she asked.

"I thank you, no, but I must write to Georgiana at Netherfield. She should learn the news from me rather than from strangers. And no later than tomorrow I must call on Bingley, as we still have some matters to resolve."

Elizabeth stood, and for a moment he feared she would leave, but instead she merely moved to perch on the side of the bed, only inches from him. "Perhaps you could dictate a letter to Georgiana to me. And we could send a note to Bingley inviting him to call on you here. Is he aware of your injury?"

Darcy's mouth twisted. "It would be hard for him to be unaware of it, as he was one of my seconds, along with my cousin."

"Then he will understand."

"He has enough to deal with, given the scandal of his broken engagement."

"Then perhaps he might be happy for a reason to leave London. He could deliver your letter to Georgiana at Netherfield."

"The post will suffice, without Bingley taking that trouble."

She raised an eyebrow. "Why, do you suppose Mr. Bingley would object to having an excuse to travel to Hertfordshire?"

"Ah." Darcy nodded. His mind must be more muddled with pain and brandy than he had thought. It was a good thing Elizabeth was by his side.

THE FOLLOWING MORNING, Colonel Fitzwilliam returned with the same man of the cloth who had performed Lydia's wedding. He was either remarkably unsurprised by the request to perform a sudden wedding for a member of the *ton* in a tradesman's house or the colonel had lined his pockets well for his trouble and cooperation.

Elizabeth decided philosophically that this impromptu wedding was a fitting conclusion to their odd courtship. It would have been almost anticlimactic to have a traditional service after the long and rocky road she and Darcy had travelled. Fortunately, she had never been one to dream of her own wedding; that had been something she left to Jane.

To no one's surprise, Darcy insisted on standing for his wedding, although he agreed to wear a sling of Mrs. Gardiner's creation. The event was lent an air of festivity by the extreme excitement of the eldest Miss Gardiner, whom Elizabeth had asked with great solemnity to do her the honour of standing up with her, making the ten year old feel very grown up indeed. Her brother Henry pouted over not being given the same privilege by Mr. Darcy, but was eventually brought to a grudging agreement that Colonel Fitzwilliam, as Darcy's blood kin, had precedence over him.

"Then I will hold Lion," he announced. "He wants to come to the wedding."

"And who may Lion be?" asked Darcy with what he thought was admirable patience.

Young Henry favored him with the incredulous look reserved by the very young for hopelessly muddled adults. "The puppy, of course."

Elizabeth had completely forgotten the puppy in all the excitement after turning him over to the kitchen maid the day before. "Lion?" she asked dubiously. It would take a great stretch of the imagination to think that the adorable springer spaniel puppy looked at all like a lion.

Mrs. Gardiner made a tutting sound. "According to Nurse, your dog spent most of the night in the nursery, since the only other choice seemed to be having the children sleep on the floor of the kitchen with him."

"Very well, then," said Elizabeth with a laugh. "You shall hold Lion, then, Henry, but only if you fetch him this very minute, because we are about to begin."

All these complications and distractions were quickly forgotten by Elizabeth at the sight of the expression on Darcy's face when her uncle brought her to stand by his side in front of the cross that served as a makeshift altar. She remembered what he had said about Lydia's wedding, that he had been making the same vows silently to her that day. Now they were before the same clergyman, repeating those same vows. They had come full circle.

She regretted only the absence of her family, though she supposed it would have been far too much for her mother's nerves. Still, she would have liked Jane to be present, and her father to give her away instead of her uncle, but afterwards, when Mrs. Gardiner took Elizabeth's face between her hands and said, "Mrs. Darcy - how fine that sounds, and how happy you will be," Elizabeth would have been hard pressed to think of any way in which her wedding could have been improved upon.

Bingley arrived as they were sharing a celebratory glass of wine - watered down to practically nothing in the case of Miss Gardiner and her brother - in the sitting room, with both Colonel Fitzwilliam and Mrs. Gardiner keeping a gimlet eye on Darcy to ascertain that he took no unnecessary risks with his arm. Mr. Bingley's astonishment at being introduced to Mrs. Darcy was only increased by the contradictory explanations he received as to why the ceremony had been performed with such alacrity. "I cannot understand a word of it," he proclaimed, "but I will be happy to join you in toasting the health and happiness of Mr. and Mrs. Fitzwilliam Darcy." If his own countenance revealed a certain degree of sadness, no one in the party saw fit to remark upon it.

Darcy took him aside to ask him if he would deliver a letter to Netherfield. "I do not wish Georgiana to learn of our wedding from a stranger, nor for her to believe that our haste had to do with anything besides impatience, but Elizabeth has been quite firm in insisting that I am not ready to travel such a distance myself. Would it be too much to ask for you to break the news to her?"

"I will be happy to do so," said Bingley stoutly.

"You have my thanks. I believe Elizabeth is also writing a letter to her family; perhaps you could carry that as well, if you do not object to calling at Longbourn?"

"That will not be a problem." Then his countenance suddenly brightened with a smile. "No, I can see no difficulty with paying a visit to Longbourn."

Darcy gave Bingley's shoulder a friendly shove with his good hand. "Good for you, my friend. And Godspeed, although hopefully when you take the step I did today, it will be in a less precipitate manner!"

Bingley smirked at him. "You do not appear unhappy with the outcome."

Darcy looked over at Elizabeth and his gaze softened. "No, I cannot complain of unhappiness at all."

Chapter 27

SOMEWHAT TO DARCY'S surprise, Mrs. Gardiner made no objection to their return to Darcy House that day, provided his arm was well supported in the carriage and that he would be careful to keep warm poultices on his wound whenever possible. He fully agreed to her conditions, earning an approving look from Elizabeth, who doubtless would not have allowed him to disregard her aunt's instructions in any case. So, after profuse thanks to the Gardiners for all their hospitality and support, Darcy finally had Elizabeth to himself in his carriage – or almost to himself, as there was an exhausted puppy curled up at Elizabeth's feet.

She sat on his left so that their hands could remain joined. It was a much needed comfort to him, since the ride over cobblestone streets sent a stabbing pain into his arm with every bump, despite all the springs and cushions that his luxurious vehicle provided.

He was relieved when the carriage finally pulled up in front of his elegant townhouse on Brook Street. Although Darcy of necessity permitted the footman to open the carriage door, he insisted on handing Elizabeth out himself. He wanted to see her face as she discovered her new home. She looked up and down the street, then smiled at him. He offered her his arm and led her up the steps to Darcy House.

As he had expected, the door opened to them immediately. Briggs bowed lower than usual, but showed no other sign that this was anything beyond a normal day, in zkeeping with the instructions Darcy had sent ahead. Elizabeth had been through enough today without dealing with a formal presentation to the servants and meeting the housekeeper. Tomorrow would be time enough for that.

Briggs took his hat and gloves. "Mr. Thomas Wickham is in the sitting room, sir. I informed him that this was not a good day to call, but he insisted that the matter was urgent and must be dealt with today."

Darcy frowned. This was not how he had planned matters. "Well, he must wait a little longer, then. I will be with him in half an hour. Are Mrs. Darcy's rooms prepared?"

"Yes, sir, everything is in readiness."

Darcy turned to Elizabeth. "I thought you might prefer to wait until tomorrow to tour the house."

Her eyes sparkled. "I will follow wherever you lead."

Uncaring for his dignity, he took her hand in his and raised it to his lips. To have Elizabeth here as his wife was such a long-standing dream that he could hardly credit it was true. "Come, then," he said.

THOMAS HELPED HIMSELF to some of Darcy's finest port as he cooled his heels in the sitting room. He had heard Darcy arrive, but realized he was apparently to be kept waiting on the great man's convenience. Finally footsteps sounded in the passageway and Darcy appeared in the doorway. No, not just Darcy; Miss Elizabeth Bennet was with him as well. Trust Darcy to ignore the rules of propriety when it suited him.

He nodded to Darcy and was about to take his companion's hand when he noticed she was not wearing gloves. Quickly he converted his gesture to a simple bow. "Miss Elizabeth, this is an unexpected pleasure. Are Mr. and Mrs. Gardiner here as well?"

Elizabeth's mouth twitched in a small smile, but it was Darcy who replied. "No, *Mrs. Darcy's* aunt and uncle are no doubt at home in Cheapside."

Thomas glanced down at Elizabeth's left hand. Yes, it bore a wedding band. Although his expression did not change as he offered the couple his warm congratulations, inwardly he was seething. So much for his assumption that Darcy would include Lydia and him in his life! He had never expected Darcy would treat him as an equal - after all, why should he? - but he had not expected to be completely dismissed, either. Now he could see that apparently he was just another dependent to Darcy. Darcy had not even bothered to invite his wife's sister to the wedding, nor even to inform her. No doubt he did not want them mingling with his oh-so-high-and-mighty family. Thomas felt an unexpected pang of sympathy for his younger brother, who had so often been a victim of Darcy's pride.

"Darcy, I do not wish to intrude upon your happiness with your bride, but I would appreciate a few minutes of your time to discuss an urgent matter."

"You may speak in front of my wife. She is aware of the circumstances."

Thomas wondered what she thought of the decision to exclude Lydia from their wedding. He had not thought her to be overly proud when they had met before, but exposure to Darcy might have changed that, or she might have only agreed to please Darcy. "If that is your pleasure. I saw him carried aboard ship earlier today. He was protesting vehemently that he was being taken against his will, and the captain unfortunately took him at his word. Understandably, he fears a future charge of kidnapping. He has agreed to keep him on board tonight, but he says George will be put off tomorrow unless he receives assurances from you that George did, in fact, agree to this. Since he is due to sail with the noon tide, it seemed prudent to inform you of this today." He spoke in a clipped voice, as if reporting to his employer, which was no doubt how Darcy saw him. The ease in his manner earlier in the month had likely been yet another effort to cajole him into marrying Lydia, and now the lord of the manor was back.

Darcy frowned. "I should have known he would not keep his word. Very well, I will write a letter."

Elizabeth said, "Or I will write it for you, and you will sign it."

Darcy bore a long-suffering expression, which earned him no sympathy whatsoever from Thomas, who said, "I tried to avoid this. I reminded him that you still hold his debts. I thought that might discourage any idea of staying in England, but he would not believe you would use them against him. Odd, given how poorly he speaks of you."

Elizabeth gave him a sharp look, quickly masked with a glance at Darcy.

Darcy did not seem to notice. "I have no doubt of it. One would think it might make him avoid me rather than seek out my family."

Thomas cleared his throat. "He still seems to be of the opinion that he has an advocate in Miss Eliz…begging your pardon, Mrs. Darcy."

Elizabeth's warm smile reassured him. "Since I have borne that appellation for less than two hours, it seems unfair to expect everyone to remember to use it."

"Less than… You were married today?" Thomas looked from one to the other. They were not dressed in wedding finery, and there was no air of celebration in the house.

To his surprise, Darcy took Elizabeth's hand. "Yes, it happened quite suddenly, which is why you received no notice. I hoped that if we were married, it would work to quell the recent gossip around me. We will no doubt arrange a celebration at some point in the future."

Thomas was surprised by the extent of relief he felt at the news he had not been excluded. With a broad smile he said, "Then I must apologize abjectly for interrupting you on your wedding day! My congratulations to you, Darcy, on avoiding all the fuss of a large wedding. I will not take up another moment of your time. Shall I inform Lydia of your marriage, Mrs. Darcy, or would you prefer to do that yourself?"

"It is not a secret," Elizabeth said briskly. "But we are brother and sister, sir, and you must call me Elizabeth, and stay long enough to drink a toast with us, as the first of my family to greet us as a married couple."

Darcy smiled down at her. "Apart from the Gardiners, who were our witnesses."

"I would be honoured," said Thomas with a bow, secure in the knowledge that he had made the correct choice after all.

BINGLEY HAD RIDDEN his fastest horse to reach Netherfield, but now that he was almost to Longbourn, he began to wish the trip had taken a little longer. He wanted to see Jane, but would she even agree to see him? Or did she hate him for leaving her so quickly for another woman? He could hardly blame her if she did. Looked at from her vantage point, it must seem beyond belief that he would engage himself elsewhere so soon after declaring his love for her. She must think him beyond fickle, and it would not help that he would now appear to be switching allegiances once more.

On reaching Longbourn, he dismounted distractedly and handed his reins to a groom. He took a deep breath. Darcy would not hesitate in this situation. Summoning all his courage, he mounted the steps and rapped on the door. A maid admitted him and showed him to the familiar sitting room, which was occupied by Mrs. Bennet and her three remaining daughters. Bingley could not keep his gaze from Jane. She looked paler than was her wont, and she frowned at the sight of him.

Mrs. Bennet greeted him in her coldest voice. "Why, Mr. Bingley, this is indeed a *surprise*. No one expected to see *you* in Hertfordshire again."

"I, umm, it is a pleasure to see you again, madam. I hope you are well."

"As well as can be expected, I suppose," she said with a sniff.

Bingley tore his eyes away from Jane, who was now staring at her slippers, her cheeks flushed. "Ah, I had not anticipated travelling here, but Darcy asked me to deliver a letter to Miss Darcy. Hearing of my plans, Miss Elizabeth gave me a letter for you as well." He fished it out of his pocket and proffered it to Mrs. Bennet.

She took it without any sign of pleasure, then put it aside on a table. "I am sorry you have been taken out of your way for Lizzy's sake. We know you are a *very* busy man with much to do in London."

So they did know about his engagement. That was only to be expected, he supposed. He shuffled his feet uncomfortably. "Actually, I am, ah, planning to spend quite some time at Netherfield." He cast a helpless look at Jane, but she was still looking away pointedly. "I believe Miss Elizabeth's letter contains some important news, and I am available to answer any questions you might have about it."

Mrs. Bennet sniffed again, then snatched up the letter and broke the seal. She read it slowly, tracing the lines with her finger. Suddenly her eyes opened wide and she gave a shrill cry, then collapsed into her seat and began fanning herself with the letter. "Oh, my good gracious, can it be?"

Jane turned to him with an accusing glance, then hurried to her mother's side. "What is it? Has something happened to Lizzy?"

"She is… she is *married!* Without any wedding clothes or trousseau!"

Jane pried the letter from her mother's fingers and perused it carefully, then said, "I do not understand."

"Darcy and your sister took their vows early this morning."

"But *why?* That was not the plan!"

His throat tightened and he felt his cheeks burning. He had to say it, and say it now. "It was apparently in response to some gossip that began after… was occasioned by the, um, unexpected termination of my engagement."

Jane's mouth opened, but no words came out.

Mrs. Bennet straightened in her chair. "You are no longer engaged to *that woman?*"

"No. I cried off after she made it clear that she preferred another gentleman." That was close enough to the truth, he supposed.

Mrs. Bennet clasped her hands. "You did? Oh, how clever you are, Mr. Bingley! Do sit down, please, and I will ring for some refreshments. Hill!"

Bingley began to breathe a little easier. At least Mrs. Bennet seemed predisposed to forgive him.

Jane still looked stunned. She said slowly, "I fail to see what this has to do with my sister, or why she would marry sooner because of it."

Bingley felt a little shaky on the rationale himself, but Darcy had told him it was the case, so it must be true. "I do not know how it happened, but there was some false information circulating that *Darcy* was the other man involved - naturally quite untrue, but it was repeated widely all the same. He felt their wedding would dispel the gossip before it went any further."

Jane looked as puzzled by this explanation as he felt. "So you are not returning to London?"

"No, there is no reason for me to return to town, and I find Netherfield far more appealing." He gave Jane a meaningful look. "There is nothing in town that could make me as happy as being here." It sounded foolish when he said it. Darcy could have said such a thing and looked dignified, but it was beyond Bingley's abilities.

Jane returned the letter to her mother, her eyes suspiciously bright. "Excuse me, I must go to share this news with my father."

Before she could leave, Bingley stepped in front of her. "I hope I will see you again soon, Miss Bennet." It was an incredibly rash thing to say, but he could not just let her go.

Jane's eyes locked with his. Bingley could not have looked away had his life depended on it. Her lips curved slightly. "I will look forward to it, Mr. Bingley." As a single tear began to flow down her cheek, she turned and left.

"Oh, do sit down, Mr. Bingley," said Mrs. Bennet fretfully. "You must tell me everything that has happened. I wish to know every detail."

Bingley sat. He could face Mrs. Bennet's inquisition with impunity, now that he knew Jane still cared for him.

Epilogue

ELIZABETH LOOKED ALONG the table at the assembled party, thinking back to the assembly in Meryton where she had met Darcy. Certainly it would never have crossed her mind then that she would ever be the hostess for a dinner party at Darcy House. Jane had just met Mr. Bingley. They had not even known of Thomas Wickham's existence then, though Lydia's predilection for red coats was already well established. But Elizabeth would never have thought the day would come when her youngest sister would be at peace and domesticated.

Thomas Wickham had been good for Lydia. He was always calm with her, but also completely immobile when he had made up his mind about something. The rules he established for his household were firm ones which could not be circumvented by cajoling, pouting, or downright disobedience. Like the soldier he had been for most of his adult life, he valued routine and expected his wife to conform to it.

Elizabeth had heard from Thomas how Lydia had revolted against his strictures in the early days of their marriage, thinking she could manage him just as she had her own parents, but that phase had not lasted long. Lydia learned quickly that her pin money and attendance at assemblies was contingent on complying with her husband's wishes, and to the astonishment of all, she had thrived under her husband's firm rule. Apparently Lydia's unmanageable behaviour had been less a matter of wildness and more that no one had ever made a serious attempt to manage her or given her any reason to learn to control herself.

Darcy was questioning Thomas about the house he had recently taken near Pemberley. Thomas waxed eloquent on the subject as only a man who never expected to have a house of his own could do, while Lydia looked on with a contented smile. A year earlier she would have been sulking because she had hoped to live in Meryton, but now, as she often said, anything that made her dearest Thomas happy would make her happy as well.

Bingley said, "An excellent decision. I could wish myself that we lived in Derbyshire. Sometimes Netherfield is a bit too close to Longbourn. *You* will at least be free of daily visits from your mother-in-law."

Elizabeth said, "Would you like an escape? We were hoping you would come to Pemberley for Christmas – all four of you. The Gardiners will also be there."

Jane's eyes lit up and she glanced at her husband, who nodded. "I can think of nothing I would like better."

"Nor I," Thomas said.

Elizabeth looked down the long table to Darcy, and their eyes caught and held as she smiled her agreement to his unspoken question.

Darcy pushed his chair back and stood. "I can think of one thing *I* would like even better than your company at Christmas, God willing, and that would be the opportunity to introduce you to the heir of Pemberley."

Jane gasped and covered her mouth with both hands. "Oh, Lizzy, how marvelous! I had wondered these last few weeks. I cannot tell you how excited I am to be an aunt!"

Lydia complained good humouredly, "Bah! I did so want to be first."

Thomas reached out and took her hand. "This would perhaps be a good time to mention that although my own filly will not be first out of the starting gate, I believe she will be running a close second, early in the New Year."

Congratulations flowed around the table. Elizabeth glowed with happiness and Lydia beamed.

Bingley cleared his throat with a broad smile. "Just for the record, I do *not* have an announcement to make. Not yet, at least."

"I would hope not!" Elizabeth laughed. "I have barely recovered from your wedding breakfast."

Jane protested, "That was a month ago, Lizzy."

"It was a very hearty breakfast! Although truth to tell, I could not touch a bite of it."

Bingley rose to his feet, lifting his wineglass. "I would like to propose a toast. To good friends and family, may they continue to increase in number!"

The toast was drunk. Darcy, rather than returning to his seat, crossed to stand behind Elizabeth's chair, his hand lightly resting on her shoulder. He still had moments when he could barely believe she was his wife.

He bent over and whispered in her ear, "In vain have I struggled. It will not do. You must allow me to tell you how ardently I admire and love you."

He felt a frisson run through her at his words.

"Is that so?" Elizabeth said, in a low voice just for him.

"Indeed it is true, Mrs. Darcy. But if you have any doubts, I will be happy to elaborate on the topic later tonight."

She laid her hand atop his and gave him a luminous smile. "I will hold you to that," she said.

About the Author

Abigail Reynolds has spent the last fifty years asking herself what she wants to be when she grows up. This month she is a writer, a mother and a physician in a part-time private practice. Next month is anybody's guess. Originally from upstate New York, she studied Russian, theater, and marine biology before deciding to attend medical school, a choice which allowed her to avoid any decisions at all for four years.

She began writing *Pride & Prejudice* variations in 2001 to spend more time with her very favorite characters. Encouragement from fellow Austen fans convinced her to continue asking 'What if…?', which led to seven other Pemberley Variations and two modern novels set on Cape Cod. Her most recent releases are WHAT WOULD MR. DARCY DO?, A PEMBERLEY MEDLEY, and MORNING LIGHT. She is currently at work on some book or other, and will let the world know if she ever figures out what it is. A lifetime member of JASNA, she lives in Wisconsin with her husband, two teenaged children, and a menagerie of pets.

www.pemberleyvariations.com
www.austenauthors.com

THE PEMBERLEY VARIATIONS by Abigail Reynolds

WHAT WOULD MR. DARCY DO?

TO CONQUER MR. DARCY

BY FORCE OF INSTINCT

MR. DARCY'S UNDOING

MR. FITZWILLIAM DARCY: THE LAST MAN IN THE WORLD

MR. DARCY'S OBSESSION

A PEMBERLEY MEDLEY

MR. DARCY'S LETTER

Also by Abigail Reynolds:

THE MAN WHO LOVED PRIDE & PREJUDICE

MORNING LIGHT

257

Printed in Great Britain
by Amazon.co.uk, Ltd.,
Marston Gate.